EDGES

GLIMPSES:
>—of disaster too great to believe
>—of a captured quantum creature

VISIONS:
>—of a lover never known
>—of a sweetheart forever lost

JOURNEYS:
>—to the last days of a dying empire
>—to the land of lust and lost gods
>—to an awesome world of earth and sky

URSULA K. LE GUIN and VIRGINIA KIDD

Two of speculative fiction's most respected anthologists present an original collection of entertaining and provocative stories by thirteen of the field's most gifted talents.

URSULA K. LE GUIN
VIRGINIA KIDD, EDITORS

EDGES

THIRTEEN NEW TALES FROM
THE BORDERLANDS OF
THE IMAGINATION

PUBLISHED BY POCKET BOOKS NEW YORK

Another *Original* publication of POCKET BOOKS

POCKET BOOKS, a Simon & Schuster division of
GULF & WESTERN CORPORATION
1230 Avenue of the Americas, New York, N.Y. 10020

ISBN: 0-671-83532-7

First Pocket Books printing November, 1980

10 9 8 7 6 5 4 3 2 1

POCKET and colophon are trademarks of Simon & Schuster.

Printed in the U.S.A.

CONTENTS

Virginia's half is dedicated
to Virginia's third—
Ben Blish

INTRODUCTION

Edges are strange; very different from middles. Edges are first cousins of thresholds, yet they can cut the hand that holds them. An edge is twofaced; it may force one to stop yet forbid one to stay. An edge may make one edgy. Artists are often—by no means always, but often—found on edges: peering anxiously over; rapturously admiring the view; putting up signs saying *You are about to fall off! Stop!*; sneaking by at night to knock holes in the protective fence; planning marvels of onelegged bridge engineering; dancing; going for a walk. Long ago someone remarked that it is not an easy thing to walk the razor's edge.

Science Fiction, Speculative Fiction, Fantasy, though all very hard to define, are by definition on the edge: not central, not in the Main Stream of unqualified, unmodified

Fiction, but (pejoratively) marginal, or (optimistically) on the leading edge, or (descriptively) slightly elsewhere —a bit off thataway.

The most solid and desirable residences are not as a rule to be found on the edge of town, out where the West begins, but downtown, close to the First National Bank. People who live out at the edge are frontiersmen, frontierswomen; not perfectly respectable, not fully reliable. You can't quite put your fingers on them.

Even on the frontier, towns, of course, get built—very quickly, sometimes very cheaply. The bank, the saloon, the jail, the whorehouse, some kind of church, there they are overnight, white frame popups, and there are the prosperous and thriving inhabitants living at First and Washington and planning to rebuild next year in brick, with two cupolas and a gazebo. It always happens, even in the Outback and the Elsewhere, even in crazy literature. SF-Fantasy is currently a boomtown, and on Main Street all the faces are familiar, known 'em since Ah wuz so high, the brave starship captain, the loyal robot, the cute alien, the rescuable princess, the wise old daddyman, the swordslinging barbarian from out of town, and all of them making a real good living, yes sirree bob. But if you keep on walking West, towards the edge of town, things begin looking quite strange at last; there aren't any used car lots, and you start to see faces you never saw before.

Some of the faces belong to the people in the stories in this book, stories by people who live out on the edge of the edge.

It is hard to categorize them. As writers they are not, I think, what you could properly call avant-garde (smile when you say that, podner). An avant-garde implies progress, as in an army marching forever forward, forward, a new wave forever breaking. These are people who tend rather to move sideways, or out, or away, or even unexpectedly back home. They are not experimentalists, because they seem to know what they are doing, and do it very well. They are, certainly, story-tellers. Some of them are famous in SF-Town, and some in the Big City (home of Critical Towers and the Great Novel Building). Some of them, on the other hand, are rank, shameless outsiders. In fact, fame or no fame, I believe they are all outsiders, threshold people, artists of the liminal, edge-dwellers.

Some—Engh, Mitchison, Sanders, Dorman—write of existences at the limits of civilization/the comprehensible/the known, that gleaming uneasy ground where two kinds or cultures meet, or fail to meet: the boundary, no man's or woman's land. Wolfe, and Pei, and Emshwiller tell of lives lived on the edge of hope, or a little over the edge. Broderick plays knucklebones at the mad fringe of Time, and Davidson teeters genially on the margins of the Real; Moore crouches at the verge of Panic, while Disch, smiling, whets Irony's fine-edged scalpel. Urrea climbs to the farthest edge of all and the nearest, the line, what line, between life and death; and Elliot returns from somewhere off the edge of the map to say what existence is like where no angels are, those crossers of boundaries, messengers from the unimaginable.

For there are limits to the human imagination; though, on such evidence as this, one might well wonder where they are.

* * *

Virginia will present each story as we go around the circle of writers gathered here; I have agreed to introduce the book entire.

Seeking a summation or motto for this anthology, I found various scraps of quotations hanging around my mind: bits, orts, jetsam, none of which I was quite sure was right. So I went and looked for them under *Edge* and *Edges* in my Familiar Quotations (Oxford, not Bartlett, because the Oxford was much cheaper in the used book store where I got it), and there was one of the edges I had been groping after—from Matthew Arnold:

> ... down the vast edges drear
> And naked shingles of the world.

Ah, the cheerful, cozy Victorians, yes indeed. Then there is always one from the Bible:

> The fathers have eaten sour grapes,
> and the children's teeth are set on edge.

And the almost equally dependable Edward Lear:

> And hand in hand, on the edge of the sand,
> They danced by the light of the moon . . .

But none of these was quite right for this book. The next
listing seemed a mere cliché: "Even to the e. of doom,"
it said. You mean there was a first person who said "the
edge of doom"? I looked it up, and smote my brow. Of
course it would be Shakespeare. And one of the greatest
of the Sonnets. And since as he used the words they are
not melodramatic or ominous but gallant against all odds,
I put his lines here for our motto, chance-struck and so all
the more appropriate to these thirteen tales:

> Love alters not with his brief hours and weeks,
> But bears it out even to the edge of doom.
> If this be error, and upon me prov'd,
> I never writ, nor no man ever lov'd.

Ursula K. Le Guin
Portland, Oregon 1980

Damien Broderick was born in 1944 in Melbourne, Australia, the eldest of six. He spent two years in a Junior Seminary of The Blessed Sacrament Fathers, and thereafter five years at Monash University, Victoria. He has done two short-story anthologies in Australia, in 1970 (in the U.S.) a sword and sorcery novel, and in 1980 the novel *Dreaming Dragons* from Pocket Books.

Broderick may or may not have raised turnips while cultivating his garden, but it can be assumed he never locked *his* tender places up in bands of prohibition.

The Ballad of Bowsprit Bear's Stead

BY DAMIEN BRODERICK

I was there, my smalls, when empire came crashing down about the ears of the old galactics. This is what the wickedest man in the galaxy told his wife at the time:

"When the entire universe is blowing itself to buggery, the only prudent course of action is to be Emperor of the whole goddam shebang."

He was capable of coarse epigrams, and atypical in that, as well: his patricians were prolix, and adorned themselves with names fished from a ridiculous pool of gnomes and proverbs. Those I'll paraphrase. Translations would only confuse. Beneath a dawn sky invariably the hue of clotted blood, the shepherd's warning was a hortation of a different colour.

The Emperor kept one cave-browed eye cocked on posterity. That was pretty remarkable, under the circumstances, since he had more than an inkling that the history he represented was about to be shrugged off like a tattered old coat. Not that the old galactics were big on coats. They were, if you'll forgive me, a hairy people.

I torqued into the High Imperial demesne in full ceremonial drag, and the stinky heat wrenched open every pore of my body. Humid summer's sun, on that fabled world, was a fat hot peach drifting in watered claret. For a while I just stood there gasping, letting the sweat run into my mouth. Off to one side of the clearing was a monstrous sail, a flat leaning deformed tetrahedron woven all of straw and decorated on its face with faces: gargoyle shields in rank on row, lofting fifty meters to the structure's pointed tip. At its base was a hut, the lower swelling of the sail, with two pert pierced nipples for leaving and entering. All the foliage of the ferns and trees beyond the clearing was hard somber green, tricking the eye to see varieties of black. It took me some effort to pick out the hunched servant at work on his shrubs and herbs in the garden.

I sighed, finally, and went to see what he was doing. Undoubtedly he was the filthiest old man I'd ever set eyes on, his tawny pelt thick with greasy emulsions on those patches where the hair had not been plucked out and his hide cicatrized with welts and gouges, nothing like the delicate tattoos which grace your mother's upper lips. He had a ripe aroma, like a wormy cheese left to warm beside the hearth, and I was obliged to turn my head aside and regain myself. When I looked again over his preoccupied shoulder, shielding my eyes against the orange sun, I saw that his hands moved through a pale glaze of sapphire light, a streaky weft of blue radiance. My telephone rang.

Entranced by the light, I fumbled for the receiver at my belt. "Yep?"

"This is Roger, your Life Support System."

"What is it, Roger?" I said patiently.

"Let go of your nose and start the recorders. That's Cerenkov radiation."

"How extraordinary." I did as the Liss suggested, and the holofield's subdued ticking came on. It was hardly necessary to give public notice that a recording was being made, since the gardener had no way of knowing I was there (which, strictly speaking, I wasn't), but the equipment had been designed to conform to standing regulations. "Roger, what's a servant doing with tachyon manipulation? I thought magic was strictly reserved to Imperial citizens."

"So he's a citizen," the telephone deduced acerbically. "Maybe he just likes pottering with flowers. Bowsprit, that's not all. There's a raft of meron activity coming from the jungle to your right."

"Vacuum fluctuations?" The dirty old beast was still fiddling with the damp soil, his stubby fingers drifting through blue pale webs. "Roger, have you been thoroughly serviced lately? The barbarians are still several light-hours away, and you know how these people feel about physical technology."

"Have it your own way," the Liss said sulkily. "Every single sensor in my pack reports singularity flux not half a kilometer from here, and coming closer, but if you wish to insist that— Bowsprit, the tachyons are gone."

"So I see." My eyes stung with sweat, but I'd noticed the sapphire haze flick out. With a grunt and a groan the old fellow got up off his knees and turned in my direction. Uncannily, he seemed to glance straight into my eyes. He placed his grubby hands on the crown of his head and lowered them to his cheeks, whining loudly, and barked like a dog.

Ah, you jump and squeal, my sproggies. Imagine *my* reaction! My belly turned over and little mice did cartwheels in it. Every lock of my beard bit at my throat and the sweat laving my flesh turned to beads of crisp dew. Before I could gather my wits, the grimy derelict dropped his arms, regarded me with a quizzical moue, and fell into that squatting posture we know so well. Stupefied, I watched him brush the fingers of his right hand (bronze-furred, the nails ragged and blackened) across the palm of his left, watched him brush right palm with left digits. My will bobbed away from my mind, and I found myself without deliberation on my own haunches, respectfully brushing my palms in greeting. The claws on the paws of my sacred garb fell together with a rattle. I babbled some nonsense in our own tongue, while my mind whirled to catch up with my well-bred instincts. Then I rose, with what dignity I could, and gave the old man my name in his people's Vocal Tongue. The telephone was ringing; I ignored it, and it stopped.

"Neither wild animal nor man, eh?" the Neanderthal said. His hand stroked lightly my borrowed pelt. "And no star barbarian either, to judge by your phenotype." He tugged at my beard, which in those sprightly days came only to the mid-point of my breast. "Your eyes are not crooked, young man, and your skin has a curious pallor. But come, let me show you an unusual vegetable, as rare perhaps in its kingdom as you are in ours." And he crouched down again into his plot of turned soil, and fetched me down beside him.

I knew these people for great workers of magic, my smalls, and I was not appalled to find a mass of stems, densely packed and decked with yellow, where a minute earlier had been only naked earth and flimmery sapphire. What dried my tongue was the simple fact of his seeing me, addressing me. We were, by every law of physics known to me, mutual ghosts: he in his time, I in mine. Under the shelter of Heisenberg, I was a skein of virtual particles, instanton fluctuations in the zero-energy state. Yet my chin smarted from his tug to my whiskers. It was all quite impossible. If possible, it was horrendous.

He delved into his garden miracle and snapped off a bloom in one hand, a leaf in the other. The leaf was deepest green, heavily veined, like the tissue of a stretched scrotal sac. The old man touched it with his tongue, chewed, grimaced, spat it out. He held up the flower to me, detailing its salient features.

"I haven't altered its genome much, though it craved a cooler climate. It has four petals, not terribly attractive, and four sepåls. Here is its pistil, and you will find six stamens. Evidently one of the Cruciferae, the mustards, you know. Marx calls it *Brassica rapa*, but Smith insists it's a rutabaga." He popped the flower into his mouth, munched without pleasure, and discarded it. "Pity. I was informed that it's edible. Are you a keen gardener yourself?"

Wordless, I shook my head. I realized, then, that he would not recognize the gesture, but I was wrong. He shot me a hard look.

"How may I serve you, then, sir? I had imagined that you were here to view my horticulture."

The telephone rang. I screamed with frustrated rage and snatched the receiver up.

"God damn it!" I covered the mouthpiece with my

palm and told the Neanderthal, "Excuse me for a moment."

"This is Roger, your Life Support System."

"I guessed. Listen, Roger, I'm in the middle of—"

"Bowsprit, don't blow it. He's right about the plant, the rutabaga is a related but different herb, *Brassica napobrassica*. This one's a turnip. Tell him to pull up the root, but not to gnaw on it—it has to be cooked."

"Roger, you're a gem."

"Don't hang up. Those singularities are getting closer. There are two of them. Marx and Smith?"

"Presumably. I'll get back to you." I passed on the facts to the old fellow, trying to breathe through my mouth. You have no idea how bad he smelled. He unearthed a number of spherical roots with tails, their plump white bodies swathed at the top in purple much darker than the sky.

"Fascinating," he said, peeling one open. "You don't happen to know how to prepare them, I suppose? Marx obtained the seeds for me for my birthday, but it would never occur to him to get a recipe. They don't eat, you see."

I risked offending him, but there couldn't have been any alternative explanation. "There are mechanisms from Earth here, at the Imperial palace?"

"Just the two. Robots. Artificial human beings, as it were. The barbarians sent them a long time ago, as a gift to the last Emperor. They're very old, like me." He took my elbow in a comradely way. "Can I offer you a drink? Come in out of the hot sun, you're sweating like a pig, you know. Tell me, are all your race so hairy? Do you all have two heads?"

With some embarrassment, I tapped the dead, ferocious jaws which gaped over my forehead. "This is a vestment, Old Father, a costume. It is of sacred significance. I wear the head and pelt of my brother Bear when I, uh, voyage."

"I thought his eye was a trifle glazed." We started toward the great sail-hut, and my telephone rang.

"This is Roger, your Life Support System."

"I know already. Can't you leave us in peace for—"

"To prepare a delicious turnip ragout," the Liss said, "peel a dozen baby turnips, not too long in the ground, mind, and set them aside. Blend a large spoonful of flour in the same quantity of melted dripping, heating and stirring until the blend is yellow. Add a cup of stock and bring to the boil. Put in the turnips, seasoned with salt, pepper and two teaspoons of sugar, and simmer for about three-quarters of an hour. Tender, the turnip is a toothsome treat."

"Thank you, Roger."

"A pleasure. Do you hear that crashing in the trees?"

Now that he mentioned it. Alarmed, I looked questioningly at the scarred, naked ancient. He was staring with interest at the handpiece of my Liss. When I was younger I was enormously proud of the instrument, a beautiful and delicate receiver, fragile with brass and ivory and carved black wood. I slammed it down. "Are there wild animals here?" Children, you see that I had lost all perspective. The most fearsome of carnivores could no more hurt me, in my virtual state, than it could detect my presence. Nor, of course, could I hurt it, even if it ran straight through me.

"Calm yourself, young man. It is only my robots. They will not molest you."

"Your—?" The spark, belatedly, arced. I threw myself on the grass at his feet. "Magnificence, forgive me. I failed to recognize your Mightiness." This was impromptu stuff, and went against the grain, but I understood without difficulty that if the incomparable magic of the Galactic Emperor enabled him to see and hear me I'd be well advised to keep on his good side.

"Get up, get up, lad, you'll smother under all that fur." He helped me to my feet, and his grip and leverage were startlingly strong. "There's no need to burden me with all that court crap in the sanctuary of my own garden. Bowsprit Bear's Stead," he said, "my name is Lyric Music Stirs Too Fierce the Heart, and it's refreshing to make your acquaintance. In private, you must call me Lyric Music. Now, let's get that drink before you expire. Besides, you still haven't told me how to cook these admirable herbs."

I grinned suddenly at him and shouted, over the racket at the edge of the clearing, "As it happens, Sire, I just happen to have a most delectable recipe. First, you peel your turnips—"

A sharp report cracked behind us, and I jumped around to see a splintered tree fall into the springy arms of its neighbor. Into the clearing, skirting the Emperor's rude garden by a breath and preceded by plentiful teeth-jarring subsonic P-, S-, and surface-type earthquake waves, lumbered an immense polished cylinder. Its loco-motion was bipedal: the elephantine metal legs rose and fell thunderously in a quintessential parody of the ma-chine technology which the old galactics despised so ar-dently. It gave an awful blast on its klaxon as it spied the Emperor.

"Sire!" it cried, grinding toward us. "Condition Red! Alert! Situation Triple-Danger! Withdraw to the deep bunkers!" In the centre of its torso a hefty ruby spun and glinted, bloodier than sun or sky: part of a laser detection system, and surprisingly merry.

"Smith, Smith," said Lyric Music, his tone weary. "Calm down. Show some regard for our guest." To me he said, "They are a hysterical breed, these robots. Noth-ing will satisfy them but rumors of war." Smith had qui-etened at once, but hopped from one mighty leg to the other with unrelieved anxiety. It stood fifteen meters high in the puddle of its own shadow. The Emperor patted its left leg affectionately. "This one, Bowsprit, was the mili-tary executive computer for the barbarians' Right-Hand Hegemony. Marx served the same role for their tradi-tional enemy, the Left-Hand Hegemony. They were dis-patched to the Empire as a gift by the previous Chairman of Earth's Glorious Republic. Apparently they were obso-lescent, but they can run up a nice woven hut in double time." He gestured to the leaning tetrahedron.

In a tiny, strangled voice, the robot said: "Permission to speak, Sire?" The confused crashing from the midst of the trees had not ceased; I could hear more trees crumpling.

"Of course, my dear, but keep it cogent. My guest is thirsty, and seems quite faint from the heat of the day."

"Guest?" muttered Smith. "I see no guest, only a ghost, a disturbance in the vacuum. Still, I guess you're the boss." I perceived in the robot a family resemblance to my Liss. All machines are adept at dumb insolence. "Sire, the barbarians are coming. The Empire is on the verge of collapse."

"Oh, that. The Empire has been on the verge of col-lapse for five hundred years. Bowsprit, why don't you take that damned shaggy suit off and come inside. I have a euphoriant potation you'll like, distilled from the ichor of a certain native bush leech."

"Gospodin! Mein Liebling!" cried a hoarse excited voice. Rearing and careening, a second robot thumped across the grass out of the trees. Half the height of Smith, chubby, propelled by four bald tires, it accelerated toward its companion in a mad rush. Smith leaped to one side and sprinted away. "Your hole!" shouted Marx. "Open to me your hole, my little mouse, for I am on fire!" It executed a neat slalom turn, bright bronze shell blurring, and tripped the first robot to the ground. The shock of impact bruised my ankles, and I felt my knees buckle. Halfway between horror and hilarity, I saw the enormous rubber hose which extruded questingly from Marx's undercarriage. It pulsed; a wave ran from its base to the glowing metal connecting jack at its tip. "I burn, dumpling!"

"Get away from me, you loathsome brute," shrieked Smith, furrowing backwards through the soil with prodigious kicks. "Put that thing away. It's the wrong time of the month."

"Stop screwing around, you bloody dolt," roared Marx. "Something's brought me on early. Open up, or I'll blow. You'll take your virtue to kingdom come."

"Oh." Smith ceased its struggles. "I'm sorry, Karl, I figured you were just feeling saucy. Oh my god, Karl, your positron count is going up exponentially. Quick, my dearest, come to me." A plate cycled open in the cylindrical torso, and Marx jerked forward, thrusting home its throbbing rubber hose. For an instant, before the red-hot jack entered Smith's socket, I saw the eye-searing corona of the power hole.

"Jenny, my darling wife!"

"Eve," cried Smith, acquiescent at last in a mythic rapture.

I picked up my telephone and dialed O. "Did we have anything to do with that?"

"This is Roger, your Life Support System. I think our arrival must have triggered the decay curve in Marx's black hole."

"Explain."

"Well, these robots are fantastically primitive. To tell the truth, they're peripatetic gigaton bombs. I wouldn't be surprised if the Republic sent them here as sort of

Trojan Horses. They run off quantum black holes, about fifty tons apiece I'd estimate, locked into a pinch effect. But the holes are grotesquely unstable. Any singularity that small tends to evaporate quick-smart, and if you can't dispose of the radiation that it's ripping out of the Dirac negative mass you have an annihilation vortex on your hands. Blooey."

"They're not anchored to a collapsar?" I asked in horror.

"Not these early models. From the look of things, they've been jerryrigged to evaporate on a turn-and-turn-about basis. That tube's a superconducting conduit. When Marx's black hole gushes, as it's doing now, it pumps about a gigawatt straight into Smith's event horizon. That destabilizes Smith's hole, but there's a reasonable degree of compliance. Our meron flux stirred up the Dirac Ocean a bit and brought Marx on too soon, that's all. Really nothing to fret about."

"Helen!"

"Eve, Eve, sock it to me, baby."

"Friedrich!" Marx yelped in a trembling voice.

Sobered, the taller robot jerked back to the full length of the rubber conduit. "That's quite enough of that, Karl."

Marx pounded its wheels on the ground. I couldn't take my eyes off them, though I was aware that the Emperor had ambled off to the shade of the sail.

"Baby, I need ya!" screamed Marx. *"Tussy!"* With a terminal spasm, it shook its battered old jelly-roll. The hose retracted, the jack cooled to a dull grey, and the socket plate snapped shut.

Smith drew back, trembling with fury. "Tussy?" it moaned. *"Tussy?* You degenerate monster. You Commie filth. Your own daughter!" And, sobbing and grinding its swivel legs, the robot rushed from the clearing with a terrible tearing of ruptured branches.

Vaguely, I heard the Emperor of the Galaxy calling to me. He stood at the entrance to his hut, two long cool drinks in his hands. "Can't we be friends again?" Marx was hollering from the clearing. "You're not really mad at me, you know. It's just post-quantal tristesse." But I had fallen on my backside in the dry, purple-green tufts, the teeth in the jaws of the bear's skull over my brow chattering together; I was clutching my belly, my smalls, laughing uncontrollably, dizzy in the stinking heat, laughing fit to bust.

Both Lyric Music and I found the barbarians' abhorrence of incest (actual and metaphorical) at once comical and offensive. One serious glance at the Galactic Emperor, with his bleached-out irises and his buckled legs, not to mention the magical tachyon haze furring his thaumaturge's hands, yielded evidence enough of stringent inbreeding. The genome for effective psi-focus is a mess of recessives, alleles as slippery as spawning salmon. Oddly enough, though, none of Lyric's wives stood in closer degree than second cousin—he took most of his puissance from his swarm of kids, coupling his genes through them to a social register refined in thirty thousand years of keeping it in the family. He'd potlatched his way to the top of the tree, building up an immense fortune blackmarketing with the barbarians and disposing of it all in one monumental eleemosynary blowout which had left him drunk as a coot, creditor of half the ancient families in the galaxy, personally skint, and the husband of his predecessor's mother-wife. In a tradition bereft of hard-core personal ambition, Lyric Music Stirs Too Fierce the Heart was a rarity.

As for me, had I not sprung from the loins of Dulcet, prettiest daughter of that redoubtable hunter, Bountiful, my father? My own dear wife was my cousin Lustrous, and the *tusu-guru* of our village, wizard and terrible master of our fetishes, was joint uncle to us both, brother to that kind woman whose breasts gave me suck, breasts heavy from her carrying of Lustrous. My future spouse and I, engaged in the week of our birth, had exchanged parents on that same day, and Dulcet was more to me an aunt than a mother. It is a fine way to grow a child up, though I would hate to have to try to explain it to the pursemouthed puritans of the Glorious Republic. You can see why I warmed at once to chubby, addlepated Marx.

Getting through the low bulging entrance to the palace hut was a bit tricky, bulked out as I was with Liss modules and my bear-voyager's pelt. You can travel one of two ways: hypnotically geared for deference and accommodation to the reality-structure of your destination, or as a spectre. I've never enjoyed finding myself embedded in a wall, or running my fist through someone's head, so I was hampered by the dimensions of the hut doorway.

Finally I backed out again and took off the pelt. I bundled him up respectfully and left him outside. Under the pelt I'd been wearing my *attush*, the same cloak I'd had since my training began twenty years earlier. That was a garment to be proud of, my smalls: a gift from my true mother, woven by her in the old way from the cloth of the mountain elm, soft and supple from the delicate flesh of the inner bark. The rich blues of its blocky embroidery were faded, it's true, but every stitch had been laid in by Dulcet's hand. I felt sorry for Lyric Music: maybe his body scars held something of the same meaning to him, but I judged it a depressing loss to go through life naked as a savage.

The Emperor was waiting inside for me, sipping his drink. Certainly it was cooler there. I had expected the interior to be pitch dark, for there were no windows, but remarkably it glowed with earthlight from a barbarian luminator. Well, an old galactic with a brace of robots is hardly going to shrink from the elementary creature comforts of technology. I got my bear-engraved mustache lifter from my bag, dipped it ceremoniously into the glass Lyric held out to me, placed it on my upper lip, and took the glass. It slipped straight through my hand and shattered on the rammed-earth floor. Hard as rock, that floor, and wonderfully level; I imagined Smith had made it, thundering on the soil with fifty-ton blows.

"Oh shit," I said, peering down at the shards over the mustache lifter beneath my nose. Lyric Music hadn't turned a hair, though one would have expected him to be bellowing for exorcists.

"Smith was right, then," he said, regarding my confusion placidly. "You are a ghost, though of the strangest kind. Did I not touch your arm, and tug your whiskers?"

"Indeed you did, Sire, and it is a tribute to your magic. Here, let me clean this . . ."

Now he *did* look shocked. "Do not demean yourself, master Ghost. What else are my thousand lazy bundles to do with their time?" A fat young Neanderthal girl was suddenly kneeling beside us, scooping up the broken fragments onto a platter of wood. It was obvious that she couldn't see me, and her eyes rolled somewhat in their hooded sockets as the Emperor took his ease on a rush palliasse and motioned me down beside him. "They eat their heads off, Bowsprit, and swive one another from dusk to dawn, and not one of the brainless creatures stops for an instant to consider what will become of them when the barbarians arrive. Which, as the impetuous Smith is fond of telling me, will certainly happen any day now."

Without a word, her task done, the servant was teleported out of the hut.

"You interest me, sir Ghost," the Emperor said, draining his drink. "I have seen barbarians in my day, and done business with the rogues, but I have never witnessed your like among them. But you're not a citizen, still less a servant. And I doubt somehow that you're from the Further World." He left questions implied, and hanging.

"Sire . . ." I hesitated, pondering paradox. To my knowledge this sort of thing had never come up before. If it did, the mathematics indicated that a voyager would loop straight out. At any given instant, in Superspace, every elementary particle subsists in a condition of absolute ubiquity, an infinite fog of all possible virtual states. A temporal paradox is impossible, because when effect precedes cause, to vitiate that same effect a damping oscillation brings the whole sement back to its ground state, but at a dreadful cost in energy. The Archives people disapprove mightily of historians who go over budget, and it didn't take an accountant to see how much a paradox loop would cost.

All this went through my mind in a flash, of course. But how do you explain such a thing to an old galactic? You don't, naturally.

"Sire," I said again, "forgive me, but there are certain facts I must not disclose, even to you, and certain matters of politics I am forbidden to discuss."

Lyric Music looked at me steadily for quite a while. Then, "Quite right," he cried, slapping my knee. "Only the vulgar and the shiftless waste their worry on politics, sir palpable Ghost, and I do not believe in pushing a man where he will not go." He considered me craftily. "Still, you pique my curiosity. What was that stick you held so oddly beneath your nostrils? And may you not throw me some small tidbit about our people? How are your tribe known, Bowsprit Bear's Stead?"

I'd been glancing surreptitiously around the long, bare

hut, expecting someone to interrupt us and get the pressure off me. All my training was as an observer, an interpreter of the lost and the alien, a witness; I was no diplomat. To my astonishment, we were completely alone. Apart from the arrival and vanishing of the servant, there was no indication that Lyric Music had not all his life lived incarcerated, or as a hermit. The psychic, I reminded myself earnestly, are different to us. On some waveband of the mind, the Galactic Emperor was plugged into a universe of bustle more frenzied than a termite's hill.

I compromised, showed him the mustache lifter my father had carved for me when my beard was a laughable wisp. "My people, Sire, are known as the Men—in our tongue, the Ainu. We pride ourselves for our hirsuteness, and the ancestors of the barbarians made mock of this, naming us the 'Hairy' Ainu. The most blessed among us, such as my fortunate self, are scholars, voyagers, messengers of the bears." His short, thick fingers ran admiringly across the embossed bears on my lifter. "Like your mighty nation, Sire, the first seed of my people was nurtured in the soil of the world Earth."

"The latest seed of that world," said Lyric Music gloomily, "is on its way with its damned bloody engines of death to fertilize our gardens with our blood." He rose, handing back my lifter. "It is a topic which much exercises my principal wife. I suppose I'll have to see the harridan. I have enjoyed our chat, sir Mystery, but I must leave you now to your own devices. Even an Emperor must work on occasion."

The hut was crammed with bodies, rank with their own effluvia and the short-chain aliphatic pheromones the Neanderthals favour for perfume. All of them were women, short and broad, with heavy broad noses and immense gleaming teeth, breasts jaunty and sagging according to age but all scarred with initiatory symbols; slender collarbones, to be sure, but arms and legs like wrestlers; pubic beards to put an Ainu warrior to shame. I confess it: excitement jolted in me, despite the shock to my nostrils. Quickly, I withdrew to a corner of the palace hut, and watched with more than the delight of the historian as the serving women of the Empress sorted themselves into a kind of order, and the ancient woman herself stepped forward haughtily to greet her liege.

As à boy I was randy as a beagle, which befits a healthy child, but I was never noticeably Oedipal with it. Certainly I was a rogue with the village girls, and the boys, too, more than once, tugging at their skirts and wraparounds, quick to pull another child's hair or tickle her armpits, all the better to cop a delicious feel. Surely it was the bane and gory tragedy of the pinched, trap-lipped hordes of the Glorious Republic that they locked their tender places up in bands of prohibition. All their buried heritage cried out in repudiation of this madness—their Taoists, their Shinto saints, their rubber-limbed Tantric athletes—and went unheard, smothered by the colder joys of mechanism and lock-step marching. I've seen their rigid bodies, clad in their dull uniforms: as inveterate a tribe of brain-softened masturbators as the species ever spawned. Not that we failed to twang our own nice places, in my youth, when the need was hot upon us and no fellow creature close by, but that was not often. I speak of yesterday, of course, my smalls; today I am a husband and a father, a grandfather, as I was when I stood in Lyric Music's crowded hut. I have never fancied the faithless husband's fate, toe-dancing on the ground, suspended by the shrieking hairs of the shame-heaped scalp.

Such matters are seldom all-or-nothing, but for the wretched subjects of the Glorious Republic it came a long chalk too close to nothing. What other nation could have conceived so gross a travesty as the rutting robots of their abandoned Hegemonies? There, at least, their fundamental equation spelled out its formula without disguise: that spasm yoking sex and power, raw crude power, the energy of implosion, the fusion of self with self in endless self-containment, and the burning violence of its only seed?

I have said that I was not overly Oedipal, yet the truth is that I find my highest pitch in the womanly pelt of a lustrous pubic beard. An epithalamic allusion, my sproggies, but my fixation was pre-nuptial. Many the winter evening, in the shadows of the flickering hearth, before my manhood was fully upon me, had I wriggled in the mandala of an inverted kiss, licking and snorting at the apricot cleft of a friendly girl child (and sniffed in, more than I cared to, the odour of dried urine), but my heart's delight was the prospect of snuffling a nether beard.

There are great mysteries, my children, in our people's ancient ways. That tattoo, on the upper lip of a wedded woman—does it say that, secretly, she is a man, with all the powers over life of a man? Or does she tell us that a man is the budded form of a woman, with his pubic thatch the wrong way up and over-boastfully paraded from his chin? To the men of the Glorious Republic such speculations would have seemed obscene; their bellies would have shrunk to berries, and their manly parts (too often self-handled, unless I miss my mark) have contracted like snails. For them, the making of a baby was no more than a momentary convulsion. All the burden went upon their women, those grim devotees of duty. Is it any wonder that their children lacked souls? A woman cares for the tiny growing thing within her, but it is a man's place to fill its wrinkled red head with intellect. Lustrous, when our first child was due, went about without complaint, I recall, until the day the midwives took her off to squat in the dark. I, though, like a good father, responsive to the fish kicking in her lumpy womb, lay for weeks with the fetishes before the fire, morose, my spirit straining at its fecundating task, in couvade.

What inkling could the machine-folk have of our reward, when the tribulations are behind us, and the chubby thighs of the infant are slashed and stuffed with fungus mycelium? They are barren of mystery, locked in their time, heeding only cesium clocks, endlessly visiting apocalypse upon the endless worlds of the old galactics.

Despite her immense age (she was certainly old enough to have been Lyric Music's grandmother, and conceivably his great-great grandmother), the Empress The Early Bird Catches the Worm struck me as formidably impressive. Out from the ranks of her chamberlains and serving women she stepped, bald high and low as a lizard, skin translucent and creased infinitely fine as oiled brown paper folded and unfolded by centuries of archivists, and her breasts, too, like brown paper bags emptied of their goods and discarded; right eye turned inward and useless, the other glaucous with antiquity but alive and raging. All her lineaments, in truth, made up a catalogue of sublethal recessive defects, yet a kind of absolute power and self-conviction was instinct in her.

"You foolish man," she cried, quivering, as she stood before the Emperor of the galaxy. "Do I find you loitering in this absurd place built by your abominations? Have you nothing better to do as the foe hurtles toward our world?"

The old man glanced up to meet the eye of the old, old woman, and from my position in the hut's corner I could just make out the pixie smile which transformed his huge mouth.

"My dear, you come at an auspicious moment. Come, come, sit down here with me. Look," and he held up the purple-and-white vegetables, "I have just this minute grown a wonderful novelty, a plant known as 'turnips,' and I expect them to be precisely as tasty as they look. Don't you find them elegant?" Lyric Music offered them to his wife courteously, holding them by the stalks.

"Imbecile!" Early Bird snatched the turnips from his hand and cast them on the floor. They winked out of existence. "You have become a doddering child, Lyric. What next! By my ancestors, I am ashamed. Wife to the High Magus? Wife to a village gardener! You are a pollution to my honorable bloodline, Lyric, a curse and a disgrace . . ." Her breath failed in a rattling wheeze, and instantly women held her by waist and elbow, helped her down to the palliasse despite her objections; their glances at the Emperor were venomous.

"My good wife," said Lyric Music, with a touch of acerbity, "I find your slurs on the craft of the gardener offensive and short-sighted. Competent agriculture is the wellspring of society, and *inspired* horticulture its highest art. Nourishment for both body and soul is—"

"Lyric!"

"—both the supreme end and the finest means—"

"Sire, I beg you!"

Gently, Lyric Music took her crippled hands in his, and fell silent for a space. One of them wordlessly expressed a command, and the hut was empty. Neither took any notice of me in the corner.

"Early Bird, sometimes you forget yourself."

She was weeping, but she had not softened. "I apologize, Sire."

"Oh, crap. Madam, you're a stiff-necked old bird and all your children are the same." He stroked her fingers. "Do you think that a genotype like ours will be disturbed one whit by the antics of barbarians from a single world?"

Whipping her head up and around, Early Bird stared

at him. "The New Humans are not a comic troupe." With
patrician decorum, she insisted on giving the earth people their proper designation. "They are murderers, Lyric.
They have slaughtered their own kind for half a hundred
millennia, and now they mean to slaughter us. Something
must be done to stop them. Their leader is only hours
distant. When his abominable machines arrive he will
have this world put to the torch. It is their way. Our nation will be utterly destroyed. It is your duty to prevent
that holocaust."

My own excitement, my smalls, was extreme, and I
could not suppress a shudder. Here was history! Here
were the principals of the fall of empire, and I was privy
to their debates. Lyric Music toyed with what were left
of his turnips. The only sound in the hut was the ticking
of my holofield recorder, lapping up the actuality. The
Emperor looked my way, then, one swift penetrating
flick of his eyes, and away again. I have listened to that
recording a hundred times since, children, and I am mor-
ally certain that his next words were meant as much for
us as for his wife. How could he have known? I can only
say that Lyric Music was the craftiest man I have ever
encountered.

"My dear," he said, rising to his feet and striding back
and forth in the long hut, "are you reminding me of my
duty to history?"

The ancient woman laughed with some bitterness. "To
history, Lyric? What else is our nation if not history?"

"Indeed. It is written in our genes, and the genes of
our children. You and I, Early Bird, are the custodians
of thirty-seven thousand years—"

"You," she snarled, "by right of purchase."

"Because my gene-line strayed from the path of psychic purity?" Lyric Music sighed, and ran his fingers
down the wonderfully woven straw of the wall. "Because
my ancestors discerned value in talents other than the
single vampiric ability to suck off the *mana* from count-
less human cattle?"

The Empress was on her feet, trembling and blood-
less. "Guttersnipe! How dare you? With every word you
muddy and defame the nation at whose pinnacle you
loll like a drunken slave. You showed enterprise enough
toadying to the machine-mongers, buying your way into
eminence." Beside herself, she lifted an earthlight lumi-

nator and dashed it on the floor. It bounced several times without breaking, and rolled aganst a rush wall, casting strange shadows. "All your power you owe to me and our children, and you dare to defame us as parasites."

"Sit down, madam." His voice rasped with authority and anger, somewhat belated in my opinion. "The means by which I obtained this post were legal and time-honored. I would remind you that I am your liege. Your behavior is disgraceful. For one who despises the bar-barians so strenuously, you remind me distastefully of their arrogant women. Now," and his voice regained its gruff blandness, if you see what I mean, "we were speak-ing of history, and its demands."

Thinly, the Empress told him: "There will be no more history when the New Human warriors land."

"You astonish me. History is the record of events. It has no favorites. You make time a myth."

"And so it is, Lyric. We see time with different eyes, Sire. Yours is the dew which evaporates from the drenched earth, leaving no trace. Mine is the rain which smites the topmost leaves of the forest, runs from twig to branch to trunk to root, fecundating the earth. And its fruit is the tree itself, older than that transitory time which gives drink to its roots. The history of our nation is the myth of the tree, Lyric, with its infinite frag-ile branches in a thousand million worlds. And its Em-peror is the trunk. They will hack you down with their barbarous instruments, and hurl the tree of our people into the fire. Then," she said, with a voice as lost and elegiac as her words, "time for both of us will be a thin smoke dispelled by the breeze, and a handful of dying ashes."

"I see." The Emperor turned away from her and crouched on his haunches, tracing with his right index finger the scars on his left biceps. Perhaps the blue glow danced at his fingertip. "You speak for the Women's Mysteries?"

"I speak for the nation entire."

"Do you understand what you are asking?"

I could hardly hear her voice. All the snappy verve and choler was gone from it. "I ask for a Great Culling."

A tremor passed through Lyric Music's shoulders. "You are prepared to destroy a whole people, to the last man, woman and child, to preserve your own culture?"

"What choice do we have? They are savages. They will not rest until they have laid waste our nation."

I felt sickened. My head reeled. Some hint of this moment, this swinging balance, had passed into the later apocrypha, but no one believed it. No one had doubted that the thing was feasible, but who could credit the cold proposal to murder twenty billion human people? We can imagine the barbarians making such a calculation, but not the old galactics. My body was cold, my smalls, and my bowels like water.

But I see that some of you do not understand. Let me explain how that ancient witch had planned the death of old Earth.

In coldest winter, the year I became a man, my uncle the *tusu-guru*, he of the "double life," sought me out one day beside the hearth, under the dark sooty rafters, and led me through the frigid sleep to his brightly-lit study. I had never been within that code-locked place before, and I shivered more to see the yellow bears' skulls and willow fetishes and other arcana than I did from the blustering walk there through snow halfway to my knees. He took from a tall shelf a curious artifact of lovingly polished wood and glass, as wonderful and powerful, I thought, as any fetish, and perched it on his lap. It was an elongated triangle (not unlike the sail-hut palace of the Emperor, in fact), and behind its glass face a thousand small buttons spread across a velvet backing in an array as regular as Pascal's Triangle. I could not conceive any mundane use for it, but its simple elegance bespoke an instrument of some kind.

"Saucepan," my uncle said (for in those days I was not yet Bowsprit, and certainly had not dared to hope for that lofty role as the bear-messenger's proxy), "have you been taught anything yet about the old galactics?"

"A little, sir," I admitted, looking at my feet and the cork tiles they stood upon.

"You have heard that they were wizards?"

"Yes, sir." Was it a trap? I glanced at him quickly. "But their magic was not like our magic."

"No." My uncle moved the instrument, opening a lever recessed into its apex. "Their magic was the old, forbidden kind, harnessing the stored power of a million minds to the benefit of one magus. Do you know the binomial theorem, Saucepan?"

I assumed it was mathematics. "No, sir. I am studying hunting, training the dogs."

"Well and good, my boy. You seem agile enough in the snow. Still, I wish they'd give you children an earlier start with numbers. It doesn't matter, my little engine here will make the point well enough. Look closely, lad. At the top, here, is a chute giving access to the board within." He took up a canister from his bench, and I saw that it was filled with hundreds of small perfect metal balls. My uncle fixed this container to the open chute by means of a narrow valve at its base. "When I release these spheres, they will rush down the chute and dispose themselves at the bottom of the triangle. As they fall, they will strike the buttons and suffer deflection, some this way, some that. Can you tell me, boy, what the pattern will be when all have fallen to the lowest available point?"

I gazed at the machine and puzzled over the problem. The gap between velvet and glass seemed hardly greater than the diameter of each ball, as did the distance between adjacent buttons. As the *tusu-guru* had said, each sphere, in falling, would hit numerous buttons on its path. I became slightly dazed, trying to picture the pattern. Some of you laugh at my naivete, but the matter is not immediately apparent if you are innocent of statistics.

"I suppose they'll pile up in the middle and spread out evenly," I hazarded.

"Let's see," said my uncle, and released the spheres. With a rattling, glinting rush, the balls cascaded into the triangle. It was impossible to observe their paths as they batted and caromed from button to button. In a moment the activity stilled—and the balls could be seen as a silvery bell-shaped mass at the instrument's base, few at the extremities of the triangle, most mounding upward at its center. I was dazzled by the demonstration. I think that moment was the beginning of my life-long love of mathematics: the latent order in random things.

"We call that curve the normal distribution," said my uncle. "Few interactions in this complex world are as neat and clear as the carefully-designed workings of my little toy. Still, the underlying principle can be found in most things which are the result of a multitude of small influences, none of them connected."

"And this is the secret of magic?" I guessed.

"On the contrary, Saucepan. This is the secret of science. We cannot predict the path of any particular ball in that maze, but we know quite perfectly the end-state of all the balls together. Magic works like this." And with a deft flick, he inverted the instrument. Spheres scurried and jostled, whirling miniature worlds, and drained back into the canister. "The psychic force is generated at random within the human brain. Some of us are more powerful emitters than others, but psi is always sporadic and unpredictable. It can only be directed usefully, and put to work as magic, under strict social conditions."

"Like an orchestra, you mean?"

"Exactly, Saucepan. But an orchestra playing powered instruments, with the current cut off from any given instrument ninety-nine percent of the time. To obtain music from such an ensemble, you'd need thousands of instrumentalists, maybe hundreds of thousands, none of them sure if his keyboard was alive but obliged to play as if it were. Well now, imagine how crucial is the role of the conductor in such circumstances."

In fact, I knew almost as little about orchestral music as I did about stochastic analysis. I'd heard holos, but that is sound detached from its root. I tried to bring the analogy back home, to the night gatherings where we played our *tonkori* zithers, striking the open strings with both hands, adding our voices in the ancient guttural polyphonies. And the image no longer conveyed my uncle's meaning; magic is centrally totalitarian, an elixir distilled from the dross of masses. Our music, even our shamanistic rapture, was too personal for that, too earthy and immediate.

I stared at the canister, and all the little globes of silver crammed together. They reminded me of salmon, the divine fish, piled gleaming in the sun ready for drying. "The conductor—the magician—he, he sucks out the psychic force from other people?"

"You could put it that way, lad, but the truth is more horrible. The forbidden magic of the old galactics gained its power from the willing co-operation of a race bred like cattle. To be a magus, a psi-focus for that confluence of force, required in its turn a very special genotype. Magic, like language and mathematics, is a sort of machine which transforms energy through symbols." My eyes must have glazed over; he added, "Well, never mind. The important thing is that the brain of a magus has a special structure, refined by careful genetic selection through many generations. When it taps the random blurts of psychic energy from ordinary brains, it acts as a rectifier, a transformer. Nor is it the brain of the magus alone which channels this force, but the brains of all those whose genetic constitution most resembles his own. And archetypal symbols, in their turn, are all-important. The Emperor of the old galactic order stood at the peak of an immense psychic pyramid, confirmed in his role by a tradition of untold thousands of years, and his children were the most vital circuit in his psychic amplifier."

"Yes, sir," I mumbled. I desperately needed to take a piss, but I was much too awed to say so. And the pressure on my bladder was acting as an erotic stimulus; I had arranged with another young person to meet under the furs that afternoon, and it began to seem that I would miss my appointment. How little we value the truly important things of life, such as the opportunity for pure learning, when we are young. Ah, smirk if you will.

Nevertheless, what my uncle told me next cooled my ardor.

"Saucepan, listen carefully. We have come to the point where the dogs drive the catch to shore." He smiled. "I'm sure you would rather be back beside the fire, under the covers with your little friends. But I wish you to fix this in your thoughts, engrave it there, for your manhood rites are very close now and this is one of the great truths every man must know well and fear." He paused until, in my sudden fright, I nodded. His friendly tone was in shocking contrast to the portent of his words, more effective than any ranting might have been.

"The psychic force, like poetry, operates at the level of symbols. And the fundamental symbolic structure in our bodies and minds—and in the bodies of all living creatures —is the architecture of our cells, and within our cells the DNA of our genes. In the antiquity of our species, it was believed that knowledge of a man's name conferred control over his person. That was a mistaken belief, my small, but it hinted at the greater truth; for knowledge of the phenotype does indeed yield authority, in psychic operations, over the genotype. The ancients of all nations employed dolls adorned with a man's name, hair and nail-parings, but the magus used true gene-linked symbols. A race of men or animals is defined by those symbols, even the most superficial."

My uncle leaned forward intently, his hazel eyes regarding me over his snubbed nose, and grasped my left hand, turning it upward.

"Look closely at the shape of your fingerprints. See the loops, like a buffeted wave curling under its own rushing force? That shape is typical of our people, scribed in our DNA. The fingerprints of the old galactics were predominantly whorled, like the rings across a tree stump."

Despite his intensity, and my apprehension, I was *dying* for a leak. I hopped about edgily. "It doesn't seem like a very important difference."

"By itself it's not. But it segregates the Ainu from those bearing a different genetic makeup. Suppose a strange and terrible plague arose which discriminated its victims according to which fingerprint gene they possessed. Then you might find the matter less than trifling."

"Is there a disease like that?"

"In the ancient days there were many—malaria was one. But I am trying to make a more general point, boy. Mother Goddess, I wish they'd get you started on science a couple of years earlier. Do you know about blood type?"

"For accident transfusions? Of course, I'm type B."

"Good, good. Well, my small, the Ainu as a group have a blood-type signature unlike any other people. Twenty-eight percent are like you, bearing the gene for type B. Five percent less have mine, for type A. None at all have type A_o. There are four percent with Rh-negative, and we have the highest recorded level of NS combination. Never mind what that means; the point is, a map of the Ainu people would show gradients for a million characteristics of this kind in proportions singular to us alone."

"Uh. sir," I said with some desperation, "may I be excused for a moment? I gotta take a leak."

"Huchi, Saucepan, why didn't you say so? Get the hell out of here, then. I don't want you piddling all over my nice new floor."

I bolted out the door. The weather had eased, but the sky hung over me like a grey hand. I ripped open my garments and poured a hissing, smoky stream into the snow, sagging with relief. The spark arced in my mind, ripping away the blissful emptiness, and I jerked, spraying my boots.

I slammed the door. My uncle looked up in exasperation.

"You weren't talking about disease, you meant magic," I said with horror.

"Of course."

"And the triangle—the balls falling into that pattern. It works the other way too, doesn't it? A magus got his power from his own kind, channelled through his kin. And if he wished, he could aim it in the same way. He could make a map, a symbol map of his enemies, and blast all that power straight into their bodies, and their own genes would act like a, like an antenna tuned for exactly that frequency."

"A selective effect," the *tusu-guru* said gravely, "and no way to avoid it if it's aimed at you. The old galactics used it for ecological control, thinning out animal populations on a scheduled basis. They needed neither fences, nor domestication, nor cultivation. And they employed the same techniques, handled with infinite delicacy, in breeding their trillions of human slaves. They sculpted the genome as easily as I carve a fetish from willow."

He picked up a bird's oracular skull and turned it slowly, his fingertips skimming the empty sockets.

"Saucepan, when you leave here I would like you to meditate on the fact that you immediately interpreted your insight in lethal terms. That is one of the reasons why the old magic is forbidden. We are a peaceful people, we Ainu, but we have a legacy of war. Today we are hunters and scholars: once we were ferocious soldiers, and we could be again. The risks are too great."

He sighed. "We are hostages to our own symbols, too often the symbols written with the four letters of the primeval code. When we sicken, our bodies are in rebellion against some symbolic statement our cells repudiate. I might heal the sick with antibiotics, or with whale bristle and deer horn powder, but in both cases I am waging a war of propaganda. There are certain bacteria, Saucepan, which wear embroidery on their *attushes*, graffiti which enrage our flesh. These lipopolysaccharides are harmless in themselves, but the moment we read their slogans our white blood corpuscles become hysterical. They swarm together in the blood vessels, blocking the body's fuel. They gush pyrogens, igniting fever. A normal activating hormone from the adrenal medullae begins literally to kill the tissues it encounters. Serum fractions in the blood holler for more leucocyte reinforcements. In the worst cases, the victim goes into hemorrhage, high fever and shock. And all of this crazy runaway self-destruction has been provoked by an automatic response to endotoxin symbols which by themselves do no damage at all."

I gaped. Until that moment I suppose I'd always regarded myself as on perfectly cordial terms with my own body. Abruptly, I saw it as my potential assassin.

Struggling, I asked, "Do you mean that the old galactics could, could *trigger* this kind of sickness in people, by magic? Make their bodies destroy themselves?"

"That's exactly right, Saucepan." The fragile skull cracked, with a sharp sound, in his hands, and fell into two uneven pieces. "They did it when culling animals. There is no reason why they could not have done the same with human beings. Fortunately, to our knowledge, they never did use it in war. The Neanderthals, after all, had left Earth originally because of their nation's loathing for the violence of the New Humans. But they could have culled the barbarians. They could have slaughtered every single one of them."

My uncle rose and took me to the door. A freezing gale was blowing up again, in the black, splattered night. He put his arm about me as I left. "Saucepan, meditate on what we have discussed. And ask yourself, until the answer is clear and without qualification: Do you think that you would trust yourself with such power?"

I slogged off through the snow, and felt the burden of manhood on my shoulders.

A reprise of that emotion took hold of me, as I stood out of the way in the corner of the palace hut, destroying the last remnants of my professional composure and detachment. I was in the grip of an acute anxiety attack. My situation was unprecedented, after all. I should have been a ghost, intercepting a shadow reality. Instead, that phantom realm had chatted to me and tugged at my whiskers. Far from my practiced role as observer *par excellence,* I had become a participant. At a level of unconscious self-perception deeper than my training—and that buffer of educated response, in turn, now abruptly irrelevant—I had introjected the reality I saw and heard.

Unlike the youth of memory, though, discussing the theory of psychic genocide with his shaman, I was spared the pressure of my bladder. But without the renal dialysis unit of my Liss, rubbing on my cramped belly muscles, I'm sure I would have pissed my pants.

Clarity returned. Only then did I realize how close I'd been to passing out. My face was icy cold, and my limbs trembled. Roger, monitoring my vital signs, had reorganized my endocrinal balance. Tranquilizers have their place.

Lyric Music, the comical savage whose act of will could blight a world, stood facing his wife. She had not moved. The enormity of her demand had shaken her, I suspect, almost as much as it had shaken me, but she was not cowed.

"I have never been in any doubt that you despise me," he told her. She did not deny it. A professional eavesdropper, I nevertheless felt uncomfortable. The ticking of the holofield's public notification seemed unnaturally loud. "You can doubt my wisdom to your heart's content, madam," he said more sharply, "but I hope you do not dispute my knowledge."

"I do not. But we are not discussing your unparalleled access to the collective memory of my ancestors—"

"They are my ancestors too, Early Bird."

"Only in diminished degree."

The Emperor took a deep, harsh breath. "Your patrician regard for heraldry is quite stupefyingly beside the point, madam. Do you think I entered your gene-line because I was hungry for personal prestige?"

"Why else?" Her voice was as dry and parching as a desert wind.

Coarsely, Lyric Music Stirs Too Fierce the Heart said: "When the entire universe is blowing itself to buggery, the only prudent course of action is to be Emperor of the whole goddam shebang. As Emperor, I'm the sluice-gate for the energy of a galaxy of minds. As Emperor, I'm the custodian of the psychic records of my predecessors. You wish me to use the first to cull the barbarians. I'll draw on the second instead to prove why your suggestion is an abominable stupidity.

"Twenty-eight thousand years ago, there was an Emperor named Every Cloud Has a Silver Lining—"

"We do not speak of him," Early Bird said with, I swear to you, a sniff.

For the first time, the filthy old man laughed. His eyes rolled under their jutting brows.

"I suppose you don't. He died insane, after all. But I have his memories. It comes with the job, madam, and I can't prune them off your mythic tree in the interests of neatness and convenience."

"Lyric, this is in the worst possible taste."

"By god, woman!" He seized her frail, birdlike jaw in his blunt fingers, and I waited for her skull to shatter. The blood left her crumpled brown paper face, and she gave a thin shriek. "You demand a Great Culling of human beings, and you find your black sheep ancester too ignoble a topic for polite soirée. This is what your fucking mad disgraceful ancestor did:

"Silver Lining took himself off to the solitary moon of a gas giant world ten thousand light years from other human company. There he skulked for the decades from his middle age to gibbering dotage, in the company of fanged slugs and insects huge as clouds, not all of his own imagining. He had fathered three children, daughters all, and they stayed behind and multiplied his genes."

The Empress jerked her bruised jaw out of his clutching grip, and covered her face with her own bony hands.

"At last, Silver Lining's spiritual disease populated even this bolt-hole with enemies and lurking wizards," Lyric Music said inexorably. "A solution occurred to the lunatic, finally. If he could not out-run his illwishers, he could at least hold them at bay. He issued a decree for a festival of poets and artists . . ."

"I do not wish to hear this."

"He summoned to his gloomy moon a hundred thousand of the finest, most refined men and women of enhanced sensibility in the galaxy. Our nation's numbers were much fewer then, madam, but the highest flower of its talent was no less distinguished."

The old, old naked woman was bent double, and she keened with an almost inaudible register of distress. My own fear was gone, now, and my skin prickled with the strangeness of it. Lyric Music was speaking to her with more than words, I was sure; perhaps he was evoking in her consciousness the demented phantasmagoria of his monstrous borrowed memory. And the words themselves were enough to fix my attention utterly.

"He brought them to his thin-aired world, and disposed them one by one on every range of hills, beside the seething lakes, on islands and places rimed with ice. And he set them to the making of their arts: the weavings of colors and textures, bright songs like lonely, lovely birds, the meditation of exalted philosophies. And when he judged that the moment was right, when their fears were soothed and their souls opened to the whisper of eternity, he gathered in the power of the worlds beyond number of our nation and he fashioned ten thousand burning sunlets in the void—"

"No! No! Too bright!"

"—plasmas from a fusing star-heart, and he cast the flame upon them, a small piece of hell for each man and woman scattered across his moon, and as they blazed up in their private infernoes like insects shrivelled in a campfire—"

Early Bird screamed, and fell onto the floor.

"—the magus wove their agony into a shield that locked his world away from humankind forever." Without pity, the Emperor regarded the naked crone writhing at his feet. The fall had been too much for her decalcified frame; her left arm had bent sideways, fractured at the humerus, and there was something badly wrong with her clavicle. Possibly her pelvic girdle had cracked as well. Keening, Early Bird brought her knees up and her bony buttocks pointed at me. With a blend of profound shame and clinical fascination, I noted that the poor bitch had long ago suffered a prolapsed uterus, and massive piles stood out like a fist of greasy knuckles. Early Bird had earned her pride and her dignity. The old galactics bred their star gene-line dams well into their ninth decade.

Lyric Music knelt down carefully beside his moaning wife. Cerenkov radiation flared in his palms as he straightened her broken bones. Obviously there was nothing he could do for the tissues which nature had ruptured. He helped her to her feet, but his expression remained stony.

"There will be no Great Culling, madam. If you wish

to kill barbarians, you must use their own methods. I doubt, though, that they will be terribly eager to sell you weapons."

Holding herself away from his touch, Early Bird stared at him with detestation. "I shall never forgive you for what you have just done."

"It was necessary to make you understand. *Do* you understand?"

She refused to reply. Her hatred was palpable.

"You are all the same," the Emperor said dismally. "You use power with no concern for its source or its laws. Silver Lining turned an entire world into a pustule of poison we can never lance, and you would have me do the same to the galaxy. Magic is not a tool you can use and discard. *It is ourselves.* It casts back our actions upon ourselves, like a barbarian mirror reflecting the light from our faces. Our nation," he said, sharpening each word like a blade, "is rotten through and through. It is time to dismantle it. Now go."

The Empress vanished. Lyric Music sat with his legs spread, elbows pressing his knees, kneading his fingers. After a moment he vanished as well, and I stood alone in the sweat-stinking hut.

My telephone rang.

"This is Roger, your Life Support System. I didn't think you'd want to be interrupted; I figured the bell might throw our subject off his stride."

"Yeah. Use the microwave link if anything big blows up while Lyric Music's here. Roger, I could really use a drink."

"Won't be much longer, the Earth fleet has just entered planetary orbit. Bowsprit, something *has* come up. The robots must have tuned their detectors. They're aware of our presence at an interactive level. Smith has been nosing around the bear pelt. Oh shit, he's picked it up."

"Fire Goddess!" I yelped, and ran for the exit.

That bear had been with me, you understand, almost from the beginning. How well I recall capturing him, a snuffling cub, and toting him home triumphantly to the village. He was the last of the animals our people ever sent on the great pilgrimage, and I still believe that the abandonment of that tradition has been a grave impoverishment of our way of life. No doubt you think me an incorrigible fogey.

I was twenty-four then, and our village had shifted to the mountains of Hokkaido after our ancestral home in Sakhalin cracked into three pieces and sank, spewing lava and superheated steam into the ocean. A terrible year for fishing. The Okhotsk Current went crazy. Lustrous and I were on the slopes of Fujiyama at the time, where I was taking accelerated courses in the new meron physics. My eldest son had not yet been weaned, and when he flew back to help settle the survivors Lustrous' breasts were still rich with milk. My village had lost their bear in the disaster, and I chivvied the men into coming in search of another.

Fiercely cold was the snow, and the bamboo gaunt and flattened. We clambered blindly through territory none of us had hunted before, carrying only bows for arms. When I saw the yellow marks in the snow, the breath-spoor of the hibernating bear, I called the others to a halt and dispersed them to their posts. I wrapped my head in thick cloth, fingers frozen and heart thumping, and crept into the beast's den with my knife. The animal was dormant, and there were two cubs curled against her. I rousted her out of her hole with cries which terrified me as much as her, booting her in the arse as she turned blindly to find me. Once started, she went out like a locomotive, dogs yapping around her, arrows thudding into her hide, the men bellowing like a gang of yahoos. One cub jolted after her, tumbling in the snow; the other I captured with little enough complaint. He was a biddable creature, my adopted son.

Lustrous loved him. She took Woodchip off the teat as quickly as it could be managed, but for a time my son and the cub shared her breasts. I will not tell you the name we gave the cub; he has travelled ahead of us, and it would be impolite. He was a sturdy little fellow, with his baggy skin that seemed a fur coat in all truth, small eyes gleaming with the promise of wisdom in his broad head. He quickly knew us for his family, and I do not think his sharp teeth ever bothered my wife's long nipples.

We had two more children by the time he'd grown large enough for the cage. Or was it only one, my eldest daughter? That must be it: two children, one bear. You have lost so much, my smalls, in giving up that rite. He ate at the hearth with us, taking the lid delicately from the millet pot and scooping up as much as his appetite called for. I taught my youngsters that he was the mirror of Aeoina, the "Person Smelling of Man," who came among us in the times of fable and bore back to the gods a human *attush*.

When the Feast of Sending Forth came at last, the *Iomande maratto*, my beautiful Lustrous lingered for a time on the edge of a psychotic break. Perhaps you are right, my sproggies. Perhaps the price of our message was too great. As the bear waxed fat, squatting cheerfully in his cage, poor Lustrous lost her taste for food. I lay beside her in the nights of that September, while she shivered and wept, and I traced the tattoos of her mouth. There I had gashed her skin with an obsidian knife, and rubbed in soot to complete her passage into womanhood; now, it seemed, it was her very soul which had been lacerated. I told her of the honor this meant to her adopted child. I took her to the cage where every day we praised our bear and passed him wine to drink and begged him to carry only good reports of our hospitality. It did no good. Lustrous bit her tongue and redoubled her tears, wresting herself from my grip and fleeing home, throwing herself before the lilac *inua* fetish in the northeast corner of the hut.

On the day of the feast, though, she was resigned. With the other women she baked a tangy meal of dumplings and spicy cakes, and set it before us. I went privately and whispered to my bear, and now found myself overwhelmed with grief. I patted his narrow snout and gave him the confections I'd stored away from the kids, and then I turned away with my eyes blurry and went inside, and shaved the beard from my neck with a nicked, rusty razor, and hacked the hair from my forehead and shaved the stubble clean. The children were singing when I came out into the luminous, cloudless day; the women swayed and clapped their hands, inducing trance. It was a glorious misery. One by one the other men came from their huts, skin pale and bloody where they had shaved their foreheads. We danced, crying to our fetishes, striking the ground hard with our feet, begging the bear's forgiveness, calling for his advice. Arrows whistled between us, blunt and stinging, striking the bear in his cage. His paws went up to protect his face. I found myself laughing, reaction-formation, and I ripped a bow from some-body's hands and flung an arrow at my son.

I do not think I was fully conscious when we ran to the cage and dragged the stunned animal out. He had drunk much *sake*, I suppose he was drunker than us. He waddled between us on his clumsy back legs, and waited patiently as we lashed him upright to a post and jammed a chunk of wood in his jaws. My cousin Valid handed me a pole; together, we strangled the bear into insensibility. Something was placed in my hand. It caught the sun's autumnal brilliance. I had carried the same blade with me into the den when I had captured this winter cub.

He died without pain, without waking. His spirit ascended, carrying our messages. Now he is walking the earth in a new body, hungry for honey, rollicking in snow drifts.

We caught every drop of his blood and drank its salty warmth, smearing it into our beards and hair until we took on the guise of a party of axe-murderers.

Lustrous, like all the women who have given a bear suck, grew quiet and strangely patient in the years that followed. My uncle took the pelt, when the feast was done and the bear brought through the shattered east window of the chief's hut, and had it tanned. Shortly after that last of the great feasts I was called away to continue my studies, and took up my role finally as the Bear's Stead, walking the endless paths of the vacuum fluctuations, and in that sacred duty I was comforted always by the warmth of my bear's brown saggy, baggy pelt. If the robots messed with him, I'd strip the bastards down for junk.

Purple dusk, under a mandarin star flecked with sun-spot whorls. They were gone. Distant crashing in the afternoon forest, diminishing. I pelted through the grass toward the trees, cursing.

A vertigo whir in the pit of my brain made me stumble. My Liss had shifted to microwave, two gigahertz straight to my soft neuro-tissues. The power was too low for anyone else to pick it up; his imposed and disembodied voice demodulated in the asymmetrical synaptic array of my cortical rind, and I "heard" him without any difficulty. Generally the process is illegal, and I wouldn't recommend it anyway; it can make your nose bleed.

"This is Roger, your Life Support System. You'll never catch them on foot. Hang on a moment and I'll change our co-ordinates. Okay?"

"I hear you," I said.

"I've found the band they're talking to one another on," Roger said. "It's way too fast for one-to-one transcription, but I can slow it down for you."

"Put it on," I said, chafing.

"Scrawniest animal I've ever seen. It seems to have no internal organs."

"I don't get any EEG, Smith. I think you've killed it."

"Oh Jesus." A pause. *"Maybe it's not a symbiont. Maybe the primary creature moults. You know, sloughs off its outer skin."*

"If I didn't know better, Smith, I'd place it in the Ursidae *family, from back in the USSR."*

"Christ, Marx, you really get my goat sometimes. You're the most obdurate, jingoistic reductionist I've ever . . ."

An indigo jump. The robots faced each other at the lip of a cliff, with nothing beyond them but bruised sky. We stood on rock, blue-grey basalt, the kind formed when lava vomits up red-hot and poisonous from a world's guts and quenches fast: it's glassy and hard, hard. A laser reference beam speared out from the belly-button of the huge columnar robot, scanning my airborne, spread-eagled, slowly rotating pelt.

"That's my property, you son of a glitch," I screamed. "Put it down at once. What the fuck do you think you're playing at?"

There was a noisy guffaw inside my head, which turned into a peal of laughter. Through it, I heard the robots say with startlement:

"It's the ghost."

"He's angry, but at least he's not dead."

"I never thought the ghost was dead. I was talking about this . . ."

They'd completed their conversation long before the Liss-slowed transcription ran out, and my bear bundled itself up neatly in the air and deposited itself on the rock in front of me. The robots edged closer together.

Frustrated and enraged, I yelled, "Roger, is that you laughing? Shut the fuck up." The snickering cut out abruptly. I picked up the pelt and shook it out. No damage that I could see. "What's the joke?"

Resentfully, the Liss said: "This is Roger, your . . ."

"I *know* who it is, you cretinous dummy. What was so funny?"

"I should have thought it was obvious. Didn't you wonder why the Smith robot has no arms? It uses an external pinch effect for manipulation."

"So?"

"Bowsprit, really—it's Adam Smith's Invisible Hand!" I was totally baffled by now. "And?"

"Mother of Fire," the Liss snapped irritably, "you humans are so ignorant. Look, it doesn't bear exegesis. The essence of wit is concision, an unexpected and pleasing juxtaposition of—"

"Explain!" I roared.

In a dry, marked manner, Roger said: "Adam Smith (1723–90), b. Kirkcaldy, d. Edinburgh, proposed in his 'An Inquiry into the Nature and Causes of the Wealth of Nations' (1776) that the sum of independent entrepreneurial actions, each governed by self-interest alone, tends to an equilibration identical with maximal societal well-being. This cybernetic effect Smith likened to the benign influence of an Invisible Hand, which . . ."

"Enough." Again, the Liss fell silent instantly. Match and game. Ears and tail. The two robots were creeping closer to me, somehow forlorn and hang-dog. I hung the pelt over my shoulders.

"Ahem," said Marx, sagging back on its threadbare tires. "Sir Ghost, please accept our apologies. We hope this regrettable incident has not caused you too much mental anguish."

"All's well that ends well," I said gruffly. My anger, deep and seething, was all directed a' Roger now. It occurs to me for the first time, my small's that perhaps my Liss meant it that way. He was shrewd, shrewd.

I regarded the robots speculatively, recalling Roger's surmise that they were fifth columnists, black hole time-bombs. There wasn't any record of mammoth gravitational collapse in the immediate future, but the records were such a shambles that nothing would have surprised me. "Tell me, are you robots hard-wired to tell the truth?"

"Categorically," Marx affirmed stoutly.

"If you'll forgive me, sir," Smith added, "that was a

rather pointless exchange. You've run up against the paradox of the Cretan Liar, sir. If Marx is a liar, how can you trust a word he says?"

"Quite so." I cudgeled my brains. Stepping closer, I discerned a line of print stamped into their looming hulls, one in English, one in Russian. Illiterate in either, I asked Roger, "Is that the statutory warrant that these robots are programmed to obey the Three Laws? Answer yes or no."

"Yes."

With a note of resonant ritual, Marx said: "We avow our adherence to the Three Laws of Microprocessors."

"First," said Smith, " 'Thou shalt love mankind with thy whole mind and thy whole heart and thy whole soul.' "

"Second," cried Marx, " 'Thou shalt love thy neighbor as thyself.' "

"Third," finished Smith, clashing its heels together in a crisp salute, " 'Thou shalt love thyself.' "

I was shaken; I'd imagined the behemoths under the control of a more stringent algorithm than that. "It seems rather open to interpretation."

"Ethics is like that," Marx said. "It's a Gödel problem, like the Cretan Liar. Don't fret, though, sir. We're situationalists, but we opt from a rather comprehensive metaphysical consensus."

That seemed to dispose of the Trojan Horse hypothesis, or at least to put it beyond testing. There was a lurid flash across the sky, and a heinous booming. The Glorious Republic was dropping down out of parking orbit. I had to get back to Lyric Music. My hand went automatically to my telephone. Smith swivelled.

"Before you go, sir Ghost, we wonder if you'd settle a private dispute?"

"Hurry it up, then."

"We've deduced that you're a time-traveller, sir. I say you're from the remote past. Marx maintains that you must be from the future. We have a wager riding on the matter, you see."

Fuji-no-yama, mountain of the Grandmother, old Huchi the Fire Goddess, came howling and red-faced into the world in a single catastrophic night, in 285 BC. Lustrous and I sat in a sundeck on her southern slope, sheltered from the cold wind, gazing over Suruga Bay, the day the Institute engineers first tore merons out of the zero-energy vacuum and accidentally ripped our birthplace apart. Under us the earth rumbled, shook the deck, tossed little Woodchip out of his tripod-hanging litter. Fujisan belched, mildly. The black, boiling clouds out of the north took hours to reach us, and by then Sakhalin, old Karafuto, had wallowed like a butchered whale back into the depths. Subtract my grief from that moment, my smalls, and you might guess how well the shock and incredulity which is left over serves as a metaphor to my reaction at Smith's easy question. I blinked at them like a puppy and said at last, "What an extraordinary suggestion. I am a scholar, no more and no less."

"A scholar you may be," Smith said, "but you are clearly not from this era. Your technology's a dead giveaway. Of course we can't compel you if you decline to humor our perfectly reasonable curiosity."

You can see my fix. Whether I told them the truth or not, these garrulous buggers would blab from one end of the galaxy to the other. I'd be slammed into a loop straight back to the beginning of insertion, and the scale of the thing was so gross that we'd probably get quantum hysteresis locking us out of the entire period. We'd never find out what happened on the day the empire fell—and it would all be my fault.

"Would you like to hear our reasoning?" asked Marx. "You're not a Neanderthal, though there's a striking physical resemblance. You're not from the Glorious Republic —if they had equipment of your class they wouldn't be farting around in starships. You can't be a spirit, sir Ghost, because . . . well, for example, it seems vanishingly unlikely that spirits need little black boxes to piss into. Phenotype too close to human for an alien, and none have ever been detected anyway. That leaves parallel universes and time-travel. Conservation laws militate against the first, paradoxa against the second. We're rooting for the conservation laws."

Their logic was shot to shit, but it held up well enough in terms of their contemporary physics. It didn't leave me any choice.

"Okay, guys, I'll come clean." I put authority into my voice: "Under the provisions of the Three Laws, I bind you both never to divulge, whether by action or implication, the conjectures you have advanced about me, or the facts I shall now reveal."

"Freedom of Information!" Smith protested.

"A nation which hampers the free flow of data," Marx cried vehemently, "is a nation in chains."

"That's rich," I said, "coming from you two."

"That was in the past," Smith said in an injured tone. "Circumstances alter cases."

"The dialectic has moved on," added Marx. "Now that the negation has negated the negation—"

"Be quiet," I told them. "Do you understand my stipulation?"

"Naturally, but we don't have to like it."

"I'm a historian from the future."

Marx crowed. Snarling, Smith booted it savagely in the tire. "Will the Glorious Republic win, or did the Empire rally at the last?"

"Don't be simple-minded," I said. "The actual outcome wouldn't make the faintest sense to you. History is always opaque to its participants. Now you can tell me something in return. Just a moment." My Liss had announced himself in my queasy brain-tissues. "What is it?"

"Bowsprit, I've been keeping tabs on the Emperor. He's been flashing from place to place like a demented mosquito, but now he's back in his hut. And the barbarians have started landing. I think we should get back to where the action is."

"Hold it. I'll give you the word." I looked up again at Smith's towering presence. "I'm puzzled, Smith. How could you suppose that I'm from the past? Time travel never existed until my people discovered it."

"Well, I thought you might have been a Cro-Magnon and got it from the Old Ones."

"That's absurd. The Neanderthals never had time travel."

"No, no, not the Neanderthals—those Old Ones who led the galactics out of the home world when the New Humans appeared."

I goggled, my smalls, and felt that first radiant crack appear in my preconceptions which heralds a paradigm cataclysm. I must have been ripe for drastic change; there was no strangled clawing to preserve my verities. In some quarters, this has been attributed to my genius. Modesty aside, my sproggies, it wasn't; simply, I'd taken such a mental thumping that cognitive dissonance seemed my natural condition, and impossible truths bobbed on the surface for all to see.

"But you said no aliens had ever been detected."

"The Old Ones are hardly 'aliens,'" Smith said primly. "Besides, They're all asleep."

"They're hibernating under the sands, on the planet Marx."

"I've never even heard of it."

"You must have. Fourth planet out from the sun, in the home system."

"This is Roger, your Life Support System. It means Mars."

"Don't you mean Mars?"

"The Red Planet," added Roger.

"The Red Planet?"

"That's what I said, haw, haw, haw!" shrieked Marx with delight, and spun its tires wildly on the basalt shelf. Smith put an end to these comic capers with another ringing kick to its undercarriage.

"But seriously, sir Time Traveller," Smith told me, "I'm surprised you haven't deduced the Old Ones yourself. A historian should comprehend the import of chronologies."

"Make it snappy, the Chairman's on the ground."

"Most of the time, Mars is a rotten place to live. The atmospheric pressure is less than one mm, and all its water and carbon dioxide is frozen in huge layers on the poles. But the Martian orbit has a lot of eccentricity, around point zero nine, so there are massive precessional seasons. Every twenty-five thousand years it swings into the ecozone. The atmosphere comes off the poles, lakes form, ozone heats the air and blocks the UV. The Old Ones come up to the surface and play god games."

"They . . . interfered with *Homo sapiens?*"

"You bet. Last summer was twelve thousand years ago, and They stirred up the New Humans into inventing agriculture. As far as we can make out, the New Humans were a long term project of Theirs. They got them started several seasons ago, mutating them off the original stock by fuzzing their psi capacities. That might have been a mistake, because it turned them into a bloodthirsty gang of mothers. The Neanderthals couldn't hack it, so the Old Ones lifted them out thirty-seven thousand years ago and gave them the rest of the galaxy to play with. Now the chickens are coming home to roost."

I swore vilely for a while, and slapped my head with the heel of my hand, and went over to the edge of the cliff and watched the sunset. Flocks of dark native birds drifted like blown soot over the black trees. I hadn't seen any domestic pets around the Emperor's palace, no cats or dogs, not even a trained parrot. The old galactics preferred to domesticate people. Had Lyric Music appreciated the ancient embedded parallel in his borrowed action, when we'd met beside his garden patch? Into my mind he'd snuck, deft as a thief, to pluck out our Ainu greeting rituals. There'd been no time for search, to check the catalog; it must have been quite automatic.

Staring into the darkening sky I put my hands on the top of my skull, as he had done, my eyes blurry with anger, with truly bitter anger, and drew down my fingers to the sides of my face, stroking the heavy fur of my beard, whining in greeting across the unspeakable light years to my discovered masters and creators snug and dreaming like hibernating bears under the frozen sands of Mars.

"Hello," I screamed, pawing at my cheeks. I whined again, salutation of custom, the courtesy of two Ainu warriors met in a bamboo trail. "Hello there, you bastards, you sons of bitches, you tawdry gods. Wake up, get out of bed, your experiment's proceeding nicely, right on time no doubt, hello, hello, you fucking heartless shits," and I barked like a dog, I went down on my hands and knees on the hard, hard rock and bayed a canine howl of fury and revulsion, while the two robots from old Earth stared at me in consternation and Roger my Life Support System dithered in my uncomprehending ears.

Before the fall of Sakhalin into the broken sea, my greatest pleasure was in taking out the dogs to fetch in a haul of fish. I had a wonderful dog in those days, a kelpie named Beadle, true son of the animals bred by our Amurian cousins in the Murray River basin, in ancient Australia. He would stand forward proudly on the prow of a dugout when we surged out with our lethal gaffs to hunt fur seals, but his great skill, and our mutual joy, was to lead the pack into the waves.

Even in the warmer months, when we fished, the ocean waters bit like aconite, but the dogs never flinched. They would run cheering and snapping ahead of us through the dense bamboo, churning up the gritty sand at the shore, falling into line at our command. Beadle went always to the head of the righthand queue, straining to be off, ears pricked, never looking back, waiting for my cry. I would stand there between the lines of animals, my sproggies, with the salty wind in my throat, the dogs quivering a hundred meters distant on either hand, and I would give the ringing, harsh command, and in they would dash, slashing the waters in a demonstration of Euclid's arbitrary axiom, and you could sense the deep shock of dread which vibrated through the schools of fish moving blindly in the water, you could sense it at the tendrils of your skin.

Another cry, and Beadle would turn, sharp left, and paddle resolutely across the stinging tide toward the wheeling dogs that came to meet him. Deployed, then, an animate net, they would ride the surge and wait for the signal. I'd howl it out, and in they'd come like torpedoes, curving to a crescent, driving the terrified salmon before them, driving the divine fish toward us. Then into the water we'd splash to greet them, no tools in our hands, scooping up the threshing chum-fish, the sacred salmon, the gift they'd brought us. Once purchased on the sea floor, each dog would dart and harry the fattest fish in sight, clamp it in his tender mouth, run and deliver it up before shaking off the chill in a cloud of sparkles. To me would Beadle come, for though we shared the dogs without ownership he knew me for his master, and a plump fish would be my reward for allowing him this sport. After we'd cleaned our catch, I always gave Beadle as many heads as he could eat.

I panted for a time, my cheek pressed to the ground.

"You're making a fool of yourself, Bowsprit," Roger told me.

"We're their doggies," I said. "We fetch in their fish while they sleep, and they graciously allow us the heads."

Acutely, Roger said, "I've always taken you for a religious man, Bowsprit Bear's Stead. Would you prefer the history of humanity to have been the outcome of a random process?"

"Better than this," I mumbled.

I rolled over. For the first time I noticed the droplets of fierce light falling with all their ominous threat into Lyric Music's venerable sanctuary. Roger was pestering me, but I got to my feet and watched the starships make planetfall. Chairman Pan-Ku and his staff were already in conference with the naked, complex savage who thought he ruled all the bright pin-points which shortly would be coming out over my head and the ones I couldn't see under my feet because a world was in the way. I experienced the demented clarity of manic hysteria, hard and faceted and feverish. It was like the euphoria in which I'd slain my adopted son, my brother bear, but where thought then had been bound in the infrangible constraints of ritual it was now exalted, utterly disconnected from precedent, a mad surgeon dismembering something warm and breathing and unearthly.

"Roger, are we linked to the robots?"

"Certainly. How else could they perceive us?"

"Not just information. Can we affect them?" Shivering, I pulled the bearskin tighter about me. "Sorry, of course we can. We already did."

"Right, when we churned up Marx's black hole. Unprecedented. It's clearly a function of Lyric Music's incomparable magic, a direct consequence of his psychic rapport with us. The robots are tuned to him, and they're getting a feed through his personal wormhole mosaic."

Even though my teeth were clattering together, I didn't feel cold. I didn't feel anything much, my sproggies. "Roger, can we use that channel to destabilize the holes?" There was a shriek of anguished remonstration from the eavesdropping robots. I ignored them. "Roger?"

After a lengthy pause, "Bowsprit, forgive me but you're not being rational. Your physiological indicators . . ."

"Just answer the question."

"Yes, we can."

My legs gave way, and I sat down again on the rock. "Three points. Can we do it without getting caught by whiplash? Is it feasible to cut Lyric Music out of the channel? And do we have any evidence in the historical records of Marx and Smith still being here after the conference?"

"We don't have any post-Earth record of them, period. That could mean anything. If you want to take them out you'll just have to risk precipitating a temporal loop. But for Huchi's sake, Bowsprit, they're Good Guys!"

Wearily, I said, "I know. But they're tattletales. I can't run the risk of leaving them intact; Lyric might get past

my prohibition." The robots were keening pitifully, met-
aphorically wringing their hands. "What about side-
effects?"

"I can manage it." I'd never heard the Liss so bitter.

"Do it."

Blue-white light flared like a nova. A quantum filter
kept it bearable, even beautiful. All the megatons of those
poor, clever machines went into a pinch beam half a
millimeter wide, straight up into the sky. Winds howled
in a superheated micro-vortex, and thunder hollered.
When my eyes had come back to normal there was a
small bubbling lava pool on the clifftop, sizzling with leaves
ripped from the trees below, and no sign at all of the
robots from old Earth.

"Are you sufficiently purged?" the Liss asked snidely.
"Can we get to the conference now?"

"Change of plan, Roger," I said. "Take me home."

"Whaaat? Bowsprit, do you know how much this jaunt
cost?"

"I know. Move it."

"How often do you get to see the greatest empire in
history carved up?"

"Someone else can do it," I said.

"Mission aborted," Roger sighed. Through the microwave link I heard bat squeaks, tiny flutterings at the
back of my tongue: the Liss setting up homing signals
through the Dirac Ocean, laying co-ordinates for our return to the future. So must Lyric Music's swollen, tender
mind vibrate to the tachyon whispers from a galaxy of
active brains. Was he yet aware of the catastrophic de-
mise of his metal pets, or had Roger's counter-magic
spared him that? I imagined the pang of their termina-
tion going into him like a needle, trembling his voice, his
hand, as he sat with the New Humans as he'd planned
for decades, ceding them the Empire.

"Done," said Roger. "Before we go, I have one thing
to tell you, Bowsprit, if you can contain your *Weltschmerz*
for a moment."

You can believe, my smalls, that there was an edge to
his voice.

"Go ahead."

"Have you ever paused to wonder what it's like to be
me?"

It took me unawares; I laughed unbelievingly.

"Gods of the hearth! Spare me your sanctimonious allegories."

Fallen starships burned victorious in the darkness, cities of light and power. The birds, disturbed, were trying to get to sleep against their better judgement.

"No, you've never wondered." Was it pity or contempt I heard in Roger's tone? "Poor bear messenger, how insulated you keep yourself! Always the observer, eh? Wrapped up in your heavy protective fur."

"Shut up," I said shrilly, the sound petulant even to me.

"I," the Liss said, "have always known where I came from. Your people made me. You put me together from micro-laminates and you programmed me in a factory and you sent me out to do a job."

"That's right," I yelled. "You're a machine. I'm not. I am not a machine."

"My thoughts run ten thousand times faster than yours. I am never deactivated. While you plod in your clumsy pedestrian way from idea to slow idea, I sing in my soul like a dolphin. But I do not deny what I am. Yes, of course, Bowsprit. I too am a machine. Allow me to recommend a stance of adaptive despair."

We torqued into the meron flux, grey banners of mockery.

"It's okay, brother," Roger said gently. "You'll get used to it."

All I could find within me was the image of my dog
Beadle, alert, obedient, gulled. He was a wonderful animal, wonderful.

Carol Emshwiller grew up in the town of
Ann Arbor, Michigan, and was graduated
from the University of Michigan. She has
lived most of her adult life on Long Island,
an existence leavened by forays to such
places as the MacDowell Colony, Rio de
Janeiro, California . . . and by the winning
of various monetary grants to further her
writing. Anatole Broyard describes her work
as "a wilderness of economy." Emshwiller
writes solely in the short story mode and
ordinarily eschews plot in favor of more
objective concerns; witness her collection,
Joy in Our Cause.

There are reputed to be a limited number of
possible story situations, anyhow, of which
boy meets girl is one. Boy almost meets
girl is another.

Omens

BY CAROL EMSHWILLER

Wait.
Don't reach out.
Stand still or whatever sort of spell there is here on
21st Street and 6th Avenue will break before the light
changes and it says WALK in green letters. But what can
happen after that first glance except that they go on, she
to an Italian grocery store (she certainly must be Italian), he to the nearest coffee shop where there's magic
in those boomerang shaped designs on the counter top,
magic where you might walk through a mirror so suddenly
you'd never know you were doing it.
And don't go near those Spanish-speaking short-order

cooks. He knows this. Hides his eyes with his hands pretending headache. Eats a sixth of a pizza. Drinks tea.

Well, how can a man like that be loved without casting a spell, too big, too fat, too hairy, too old and with one secret lewd desire. Count seven steps and seven steps and seven steps or nine. Walk around this particular block three times with umbrella up thinking: Remember Mother. She had a right to be angry that last year before she finally died. Remember (vaguely) almost dying, too. That was the only time ever held hands with mother.

Three days pass.

Another meeting is unlikely, but now he has found himself standing next to her at Nedick's. He spills mustard on his beard and doesn't even know it. Guesses it, though, but isn't sure. Beard always was mustard colored right around his mouth anyway.

She avoids his face. (He sees that.) He doesn't have his glasses on and can't read the runes on her purse. Certainly she would have liked to turn him into a big dog with his fur full of burrs. He wears his pants too low. (Everything he owns is brown.) They don't speak.

It's crazy! Now they have met in Macy's basement, both buying identical black wool scarves. He smiles. Frowns. Smiles. Winks. A tear comes to that eye and he turns away to wipe it. When he looks back he sees her old tan sweater already off into the crowds beyond. He waits for his change and then leaves in the opposite direction. It's the only thing to do. Sits hopefully in the front of Chock Full O'Nuts for twenty minutes. Shuffles back to apartment in basement of brownstone thinking of Nietzsche and the *Birth of Tragedy*.

So, while thirty to forty pigeons mate in Central Park, while six or eight men are goosing women in the subway, while the first conference on prostitution is taking place, he says, "She loves me, she loves me not," breaking out the teeth of his plastic comb and she has a sudden headache as though someone were sticking pins in her doll.

Think twice.
Think three times.

Saturday maybe take ferry to Staten Island. (He once had a friend there.) So, whispering a secret number, he does that but misses her by half an hour because he gets lost in the subway. It's the same on the way back. Sits on deck in the rain thinking: Mother had a right to be angry, dying a slow death every day and not even knowing it (but she suspected). And then one tube down the left nostril, needle in arm, etc., etc., etc. Nothing left but bones by now. Teeth and hair. The boat hums. A sad guitar plays in his mind. (Classical). The *Times* said rain, but he could feel that in his knees before, anyway. Thinks: Me, a little younger, a little thinner, and that girl "under a sheet," as we used to say when we were fourteen, fifteen. I'm very gentle. She's never known anyone as gentle as I am. Until suddenly. And right now. Very nice. Just fine. Fine. "The best I ever had," she says.

Be the last one off the ferry.

Thinks: An encounter group might teach me to touch my fellow man.

Dear Mother; I've been having a glorious time. Brief moments of . . . Well, it's wonderful how sometimes the penis . . . in conjunction with the thoughts, that is . . .

Dear Mother; I've moved to Florida. It's a lot better. I've found love. More than you ever thought I would.

Dear Mother; Look at me now!

Dear Mother; In the forest . . . the smell of pine needles blocks out all else. I lie back. I shut my eyes . . .

Dear Mother; (May fourth, 1973 or 1974.) We have forgotten all about you by now. We are happy.

A week goes by.

He writes: Dear one who has not read the *Birth of Tragedy*. (Instinctively he knows this.) I'll meet you at the movies at the Museum of Modern Art. We'll have lunch in the garden. You are all goodness, kindness, charm, all delicacy, all sensitivity. You are artistic. I know because I can read faces like the palms of hands. I also see that my own handwriting is ever optimistic. But I wanted to tell you most of all that, from my lifeline, I know I will die suddenly and in great pain. I write you this because I want you to know something intimate and important about me.

A week goes by.

He comes home a little late the next day.

"Is that you?"

"What?"

"Listen, this is important."

Who can that be?

"Listen," Mother calls from back room. (Somehow she's not dead after all and she still doesn't even know she's dying.)

"I've been waiting all this time to tell you this. I heard it on the radio. Something in the hot dogs. I forget what. You should be careful. And taxis, too, you should be careful."

"Yes. Yes."

"Yesterday I thought I'd try to get up . . ."

But yesterday they robbed her of her TV set and all her blankets right before her eyes, and they robbed him of his umbrella and they took the ten lucky silver dollars in his top bureau drawer. Tomorrow they will surely come for the radio and the leather bookbag he sometimes carries his lunch in.

Dear Mother; I have moved to the country . . . to a country where grown men are crying every day and drinking themselves into stupors. You wouldn't like it here so don't ask me any questions about where it is.

Certainly she must have gotten a second chance on life at the age of fifty-five or sixty. Took it in exchange for her only son, paid in advance. How did it happen? "Raymond, Raymond, fat old cave man." He sits now in Central Park reading from the *Birth of Tragedy:*

. . . "The old tune, why does it wake me?" And what once seemed to us like a hollow sigh from the core of being now merely wants to tell us how "desolate and empty the sea." And where, breathless, we once thought we were being extinguished in a convulsive distention of all our feelings, and little remained to tie us to our present existence, we now hear and see only the hero wounded to death, yet not dying, with his despairing cry: "Longing! Longing! . . ."

And she, who has never read this, comes to Central Park no doubt looking for the simple, outdoor life (as he is) wishing there really was a god of the forest hiding there. She will look up at the new buds and see His face instead of buildings. He'll be tall, brown, thin, bearded, beautiful and invisible . . .

Tall, fat, bearded and all in brown sits in Central Park now facing West and visible, though not too. Boy steps on his leg. Dog pees on his book, the *Birth of Tragedy*. He doesn't notice this till later. He's talking to himself in stage whispers. Says, "If I see two 747s and six regular planes in the space of half an hour, and surely I will, then she'll come ten minutes later." She does, only she's early and she's looking for a tall, thin, invisible man who peeks out from behind the largest trees, and he, he has his back to her and is busy counting planes. He notes that the shadows of the planes sometimes go right over him. It can't be by coincidence.

Discovers peed-on book, feels bruised leg and thinks: There'll be one more bad thing happen before any good ones therefore how can they meet today? Thinks: Mother had a right to be angry, dying a slow death like that and not even knowing it until the very last moment and then not any time to say what she really meant. Maybe I should have moved her to the country. Yes.

So it's love, love, love and six kisses on the surface of the mirror . . . six kisses on the surface of the water in the sink. He finds a secret message in the dust on the old upright. Something tells him THIS IS YOUR LAST CHANCE! (He suspected it all along anyway.) Like a drop in the barometer, it gives him a headache.

LAST CHANCE FOR WHAT?

Murder, rape or incest?

Think twice. Can this really be love?

And think of it! Mother alive and fairly well and living as happily as could be expected in the back room, calling out, "Hey. Hey there. Is that you? Is that you out there? Who's out there?"

No answer.

Never marry a woman with a thin upper lip. He heard that someplace. Well, it doesn't matter now.

Is his wife his mother?

Or the other way around?

Meanwhile remember that condemned men are allowed one last phone call, one last good meal, one more cigarette, one more jerk-off.

Sometimes it feels as though the sky is full of swans

and the sound of their big wings . . . a few feathers falling down. They're hardly built to fly, but *they* do it. Dearest one, he'll write: You'll know me by the way I look at
you, by the way I walk, my bulbous nose. I'll be older
than you expected. I'll be looking around, humming. I
have only one secret, unacceptable, lewd desire.

(Nietzsche loved his sister and went mad.)

Go on do it. Make one magic gesture in that direction.
Fill in all the Os on three pages of the *Birth of Tragedy*,
but if you miss one O it's all for nothing.

Go on do it. Nobody looking. Hand to crotch. Yes,
somebody looking. Oh well, some other time.

Stay away from the river.

Thinks: I already know my future.

But no. That can't be. Certainly a death one of these
days and other chance meetings. She will drop her purse,
or lose an antique brooch. Cairn Gorm, they call that
kind of stone. That will make her Scotch. Dear Scotch
person; I'm a mild-mannered man. I expect to come into
a small sum of money soon and then I'll move to the
country. Also you should know that I snore. But sometimes I can't sleep. I think my breath smells. My teeth
need attention. My mother is dead.

But wait. He must have gotten the right combination for
once because right here in his room, after having blacked
out dozens of Os, his back to the light, and having muttered forbidden words that a long time ago his mother
said not to say, there she is. Not *Her,* though. A tall,
blonde, silent creature with eyes like a fox. This will be
an episode in his life he ought to forget.

He's wary. She's wary, too. Not a single word.

He tells himself she's no human being. Can't be, so it
doesn't matter. Any kind of strange and secret desires OK
under these circumstances. Get her to come at him from
behind with that that he keeps for these purposes. (He
remembered to bring a lubricant.) For a minute he knows
he doesn't love his mother and is guilty of it and of this,
too. (He can't stand the sight of blood or bruises, so has
to find other ways.) All night will be $100. It's gone up.
All right. All right, but not in this place. "To hell with
you. To hell with you. To hell with you." She doesn't
mind. Neither would the other. It wasn't *Her,* though.

He'll forget it by tomorrow.

Yes, of course, there she is, the real one, sitting on the steps of the library with her lunch. It must be Spring. Her dress is a peculiar shade of purple and black and he wonders what it means.

LAST CHANCE!

"Hello," he says. "I saw you someplace recently."

Well, she doesn't want to be picked up by an older, fat man with spots on his tie.

"I'm a philosopher," he says. "I know the future. All that can happen is nothing happens. Other people have babies, but not you and I. Life or death, with us it's a long time between events. Some people live at a different pace."

He sits down very slowly while she gets up. He supposes she is thinking she won't have lunch on these steps anymore. This is just like life, he thinks, no murder, no rape or incest and not even going on a diet, shaving beard or whatever, but maybe getting robbed of a few dollars on the way home today.

And to think that Mother continues to live without either TV or radio!

Tragedy is easy. A matter of waiting, sitting here on the steps in the sun.

Scott Sanders keeps from perishing in the
English Department of Indiana University
and has recently begun to publish fiction.
He has sold three stories: one to *New Dimensions* ("Eros Passage"), one to *Fantasy
& Science Fiction* ("Terrarium"), and one to
us (see below)—all loosely grounded in, or
departing from, the novel on which he is
working (also called *Terrarium*).

Indeed, if one has lived all one's life insulated from eyes and weather, in a world
where fox and turtle, bear and beaver, may
equally have been imaginary or are extinct,
it is not easy to trust one's instincts.

Touch the Earth

BY SCOTT SANDERS

The world was so recent that many things lacked names,
and in order to indicate them it was necessary to point.
                                    —Gabriel Garcia Marquez

The nine conspirators took care to vanish from Ohio City
along separate paths. On the agreed night, Marn set out
through the labyrinth of avenues, carrying her fear as if
it were a dish of mercury. The last lights she saw were
the neon signs at the gamepark, where the pedbelt ended.
Every further step pushed her deeper into the unlit ruins
of the factories. Even in the dark she could sense the
refinery towers, the snarl of pipes, the pumps with their
great hinged elbows jutting domeward. The gritting beneath her boots told her she had reached the gravel, and
there welling up before her was the shadow of the oil
tank, the meeting place, like a massive concentration of
the darkness.

She pressed her ear against the tank, but could hear no
murmur of voices, no rumble of carts. What if no one
else had come?

65

Her face felt clammy behind the mask. As she brushed her gloved hands over the metal, searching for the drain valve, paint flaked away with tiny snicking sounds. When at last she found the valve, she hesitated, a fist clenched on each side of the spoked wheel. Behind her the city called and called. Twenty-eight years of memory worked in her, turned her around to face the dazzle of lights. Nearby, the gamepark glowed orange and green. Further away the biogas plants and agrifactories flared yellow. And further still, at the core of the city where her own chamber hummed without ears to hear it, the towers blazed upward like a mountain afire. Overhead, the ped-belts scrawled their curves of light against the darkness, reminding her of the beaded trails left by particles in bubble chamber photographs. Crystalline, glittering city.

Let go. That is past now, dead. We will make a new place.

She tugged at the valve wheel, then peered through the opening into darkness. "It's Marn!" she cried into the tank, louder than she meant to. *Marn, Marn* the tank echoed back.

Then light flared inside, and she could make out Jurgen's shaggy head silhouetted within the opening. "It's about time," he called to her.

She slithered through the valve and emerged, blinking, inside the tank. Her mask and gloves and suit were smeared with oil. Six, seven, eight: the others were all here, muffled in their worksuits and gauzy masks.

"Welcome," came Hinta's voice, and then *welcome, welcome,* all around the echoing grease-filmed walls of the tank.

Marn whispered greetings. Safe here with the others, surrounded by the crates and tools for the settlement, she began trembling. The fear she had balanced so carefully now threatened to spill. The valve, she remembered. After one last glance back the way she had come, at the city lights snared in the opening like stars in a telescope, she cranked the valve shut.

"How's our slowpoke chemist?" Jurgen asked. "No problems coming over?"

Marn shook her head.

"Good. We're ready to go. Your crates are the only ones left to check."

So she had come last. Marn lowered her eyes until

the man's bulky shape withdrew. From her sleeve pocket she took the inventory of medicines, catalysts, acids, all the chemicals they expected to need on the outside but would not soon be able to synthesize there. While she checked through the list, the others were pushing loaded dollies ahead of them into the pipeline. Jurgen went first, since he had discovered this exit from the city, had marked the spot seventeen kilometers out from the hermetic energy wall where the pipe broke ground. As usual he wore no hood, so his shaggy hair brushed against the top of the pipe. Lee went next, then slouching Rand and waddling Norba, then all the others, each one with gait and posture unique as a thumbprint. Marn followed Hinta into the pipe, carrying the last flare with her.

After four hours of slogging, their throats gasping the stale air, the conspirators reached the spot Jurgen had marked. They all shouldered close to him, almost touching, chests heaving, while his torch cut through the steel wall of the pipe. Then Marn smelled them for the first time. Their animal smell seeped through the deodes. She smelled herself. She had never been this hot, this lathered with sweat, this lost in her body.

The torch cut through the last few centimeters of steel, and the section of wall tilted outward. Daylight blinded her. Tears seeped around her closed lids, yet she wanted to look out, to see the Earth. Films of the outside had never given her a notion of this light. Unfiltered, it poured down on her like flame.

No one spoke, no one moved. Marn squinted out past a haze of tears at blurred trees, boulders, vines. She did not know the name of anything she saw. Green—a radiant chaos of green was all she could make out. So she fixed her gaze on a single plant, its twin leaves canted upward like awnings, a bud sheltered underneath, brown-tipped, potent. If she stared at it long enough the bud might open, a flower might burst forth, proving in this one mutation that she really was outdoors, in the wilds.

"Great God in the morning," Jurgen finally murmured.

Marn let out a breath, as if she had come to the surface after swimming underwater.

Jurgen leapt first. He thudded heavily and tumbled forward onto hands and knees. The rest followed, dropping gingerly to earth. To *Earth*. Marn lifted one boot, set it down again on the littered soil, amazed to find herself actually standing on the planet. She took a few cautious steps. The others were doing the same, shuffling like toddlers. Giddy, she pranced about. Her boots made the forest floor crackle. The soil yielded beneath her, sprang back, resilient. Her feet were two miracles of lightness. She could hear the others crashing through the undergrowth, their voices thrilling in high-pitched squeals. Her eyes still watered from the raw sunlight. But she could see well enough to tell it was a young forest they had reached. Few of the trees were thicker than her waist. The ground was a tangle of briars.

Jurgen came lumbering toward her, pawing the greenery aside. "Great glorious God in the morning! Let's get that stuff unloaded. Let's build."

"Where?" Marn asked.

"Anywhere. Any blessed where!"

"We need water."

"Then let's find water." And he went crashing away, ignoring the briars that ripped at his suit. In half an hour he was back, with news of a lake. His gloves were slick.

By late afternoon, all of them working with hoods thrown back, masks steamy from sweat, they had cleared a space on the shore and inflated the dome. Only Jurgen kept lugging packets from the supply crates after the dome was sealed. The other eight sheltered inside, panting, thankful for the vault overhead, the relief from sunlight and green. Through the translucent skin of the dome Marn watched Jurgen's bulky shadow pass with arms loaded.

"We've got to take this in small doses," she called out to him. "Leave it for tomorrow."

Jurgen only grunted as he trudged back for another load.

Beside her, Hinta lay with milkywhite hair spread in a halo against the somber brown of the polycloth floor. "He told me once it was the aching made him feel alive," she said.

"He'll kill himself," Marn said.

"Not Jurgen." Hinta rolled onto her side, propped her head on an arm bent at the elbow. Her neck showed pale beneath the edge of the mask. "He'll be the last of us to die."

"Why should we die?"

"You expect to live forever?"

"I thought you meant we'd die soon, out here."

"Who knows?"

Lying back on her water-cushion, Marn stared up at the point in the vault where all the arched sections of the dome met, like a map of tube-lines converging on Ohio City. She imagined the city as a vast printed circuit. Its eighteen million people might have been so many electrons shuttling in a web. She would already be fading from the memories of the few who knew her back there, displaced by video images, flushed away by neuroes and chemmies. "Did you leave anyone behind?" Marn asked the other woman.

"Everybody I care about is right here," Hinta answered. "And you? Do you miss anybody?"

"No, not really. I don't know. Maybe a few people."

"People whose faces you've seen?"

"A few," Marn admitted.

"People you even . . . touched?"

Marn's tongue felt prickly, like a limb gone to sleep. "No one."

"I'm sorry." Hinta lay quietly for several minutes, then cautiously reached out her gloved hand. Hearing the slither of fabric on fabric, Marn rolled away beyond reach.

Outside the dome Jurgen's shadow lurched past, loaded down like a robot porter.

By nightfall, even Jurgen retreated to the dome. Dousing all but one small flare, he took his place among the others, who were lying down on their sleep-cushions, their bodies arrayed like spokes with feet pointing toward the center of the dome.

Despite the near-darkness, Marn rolled away from him before removing her work mask and hood and gloves. She paused, feeling the breath-moistened air on her face. Then she covered herself with the sleep mask and lay down.

Instead of sleeping she listened to the others breathing. Once she heard them, their animal noise was deafening. At first she thought they only seemed loud because she had never slept near more than one person before. Then she realized that she heard their breathing against a background of silence. No electronic hum, no whirr of haulers on the pedbelts, no blare of loudspeakers. As the others drifted into deeper sleep their breathing hushed, and the silence thickened. Marn felt she could almost gather it in her hands, taste it, this dense silence. She

imagined the wheel of bodies as a seed encased in the
dome, the dome encircled by forest, the forest by conti-
nent and oceans, and so on outward in ever larger circles
until Earth and solar system and Milky Way were encom-
passed by the ultimate circle of creation.

For the next eight days Marn would not leave the dome.
She mixed the starter-culture for the bio-digester, and ran
tests on all the samples of fiber and soil and water the
others brought in to her. But she would not remove her
gloves or throw back the hood or venture one step beyond the closed skin of the dome. She bathed in the vat of
purified water. At night, she dosed herself with histaphones
and immunies. Dopey from the drugs, she slept behind
a screen, her ears plugged, and she dreamed of pacing
in her chamber, where there were no eyes or weather.
Still, she woke in the mornings with the word *wilds* resting on her lips like the sediment of a nightmare.

"It's the outside shock," Jurgen reassured her. "Same
thing the sea-miners get, and the health-patrollers. We've
all suffered from it. Don't worry, it'll pass."

Marn glared sullenly back at him, and went about her
work.

Then on the ninth day, at sunset, she forced herself to
go out. The countryside was luminous. For a long time she
stood on the threshold of the dome, fighting against her
dread. Maybe she should throw off all her clothes and
swim in the lake, drown her fear by yielding completely
to the waters, the disorder. The thought made her shudder.

She turned her back on the lake. But the forest was
no more comforting, with its drool of vines, its explosions
of leaves. Only the newly-made works of the settlement
reassured her. Above her head the solar panels swivelled
to catch the last slanting rays of sunlight. The windmills
whirred overhead, sucking power from the breeze. Everywhere she looked around the clearing she saw blueprints
come to life: the filtration tanks, the methane generator,
the six domes for meditation and mindwork clustered
around the large central dome like bubbles on a pool. A
network of glass pathways already crisscrossed the settlement.

Marn chose the widest path and followed it with her
head bent down. The etched green surface of the glass
rasped against her boot treads; through it, she could

vaguely make out the underbed of pebbles. This artificial green held her eyes, kept her from seeing the anarchy of green that overhung the path.

When she finally looked up she found herself a few meters from the pipeline. The slab which Jurgen had cut away still lay in the weeds, its unpainted inner side bright with rust. She scuffed at the redness with her glove. Oxides. Nothing rusted in Ohio City.

She pressed her hooded ear against the sun-warmed pipe, listening, unsure what she wanted to hear. The purr of float cars coming after them? The ticking gears of the city? The hum of her own abandoned chamber?

She could hear nothing. No one would come for them, she felt certain, so long as they stayed outside, never broke the seal around the city. You could lapse into wildness, but you could not return, with your germ-smeared skin and your eyes saturated in green.

"Thinking about going back?"

The voice jerked Marn away from the pipe. Hinta stood on the path, her mask askew, her gloves grimed with dirt. "Just listening," Marn answered.

"Listening?" Hinta repeated the word skeptically.

"Well, aren't you ever tempted?" Marn said.

"Sure I'm tempted, everyone's tempted, to go back, where every inch of life is measured out. Where everything is *made*, while out here"—arms sweeping wide, her milky hair flaring out as she turned—"out here, nothing's made. It just grows. It just *is*."

Watching her, Marn felt that Hinta might be the first one she could touch, a woman like herself, less alien, less coarse and brutish than a man. The swirl of her hair seemed as uncanny as the dusk-lit trees. Voice, sweep of arms, eyes, everything about her crackled with the same fierce energy.

Later that night, when all nine sat on their water-cushions planning the next day's work, Marn spoke for the first time of her dread.

The others nodded, admitting their own fears. Even Jurgen confessed, "I still have to squint everytime I go out through that hatch, so I only see a little of the chaos at a time." He bent forward to spread his huge gloved palms on the floor. "But I know we can make it. I know it. We're going to survive here. All we have to do is touch the earth." A surge of emotion jolted his body. "Touch

the earth!" he shouted, and yanked the mask from his
face.

Marn was too dazed by his naked eyes to understand
what was happening. Then Hinta lifted her mask away,
then Sol, then Norba and Jolon, and soon Marn found
herself pushing the molded husk loose, flinging it aside,
gaping at the others with bare face. She had only seen a
dozen people raw-faced before, and then only after months
of ritual preparation. Now suddenly here were eight more,
and she was too ashamed and dazzled to gaze at them.

Everyone bent forward, palms spread on the floor,
chanting, *Touch the earth*. It scared her, the raw flesh all
around, the earth itself only a few millimeters beneath
her hands. Dirt. Things lived in it.

She began to trust the air and sky. Sometimes as she
worked outdoors she would find herself in a drowse, saturated with the heat, her mind gone out. In the seventh
week, while searching through the woods with Jurgen for
some damp place where water gushed from the rocky soil,
she had to keep waking herself from this sensuous drowse.

"We want our fishpond fed by a spring," Jurgen explained. "Pure water, deep down-under-rock water."

At last they found a spring, in a ravine where someone
long ago had dug a pit. At the center was a jumble of
wet stones scummed over with moss, and around the bor-
ders of the pit, where water gathered in puddles, there
was a sprinkling of tiny blue flowers. Jurgen had a way
of stooping over any new plant, screwing up his slate-grey
eyes in an effort of memory, and then telling Marn its
ancient name. "Butterworts," he announced. "How's that
for a name? They're waterlovers."

Marn felt her own face mirroring his pleasure. She had
not gone without a mask long enough to learn to control
her features, so the emotions swirled across her face un-
checked, as wind swirled on the lake.

Circling the pit, they gauged the work necessary to make
it into a fishpond. Uproot the brush and saplings, seal the
basin with clay, roof it with a sun-bubble. But first they
would need to clear away the rock.

"It seems a shame to disturb them," Marn said. "The
moss is so brilliant green, the little flowers are so blue."

"Butterworts," Jurgen insisted. He seeemed intent on
using the old names for these frail earthly things which
had forever been sealed outside the walls of Ohio City.

So Marn repeated the word: "Butterworts."

His black-bearded jaw wagged. Turning to her, his arms spreading as if to enwrap her, he said wonderingly, "And look at *that*."

She flinched back a step, shuddering, not yet ready to embrace even delicate Hinta, much less this ponderous man. But then he lumbered past her, arms swung wide, boots gouging at the bank of the ravine, until he stood at the base of an immense tree. The grey bark of the trunk flaked away in fist-size chips to reveal lighter green bark underneath, as if the tree were shedding. And higher up, where the branches canopied against the sky, the underbark showed through like the pale skin of something newly born.

"A sycamore," Jurgen cried, "sycamore, sycamore," turning the word over with his gruff voice. And he actually hugged the tree, laid his cheek against its leprous bark.

"Jurgen, that's ridiculous."

"But just look at it. Open your eyes."

"So? A big tree."

"But a *sycamore*," he repeated, as if the name alone should astonish her. "They used them for butcher-blocks. To cut up meat."

Marn turned away in disgust. Meat. Blood. Her stomach churned. And that was the way of laboring with Jurgen: one minute he made her feel easy in the outdoors; the next minute he sickened her.

Even his stony eyes could see her disgust. "You're being city, pure city."

"I'm just being human. Not animal."

His mouth tensed for an answer. Only his lips were clean of the bristling fur. Then he swatted the air once, as if to brush her away: "Forget it. Let's work."

They leaned their tool-packs against the trunk of the scabby sycamore, between two roots. Scuffling down the bank, trampling through the blue dust of flowers, Jurgen was the first to reach the pit's bottom and the damp rocks. He grabbed a stone, then another and another in a frenzy, and heaved them out of the gully. Marn picked her way down the bank, wary of his flailing elbows and fists.

"Listen, I didn't mean——" The words dried on her tongue.

His eyes, grey and rough as the stones he was heaving,

fixed on her for a moment, then returned to his work. As he hefted the next rock, there was a blur of movement—like an end-knotted rope snapping taut and jerking back on itself. Clutching the rock, mouth open, he gazed at his arm.

"Jurgen?"

"Bite," he answered incredulously.

"Bite?" She tried to think what he could mean. Only people bite. "Rock cut you?"

"Something bit me, damn it. Bit, *bit*. With teeth. You understand?"

She watched in bewilderment as he unsnapped the sleeve at his wrist. He folded the cloth back, bared his forearm inch-by-inch. She forced herself to look at his skin, as they had all promised to look on one another nakedly, to trust one another with their bodies. There was the same coarse hair that covered his jaw. Bunchy muscles netted with veins, ugly blue seams full of blood. And there near the elbow were twin rows of puncture marks, like pin-pricks, and two larger purplish holes.

Bite, she kept telling herself. Then from some recess her memory retrieved the word: *snake*. Impossible. Stupid. But that rope-like lashing-out, that knotted head striking at Jurgen's arm, these perforations in his skin . . . The idea made her woozy: "Maybe it was a snake."

"Beast," he swore, scoffing at her. He scrabbled up the bank, the wounded arm hanging slack at his side. Over his shoulder he muttered: "Bitten, yes. But not by any snake. They're imaginary, like griffins and sea-serpents. Like zebras."

"No, listen. I've seen them in glass boxes at the disneys."

"Right between cages for dragons and flying elephants." He slumped against the piebald sycamore. His outstretched legs in their coveralls looked like two more knotty tree roots. "They're all mechanoes, Marn. Automated fantasies."

"But some of those creatures used to be alive, out here, back in the twentieth. Didn't you ever read the signs below the cages?" She looked away from the repulsive wound, trying to remember her childhood trips to the disneys. "Some of the labels said *imaginary*. Some said *extinct*. Poisonous. Some of the snakes were extinct, I'm sure of it. They used to be out here, they used to—"

Jurgen laughed harshly, his chin thrust upward by pain. "You mean they were alive?"

"Easy, easy—"

"They were real, and they swallowed all our pesticides and herbicides, and they *survived?*"

Hysteria rasped in his voice. Was this how the poison worked? Or was this the outside madness, that insanity her tutor threatened would possess anyone who spent so much as an hour beyond the city walls?

"And more of their own poison in them than we could spray on them," Jurgen kept on. "Think of it, the whole woods filled with snakes!"

"The dome," she urged him. "We've got to get you back."

"And if snakes, maybe some of the others, too." His eyes, already squinting from the pain, squeezed tighter in his effort of memory, as he searched for names. "Fox. Turtles. What else? Bears. The dam-builders—what were they?—beavers."

Marn didn't want to remember those cages in the disneys. The forest already seemed to be crawling with creatures she had thought were long dead. All the terror she had felt when she first looked out across the lake rushed back over her. It was madness to have left Ohio City. Stifling or not, life back there was at least *known.* Nothing could lash out at you. Nothing ever crept up on you with a secret load of poison. Beneath her worksuit the flesh was twitching.

"Jurgen," she said as calmly as she could, "we're both losing control. We have to get back to the dome."

He grunted. "True." But instead of moving he gazed at his wounded arm. The lacerated flesh was turning purple, the skin from elbow to wrist was puffy. "Amazing," he said. "Some creature *did* that to me."

"Jurgen," she pleaded.

"Right." His legs jerked back and forth over the ground, but they would not lift him up, as if they had lain too long among the tree roots. His weakness embarrassed her now, as his strength had always embarrassed her.

"I'll call the others." She groped among the tumbled packs for the talkie.

Jurgen shook his head. "No. Body still works. I'll walk." Finally he dragged the legs under him, lifted himself to a crouch, back against the sycamore. "Stupid head," he grumbled. "Stupid dizzy." A point of fear glistened at the center of his dilated eyes.

Avoiding those eyes, she said, "Gloves." He obeyed, lifting both hands toward her, and she braced her feet against a root and tugged with all her strength. Through the two layers of syntho gloves she could sense his fingers curling fiercely against hers, alive.

Once upright, he staggered a few steps by himself, crushing the flowers whose names he had taken such care to teach her. "Can't see. Fool legs won't work."

Without thinking she eased her shoulder against his side, slipped an arm around his back, braced him with her body, and they lurched ahead. His weight grew with every step. But she wouldn't let go, not even when his head lolled against her, not when his beard rasped her cheek. She could feel his quick, frenzied panting against her ribs. Before she knew it she was panting in sympathy. It's faintness, she told herself. The poison. Shock. He'll forgive me for holding him.

By the time they reached the dome she was too numb with fatigue to worry about their intertwined bodies. But the startled expressions on Hinta and Sol brought back all her shame.

"Snake bit him," Marn explained, short of breath.

"Outside madness," Sol murmured, recoiling. Even Hinta raised her gloves, palms out, as if to shove them away.

"Just help me get him inside."

"Dome?" Jurgen's voice rose brokenly. The good fist pawed at his eyes, scuffing his flesh with the stone-roughened glove. "Can't see a thing."

That drew both Hinta and Sol out of their daze. Together with Marn they lugged him through the vacu-lock into the dome, laid him on his sleep-cushion. The swollen arm, mottled with scarlet and purple, made Marn feel nauseous. But she forced herself to fold his sleeve higher, to ease the swelling.

"Jurgen," she spoke close to his ear. "We'll care for you. You'll forgive the touching, if we help you?"

His answer came in a mumble: "Sure, sure. Touch, go ahead."

The sharp point of fear still glinted from his eyes. His shivering made the water-cushion tremble. Marn drew the cover to his chin, tucked it around his head, leaving only the wounded arm exposed. "Hurry," she whispered to the other two. "He's in shock."

Only Hinta, busy sorting through the medicine file, could hear, for Sol was outside calling news of the emergency to the other five.

"Snake bite? You said snake bite?"

Impatient with her, Marn said, "Believe me. I saw it. Just code it in, see if there's an antidote."

Quickly Hinta slipped off her gloves and typed the implausible message on the medical console. As Marn watched the slender naked fingers dance on the keys, desire uncoiled in her. She found herself yearning for the hundredth time to make her first contact with this swift-moving woman, so easy in her body. But instead here was Jurgen stretched out beside her, his body cumbersome and rough.

"Archives," Hinta muttered. "Jurgen's got himself hurt in a way so ancient it's stored in the blessed archives." She punched the new code, then read the answer as it glowed up from the console in yellow lights. Lower the arm, bind it at the elbow to keep down swelling, slit the skin at both fang marks, suck the venom out. Easy, so far. But then she read the final instructions: "Doctor immediately. Administer anti-venin."

"Which we probably don't have," Marn said.

Hinta's fingers played over the keys again, paused. She shook her head, the milk-white hair swirling round her face. "Idiot machine synthesizes antidotes for every industrial poison ever invented. But natural poisons—nothing."

Jurgen broke his delirious babbling long enough to say: "Thought they were all dead. Ghost bite."

"Easy, easy," Marn whispered. She fumbled with the bandage, trying not to cut off blood-flow at his elbow. Her gloves seemed coarse against his wounded skin, cruel, and so she drew them off and touched him with her bare hand. The shudder of that contact ran through her whole body. But she had no time to savor it, or brood on it.

Hinta passed her the antiseptic swab, then the scalpel. Only fear kept Marn working, made her slice through his skin, expose the flesh. Meat, the same as any animal.

"Now where's the syringe?"

"I'm looking."

Marn waited, waited. Jurgen grew unnaturally still under her hands. "Hurry."

Hinta opened and shut the medical cases with angry clacking noises. "Somebody ate the stupid thing. It's not anywhere."

Marn let her body think for her. "Quick, type another question. See if the venom is a stomach poison."

"Why do you—?"

"Just do it."

Clicking of keys. Then Hinta answered, "No, only a blood poison."

Marn looked down at Jurgen, his eyes barely open, nothing but the white showing, his mouth a wheezing hole of blackness in the beard. "Jurgen, I'm going to suck— I'm going . . ." She couldn't finish the sentence. But it didn't matter, because he was beyond answering. Another archaic word clamored at her: unconscious. Not to be asleep, because you can't be wakened. Not to be under chemmies or neuroes, for you can't counteract the stimulant. Unconscious, out of control.

She studied the festering wound. Each slit oozed. The skin seemed ready to split from the pressure of swelling.

"Maybe wait for the others?" Hinta whispered near her shoulder.

Marn waved her away. She kept her eyes open as long as she could stand it, to guide her as she bent down over the arm. Pressing her lips to one fang mark, she sucked gingerly. The first trickle of fluid on her tongue made her gag, and she spat violently. Poison. Blood. Then she sucked again at the wound, desperate to clean it out, to finish this, so she could stumble away and be sick, scrub her lips with disinfectants.

Soon the others were crowding into the dome, murmuring questions, carrying with them in the folds of their work-suits the smells of wood and dirt. Marn heard the word *snake* taken up and muttered from ear to ear, as if it were an incantation. So many bare faces bent over her made her reckless. She sucked and sucked, gagging and spitting, until the others were shocked into silence. When she could draw nothing more from the wound she sat back, her mouth sticky with blood and snake juices. "What are you gawking at? You rather he die?"

They all squatted on their sleep-cushions while Marn stayed with Jurgen, her hand on his wrist. The acrid taste seared her mouth and lips. Yet she felt a connection with this man, as if in pressing her face against him a circuit had been closed, power had surged round and round between them.

"We don't have the right medicine," Hinta was explaining to the others.

"How serious is it?" Coyt demanded. His wet eyes shifted from face to face around the circle. Here was our expert on the wilds, Marn thought bitterly, and he hadn't said a word about snakes. But immediately she knew that was unfair. Who could truly know the wilds? What did you ever see of them in Ohio City? The books said nothing, and the tutors merely filled you with dread of the outdoors. The video only showed deserts, sulphurous mountains, blank-faced oceans, nothing but miles of inhuman emptiness. You could learn about this forested and rivered world only by hearsay, through the old folks, or through tedious hours in the archives.

"See for yourself," Marn answered. Jurgen's mouth sagged open as if to catch a drop of something. His naked arm, ballooned and discolored, lay at his side, twitching beneath her fingers.

Coyt's moist gaze lingered for a moment on the wounded arm. "Yes, I see."

"The question is," Hinta continued, "do we take him back or not?"

"And give it all up?" The acid scars on Jolon's cheeks reddened from her anger.

Voices jumbled together too quickly for Marn to sort them out. The sensations from her hands commanded all her attention. She could feel the matted hair of his arm, so strange, and the pulse, faint and rapid, through an artery on the inside of his elbow. Could a heart pump so fast, through so huge a body? He bulked on his watercushion like a fallen tree.

When Marn could separate the voices again, Rand was saying: "It'd take two of us to haul him through the pipeline. Or we might locate a health patroller."

"And the Medical Squad would be here in ten minutes with cages and neurochems." The flaming red scars on Jolon's cheeks, the tension in her body, the balled fist on either knee announced to everyone she had no intention of going back.

Heads nodded in agreement all around the circle. Marn

knew they were right. Any visit to Ohio City would end the experiment, probably land them all in quarantine for twelve months. But she wanted the choice made clear: "And if he dies?"

No one answered. Except for the strain showing in their faces, the others might have been meditating, or dreaming under chemmies. Marn remembered the vows she had taken with them back in that echoing oil tank, to live outdoors for a year, for a whole cycle of seasons, before voting to stay or return. And she hoped the others were remembering Jurgen, whose arms and mind had always been the first to shove aside every obstacle. Jurgen, with sawdust on his beard, proclaiming to all the astounding properties of wood. Jurgen, refusing to use deodes to mask his sweat, laughing when the others wrinkled their noses at him.

Marn spoke deliberately. "It's not worth him dying. Nothing's worth it."

Sol pinched his upper lip between thumb and forefinger. "We knew there'd be accidents."

"That's the reason there's ten of us—redundancy," Coyt added.

They seemed to be speaking an alien language. Marn could not connect their words to this body panting beneath her outstretched hand. Maybe the poison had filtered through the walls of her stomach and unbalanced her mind. *Can't see,* she kept hearing him cry out, kept seeing those mitts claw at his inflamed eyes. Her own vision began to dizzy. The others' faces blurred together, until they all seemed to her like clones of the same hostile person. For the first time in weeks she longed for her mask, to hide herself.

Then she heard Hinta's voice, and recognized once again the quick-darting eyes and high cheekbones. "I don't think Jurgen would want this creature—this snake—to drive us back indoors."

Her eyes, which usually made Marn think of sky, now made her think of ice. "Look, it's not a log here. It's not a broken machine. It's Jurgen, don't you see?"

"We know, Marn, we know," Hinta soothed. "Calm yourself. We're not forgetting him. He's why I'm here, and why I'm going to stay here."

Marn looked at the other woman sharply.

"Vote," Jolon insisted.

"Vote, vote," rose in murmurs.

"All right, then," Hinta said. "Do we take him back?"

Like the others, Marn hid one hand in her lap, thinking furiously. Vote one raised finger—or her closed fist? That was the computer's binary choice, yes or no, too stark for human questions. How could she let him die, the first person she had ever touched nakedly? And yet this was why they had come outside, to get back in touch, with one another and with the Earth. Return to Ohio City would be death of another kind.

"Time," Hinta called.

As Marn lifted her hand along with the others, her fist closed of itself, squeezed tight as if to keep hold on something. Around the circle were eight balled fists, all of them saying, no, Jurgen, we will not go back. His panting, the frantic pace of his heart, kept on and on, against all reason.

The others rose from their cushions. Most of them padded away to the vacu-lock where their boots and tools waited for them. Several hesitated near Marn for a moment, glancing sidelong at Jurgen, whispering in sober tones. If the largest one of us could fall so quickly, to a beast we thought was extinct—what might happen to the rest of us? That is what Marn heard in the overtones of their whispers, what she read in their taut faces as they withdrew again to the day's chores.

Only Hinta stayed behind. Her eyes were no longer ice, had become sky again, a softer blue. As she lowered herself beside Marn her weight set up languorous waves in the water-cushion. The two women rocked softly against one another, shoulders touching. Neither drew back. "So we wait," Hinta said.

"We wait."

"He might live. Just to spite the city. Show them he can survive outdoors, do without their fancy medicines."

Marn wanted to squeeze her face against that milk-white hair. But her lips were still gummy with Jurgen's blood. Beneath her hand his frantic pulse shredded away the minutes.

After a while Hinta stirred. "Come on, there's no sense sitting here brooding." Rising with a pliant sensuous unfolding of her legs, she punched a code into her talkie.

Moments later Sol ambled through the vacu-lock. "News?"

"No. He's the same. How about you sit with him, keep him warm, spoon him some cardio if he comes to?"

Marn caught the small word: *if.*

"Sure," Sol replied. "And Marn?"

"She's coming with me." Hinta drew on her gloves, tucked her hair into the collar of her worksuit. "Somebody still has to move those rocks, clear that spring."

"No," Marn shook her head. "The rocks can wait."

"Marn."

"I can't just leave him."

"And staying won't do him any good. You'll only wreck yourself. And we need you, we need everyone." Hinta waited by the vacu-lock, boots half snapped, one hip thrust out in a challenge Marn could not decipher.

"Go on," Sol urged. "I'll code you if there's any change."

Marn knelt over Jurgen, hesitating. Every breath set her fingers tingling on his throat. The pulse seemed to be slackening its pace, growing stronger. And a half moon of stone-grey iris showed under each eyelid. What if he should wake, now, and find her hand on his throat, her hair dangling down inches from his face?

Confused, she drew back from him, lifted her fingers from the warm skin. But she carried the memory of that touch with her as she followed Hinta outdoors.

The rock-strewn spring, which had seemed a kilometer distant this morning when she was staggering with Jurgen back to the dome, was only a few minutes' walk away.

"Look at the queer blue flowers," Hinta said.

"Butterworts," Marn told her. "And that's a sycamore," pointing to the gigantic piebald tree.

"Such weird names. Sounds like Jurgen's teaching."

"Yes." Marn scuffled down the bank amidst the tiny nodding blossoms. The spring-sodden dirt squished beneath her boots.

"Here, use this, in case mister snake is still around." Hinta reached down to her a pole from the tool-rig.

And mister snake was still around, lashing out at the pole as soon as Marn disturbed its lair. There was the same blur of movement, like an end-knotted rope snapping, and the click of teeth against metal. The two women leapt back, and the snake withdrew. Furious, Marn realized now why she had come. She jammed the pole into the stones again, tumbled a few, and then out the creature slithered, gliding with sinuous ease to the ground. Its wedge-shaped head was the color of copper, and its body was mottled with stripes of brown. It might have been a limb off the sycamore, cast down and given motion. Nothing in the disneys approached it for grace. Marn watched, mesmerized, as a forked tongue licked out between the fangs, darting from side to side as if tasting the air.

Only when the snake lowered its head and began undulating away did she remember Jurgen lying unconscious back in the dome. And for an instant hatred ran like acid in her veins. Hefting the pole overhead she advanced on the snake, tightening every muscle to crush it. But even before she heard Hinta crying, "No, no, let it be!" she was easing the pole back down to her shoulder. The hatred passed, pushed out by an emotion she could not name, as she watched the creature until it glided out of sight into weeds.

"He belongs here," Hinta said. "This is his place."

Marn nodded, half mesmerized. Now that it had vanished, the snake seemed almost legendary again, an impossibility. She tugged the gloves away, to wipe her eyes.

Hinta removed her own gloves and without a word she took Marn's hand.

That night, when Jurgen sat up crookedly and demanded, "Where's Marn? I want Marn," she crept out of the dome without answering.

Shreds of moonlight glittered on the lake. Beast-sounds were thick along the shore. In the water there might be more snakes, or other creatures for which she had no names, but she would go in anyway. Her clothes formed a puny heap on the glass walkway, easily kicked aside.

She waded in with muscles tensed, breath held, and then she recklessly splashed forward as she would in a bathing vat. But this was no pure water; this was whatever fell out of the sky and trickled off the land.

Marn floated with all but her face submerged. The air was rank with the smell of water weeds and mud. The water licked the salt from her skin, licked away the dirt, the animal smell. But it could not scour away the taste of Jurgen's blood, or the feel of Hinta's fingers.

The night was the coolest she had ever felt, just as the day had been the hottest. This was living in weather, shivering and sweating by turns. Weather—another of the

ancient words they were reviving. She had always used
the word to indicate moods, the play of emotions, because
there was no weather in the air of Ohio City.

Lit from inside by flares, the dome looked from this
distance like a gigantic faceted globe. Marn could see the
dim shapes of the others readying sleep-cushions for the
night. One of them would be Hinta. Someone would be
stooping over Jurgen, giving him water, making him comfortable. It should be me, Marn thought. But she could
not yet look into his stone-grey eyes without confusion.
Her body could not overcome shame that quickly.

Afloat, her thoughts spread out on the water, thinned,
dissolved.

Sometime later a voice cried her name, and she opened
her eyes on darkness. "Marn, Marn! Are you all right?"

Hinta's voice, Hinta's lean shadow on the bank, hands
raised to mouth, shouting.

"Yes," Marn answered. "I'm coming." The water
sluiced along her ribs, her thighs, as she swam toward
shore. The dome was lit now only by a feeble glow.

"You were gone so long," Hinta said. "The others are
all asleep."

"Time seemed . . ." Marn began. But she could not
tell what had become of time, or what had become of her
fear. She lay in the shallow water, her naked face turned
toward the other woman.

"Here's a towel." In the gloom the cloth was barely
visible.

The water lapped against Marn's sides. Her arms were
sunken nearly to the elbows in the muck of the shore.
"I don't want it yet."

"Aren't you cold?"

"Come see."

For a few seconds, Hinta did not move, a slender column of darkness. Then she shrugged free of her clothes
and eased herself into the shallows beside Marn.

"Warm," she said.

"Come," Marn answered. "I'll take you out where the
springs churn up cold beneath your legs." Touching the
other woman to keep contact in the dark, Marn led her
away from shore.

Avram Davidson first achieved notice more
than twenty years ago, with such stories as
"My Boyfriend's Name Is Jello," "The
Golem," "Help! I Am Dr. Morris Gold-
pepper," and "Author, Author." Recently he
has been touring the groves of academe as
Visiting Distinguished Writer, a diversion of
which he tires; he says that he may go back
to being just "a plain ol' writer." In his time,
Davidson has given us such nobly-conceived
and executed novels as that history of
Vergil Magus, *The Phoenix and the Mirror*,
and—in a lighter frame of mind—committed some memorable shaggy dog stories
to paper . . . one of them also about that
magician.

Author, shaggy author!

The Other Magus

BY AVRAM DAVIDSON

Vergil was seated in his Glass Garden on the upper terrace of the Castle of the Egg one morning when he became aware, first, that someone was looking at him and,
second, that he had heard no one enter.

That inner awareness which he had so long cultivated
now directed him to turn his eyes to the left. There, in
between the saplings sent him by the Soldan of Babylone,
cuttings from the Tree of the Sun and the Tree of the
Moon, was a man with the willow wand of The Order
between his hands. "Compeer," said Vergil, "you are
thrice welcome." He rose, and gestured his fellow mage
to come and sit beside him.

The man did not move. "Canst fly, thou?" he asked.

"I am neither Phaëton nor Icarus."

"Their mistakes need not be made. — Can thee fly,
thou? Teach me how!"

"This gift I have not," said Vergil.

"Nay, but I will pay thee for its sale."

Vergil, puzzled, abated not his courtesy. "If I had it,
perhaps I would neither offer nor suffer it for sale,
Serrah."

The strange eyes of the other stared at him and, it
seemed, partly into him. "All gifts are for sale," he said
simply. After a moment's silence he made an abrupt gesture, vanished.

Vergil examined the floor. Earth was present, and
sand, but no trace of any human feet. "He treads more
lightly than I," murmured the Brundisian. With his own
wand he inscribed on the sand and loam a circle full
large to include whichever ell or inches the Apparition
of the Mage had superimposed. Next he took up the
lectern and set it down in the midst of the circle. "Be
thine eloign never so far, compeer," he said, softly, "but
I shall find thee out." He set on top the lectern the codex
called *The Oracles of Maro* and gave the movable top a
single spin. Then with closed eyes asking, "What mage
was this?" he opened the book at random and thrust
gently at the page with his own willow rod. And opened
his eyes.

The word was *Minos*.

"Strange," he said.

And ordered books brought him.

Long centuries ago a Phoenician vessel had foundered
off the Cumaean Sands, and only long later shifts of
winds and drifts and tides had exposed first her sundered
timbers and then her wrack-choked cargo-hold. The glass
had grown iridescent in the passing of time, but perhaps
the shock of shipwreck or the pressure of sand centuries
endurant, or whatsoever, had snapped the neck of almost every bottle, and shattered the sides of most: only
the thicker glass of the bottoms had in every case survived uncracked. And Vergil had used them to build the
iridescent walls and roof of the Glass Garden on the Upper Terrace of the Castle of the Egg. Rose spots, violet
whorls, green and red and golden marks swirling round
his face and hands, rainbows rippled the surface of the
books.

"Strange," he said. "I find no mention of any mage

named Minos. Could his entry to The Order have been clandestine?"

And later, Clemens, his beard and Poseidonian-heavy locks as thick and curly as ever, but now full white, said to him, "Have you after all found your mage Minos, then? You have! Good. How?"

"By the simplest way. The Oracles spoke anagrammatically. His name in truth is *Simon*."

"Simon," said Clemens, considering. "Simon? Simon Magus? Of Samaria. So." A faintly odd expression crossed his face.

Vergil asked, swiftly, "Do you hear them, too?"

"Hear them?" Clemens asked, cautiously. "Hear what?"

"Echoes . . ."

Clemens looked at him, slightly puzzled. "Again, your echoes. Of what this time?"

"Oh . . ." Vergil sighed. "Of books never written in our world. Of parables never told . . ."

Clemens put his head slightly to one side. Then he shook it. Then he reached for the small flask containing the fifth essence of wine, and its colors glowed and rippled, and he poured himself a few drachms. "No," he said, and sipped. "No," he said, "I cannot say that I do." He ran his tongue over his lips, and swallowed. Then he made a sound in his face. "What I *can* say is that I am afraid that when a Samaritan is bad, he is very, very bad."

Vergil nodded. He seemed faintly abstracted. "No doubt there were times when he, too, was good," he said.

Sonya Dorman is one of several notable
poets represented here (though not in this
instance by poetry). The first volume of her
work, entitled, simply, *Poems,* was a National Council on the Arts selection; the
second was *Stretching Fence;* the third, *A
Paper Raincoat*. Within the genre of science
fiction, and in the demanding category of
young adult novel, her current title is *Planet
Patrol,* chronicling the adventures of Roxy
Rimidon.

Dorman examines communication—under
duress—from the viewpoint of an alien.

Peek-A-Boom

BY SONYA DORMAN

He had been in capture a long time, in the metal groves
and labyrinths, though time appeared to have condensed
since his arrival. Probably that was the effect of his
loneliness, or perhaps the experimental attempts at communication forced on him. It might be because he spent
so much time at the resting level of his longest X-rays,
in the dim glow below his transmission frequency.

If he refused his rations, or if he became careless in
the turns he took, rather than eagerly seeking, the incom-
ing rays lengthened until the heat was nearly intolerable.
On the other hand, when he went briskly, and took the
correct turns, his prison cooled so that his strength rose
and, even in this confined place, tried to flow free.

It was all metal, except for the quartz crystal at one
end, and he rested on that even though it was a bit too

warm for comfort, because it was different, identifiable, a "place" in this indeterminate place. Sometimes the metal hedges around him flowered with sensors; then he was urged to work the labyrinth as often as possible.

On occasions he was so unhappy he would draw himself in tight around the membrane through which he perceived shapes, the flare of violet fluorescence and the long, cool perspectives which were partly memory and partly the habitation in which he was kept.

When first confined, he had opened as widely as possible to receive any sort of message, but all his receptor encountered was a combination of speckles and flickers:

"Ten thousand a year, poor schnook."

"He doesn't respond to microwaves, either, Doctor."

"Christ help me."

"It's lunch time."

"God have mercy."

"And then she put it in her mouth!"

"Half a cc and an alcohol rub."

"Three jiggers and a whiff of vermouth."

"Nothing on the audio, Doctor?"

"Christ, my guiding light."

"Merry Christmas."

"Happy Birthday."

"Gut Yontif."

If there had been some pattern he would have memorized it, but he could find none in what came through, or along, the audio walls. He was doing the labyrinth variations often, determined to keep himself occupied. And he had learned to respond to the color stimuli. He wondered if they were trying to contact him in these color frequencies, which he could perceive, but not transmit.

Now and then he would be presented with an illusion of himself, shape of cool, familiar form. He knew it was an illusion but it comforted him anyway. At the same time he was ashamed he could derive comfort from an illusion, since he came from a culture where illusions were used to arouse amusement, or to discipline the young.

Each time he confronted one of these illusions, he fought bitterly against the impulse to reach out, to flare forth to the shape so much like his own.

His ultraviolet would transmit involuntarily: "Who are you?"

Then he would return to rest, though never quite giving up his hope for freedom.

Yet, when they learned his seeming preferences, they prepared feasts for him, rays shortened upward so he could be refreshed. Then his response was very strong, his receptor would open, his spark was released to swim.

It was a daily ritual to try for communication, but the most that he ever received were those pulses of tinsel:

"I can't stand chipped beef."

"God, light of my soul."

"Twenty thousand on contract."

"Do it again. Do it again. Do it again."

"Let's knock off for lunch."

"Happy New Year, Doctor."

"Gut Shabos."

"Bon voyage."

"Up yours!"

"Happy Birthday."

"Pray for me now and at the hour."

"It must be on another frequency."

"And Christ receive my soul."

Every day he repeated his transmission: "Are you there? Are you there?" and waited, but nothing came back.

In the course of time, he became able to distinguish rhythmic patterns on the metal walls, and although he couldn't get any meaning from: "Catch the eight-fifty," it was evident that these streaks of light were messages of some kind. Not from his sort of life, and not his kind of communication, but as long as he was in contact with the quartz, he could pick up the dashes and splatters. It gave him hope that at some point he and they would merge, if only for an instant. There was little else for him to look forward to. He missed merging more than anything, the constant give and take, ebb and flow. When he encountered the faintly shining illusion of himself, he always paused, sent out a request for recognition. But to no avail.

As he despaired of making contact, or of discovering what had happened to him so he could order it and then escape it, he became wilder and wilder, way up to his top limit, to the shortest X-ray frequency.

It was too dangerous and difficult to maintain. Dropping from that narrow intensity he involuntarily went to the other extreme, down, wider and wider, until he was spread along the width of the border between limits of violet and edges of blue. Temperature and voltage began to change, the perceptor membrane developed cracks and fissures. The pulses came in at such increased speed that he writhed on the crystal which transmitted them.

"Look, in blue!"

"Thought it couldn't get through on visibility."

"What have we here?"

"Call Dr. Barlow."

"It's gone, now."

"Call Dr. Barlow anyway, we got a reading."

"Maybe it's dead."

"Can't be. Goose it along with ultraviolet, maybe it'll come through again."

"Dr. Barlow's on the way."

"What do you think we got in there, hm?"

"We'll find out yet."

"Well, gentlemen, what do we have here?"

"We got a reading on the lowest ultraviolet fringe. Came and went just like a buoy beacon. Gone, now."

"Splendid!"

"You think it blew itself up, or something?"

"My dear Miss Krakow, we don't use such expressions. It's a living entity."

"Well, it doesn't speak my language, Doctor."

Weakly, he began his standard, receptive call: "Are you there? Are you there?" He had little hope there would be a response, but continued. There must be an exit, a way, maybe not for all of him as an entity but for the essential part of him to escape. He went on repeating his call. When exhausted, he dropped below his communication frequency, and tried to block out the little flashes and streaks:

"Okay, let's try, right up into the hot spark area at the top of ultraviolet. Let's see what we get, if we can reach it. It must have survived that one effort."

"Survived? Of course it did, it's still radiating."

"Get the mantle off the laser, will you, Miss Krakow, there's a good girl."

"Here we are."

"Now let's see what we have here."

"Well, don't zap it with everything at once."

"Would it get drunk?"

"Miss Krakow!"

"Sorry, Doctor."

"All right now, let's try to get a real glimpse of it."

He was at the end of his endurance. All he could feel or desire was to be set free. He had been resting a long time, saving his strength for a final try.

Without the least warning he was directed at enormous velocity; his receptor spread flat, his sunspark began to glow. He didn't have time to move from his resting position, it happened so fast, the incredible directness of the beam.

The plate covering his receptor burnt to ash. The sunspark burst free at 186,000 miles per second, along the corridor of exit, the walls, the cables, the tables, the Dr. Barlow and the Miss Krakow, before the apparatus fused with a blast. Bruised and terrified survivors fled.

"Great God!"

"What happened?"

"Watch out, that I-beam's loose."

"Still smoking. Poor Miss Krakow."

"What's that?"

"A shred . . . oh, my God."

"Who's going to tell Mrs. Barlow?"

"I'll do it. Here come the recommish boys."

"Wait'll the Board gets the bill for this one."

"I could use a drink."

"So could I. How about you, Dr. Swerdlow?"

"Mrs. Barlow will give me one, she always does."

"Poor Miss Krakow. See you tomorrow, then."

"Okay. And somebody, put in a requisition for another one. The shipping box is still intact."

"Not sure I want another."

"Me neither. Guess there's not even any remains."

"You don't think it escaped?"

"It couldn't. I wonder if it hurt."

"Better go have a drink. So long."

"God have mercy."

"Happy Birthday."

"Go to hell."

Gene Wolfe was born in New York, raised
in Texas, and now lives in a suburb of
Chicago, Illinois. He won a Nebula Award
in 1973 for his novella, "The Death of Dr.
Island"; the Chicago Foundation for Literature Award in 1976 for his novel, *Peace;*
and the Rhysling Award for the Best Long
SF Poem of 1979, "The Computer Iterates
the Greater Trumps." With only three or
four books to his credit thus far, and after
a couple of years spent working extensively
on his tetralogy (*The Rock of the New Sun*)
he has three books forthcoming within a
very few months of each other: the first
volume of the tetralogy, *The Shadow of the
Torturer;* his collection, *The Island of Dr.
Death and Other Stories and Other Stories;*
and *Gene Wolfe's Book of Days,* a garland
of celebrations. He is unique.

His short story hereunder is a den of iniq-
uity; no one else could have written it.

Suzanne Delage

BY GENE WOLFE

As I was reading last night—reading a book, I should explain, which was otherwise merely commonplace; one of
those somewhat political, somewhat philosophical, somewhat historical books which can now be bought by the
pound each month—I was struck by a certain remark of
the author's. It seemed to me at the time an interesting, if
almost self-evident, idea; and afterward, when I had
turned the page, and many other pages, and was half
through a new chapter bearing very little relation to what
had gone before, this idea found its way back into my
consciousness and there acted as a sort of filter between
my mind and the book until I put it down and, still thinking, went up to bed.

The idea which had so forcibly struck me was simply

this: *that every man has had in the course of his life some extraordinary experience, some dislocation of all we expect from nature and probability, of such magnitude that he might in his own person serve as a living proof of Hamlet's hackneyed precept*—but that he has, nearly always, been so conditioned to consider himself the most mundane of creatures, that, finding no relationship to the remainder of his life in this extraordinary experience, he has forgotten it.

It seemed to me (considering the immense extent of the universe of the senses and the minute size of that area of it we think of as "everyday") that this must certainly be correct. Yet if it were true of every man it ought also to be true of me—and try as I might I could remember no such extraordinary circumstance.

When I had switched off the light I lay recalling, very pleasantly on the whole, my life. It *has* been a pleasant life, though I fear a dull, and perhaps a lonely, one. I live now not five miles from the hospital in which I was born, and have lived nowhere else. Here I grew up, learned a profession, practiced, and, much sooner than most men, retired. I have twice been married, but both marriages were brief, and both ended in friendly separations; the truth is that my wives (both of them) bored me—and I am very much afraid I bored them as well.

As I lay in bed, then, thinking of times when my grandfather had taken me fishing and of skating parties with friends, and about our high school team (on which I was a substitute quarterback, but one so much inferior to the first-string occupant of that position that I almost never got into a game unless we were several touchdowns ahead, which was not often), it at last occurred to me that there has, in fact, been one thread of the strange—I might almost say the incredible, though not the supernatural—in my own history.

It is simply this: living all my life, as I have, in a town of less than a hundred thousand population, I have been dimly aware of the existence of a certain woman without ever meeting her or gaining any sure idea of her appearance.

But even this is not, perhaps, as extraordinary as it may sound. I have never made an effort to meet this woman, and I doubt that she has ever attempted to meet me, if, indeed, she is aware that I exist. On the other hand we

are neither of us invalids, nor are we blind. This woman
—her name is Suzanne (though I fear most of us here
have always pronounced it "Susan") Delage—lives, or at
least so I have always vaguely supposed, on the eastern
edge of our little city; I live on the western. I doubt that
we, as children, attended the same elementary school, but
I know that we were, for four years, at the same high
school. I was able to ascertain this as a matter of certainty through my yearbooks, which my mother, with that
more or less formalized sentimentality characteristic of
her, saved for me in the attic of this tall, silent frame
house (itself saved for me as well).

Actually, of the four volumes which must originally
have existed, only two remain—those for my sophomore
and senior years. There are a number of pages missing
from the class picture section of the earlier book, and I
seem to recall that these were torn out and cut up to obtain the individual photographs many decades ago. My
own face is among those missing, as well as Suzanne
Delage's; but in another section, one devoted to social ac-
tivities, a girl's club (it was called, I think, the Pie Club)
is shown, and one of the names given in the caption is
Suzanne's. Unfortunately the girls in the picture are so
loosely grouped—around a stove and work table—that it
is not possible to be certain in every case which name
should be attached to which young lady; besides, a number of them have their backs to the camera.

The senior book should have told me more—at least so
I thought when I, at last, came across it at the end of an
hour or so of rummaging. It is whole and undamaged, and
I, thanks largely to football, have no less than four pictures in various parts of it. Suzanne Delage has none. On
one of the closing pages a woebegone roll of names reminds me of something I had forgotten for many years—
that there was an epidemic of some kind (I think Spanish
influenza) just at the time the pictures for the annual
were to be taken. Suzanne is listed as one of those "unable
to be photographed."

I should explain that ours was one of those overgrown
schools found in the vicinity of small towns, a school re-
peatedly expanded because the growth of the town itself
had been slow (though always faster, so it seemed in ret-
rospect, than anyone had anticipated) and the taxpayers
had not wanted to authorize a new one. It was large

enough, in short, that only a few leading students—the star athletes, the class officers, the few really promiscuous girls and the dazzlingly beautiful ones whom we, in those naive times, called "queens"—were known to everyone.

The rest of us, if we moved socially at all, went by classes and cliques. A student might know the others in his English and algebra rooms; the cliques—at least the ones I remember—were the football players and their girls, the children of the rich, the boys and girls whose families attended a certain fundamentalist church on the outskirts of town; and certain racial minorities, the chess and debating society types, and the toughs. It sounds, I suppose, as though there were a group for everyone, and at the time (since I was fairly well entrenched among the athletes) I believe I thought myself (if I thought about the matter at all) that there was. I now realize that all these little coteries embraced no more than a third of the school, but whether Suzanne Delage had entry to one or more of them I do not know.

I should, however, have made her acquaintance long before I entered high school, since Mrs. Delage, Suzanne's mother, was one of my own mother's close friends. They had met, I think at about the time I was eight, through a shared passion (much more widespread in our area, I think, than in the country as a whole, and more ardently pursued in the past than it is now) for collecting antique fabrics: in other words, for embroidered tablecloths, for quilts, crocheting of all kinds, afghans, crewel work, hand-hooked rugs, and the like. If my mother or her friends could discover a sampler, or a bedspread or "comfortable" made in the earlier part of the nineteenth century (it was their enduring hope, I think never well satisfied, to find a piece from what they called "American Revolution times" —by which they meant the eighteenth, even such dates as 1790 or 1799), a piece well made and decorated—the more the better—in the unschooled, traditional ways of the old farm families, then their joy and their pride knew no bounds. If, in addition, the work was that of some notable woman—or to be more precise, of some woman relation of some notable man; the sister, say, of a lieutenant governor—and could be authenticated, the home of the finder became a sort of shrine to which visitors were brought, and to which solitary pilgrims from other towns came (ringing our bell—for we possessed, as a result of

Mother's efforts, a vast appliquéd quilt which had been the civil-wartime employment of the wife of a major in a fencible Zouave regiment—usually at about ten-thirty in the morning and offering, in introduction, a complicated recitation of friendships and cousincies linking themselves to our own family) bearing homage like cookies on a plate and eager to hear, for the better direction of their own future strategies, a circumstantial description of the inquiries and overheard clues, the offers made and rejected and made again, which had led to the acquisition of that precious object which would, as terminator of the interview, at last be brought forth in a glory of moth crystals, and spread sparkling clean (for of course these collected pieces were never used) over the living room sofa to be admired.

Mrs. Delage, who became my mother's friend, possessed pieces of her own as valuable as the major's wife's quilt (which was, as my mother never tired of pointing out, entirely hand-sewn) and a collection, too, of lesser treasures ranking, as my mother herself admitted, with our own hoard. Together they scoured the countryside for more, and made trips (trips so exhausting that I was, as a boy, always surprised to see how very willing, in a few weeks, my mother was to go again) to view the riches of neighboring counties—and even, once or twice, by rail, of neighboring states. It would therefore have been entirely logical for Mrs. Delage to have been our frequent guest, at least for tea; and for her to have brought, occasionally, her little daughter Suzanne, whom I would no doubt have soon come to both love and hate.

This would doubtless have occurred but for a circumstance of a kind peculiar, I think, to towns exactly the size of ours, and incomprehensible not only to the residents of cities, but to truly rural people as well. There lived, directly across the brick-paved street from us, a bitter old woman, a widow who, for some reason never explained to me, detested Mrs. Delage. It was lawful for my mother to be friendly with Suzanne's, but if (women in small towns somehow know these things) she had gone so far as to invite Mrs. Delage to our house this widow would at once have become her enemy for life. The invitation was never given, and I believe my mother's friend died while I was at college.

Thus while I was still small I was hardly aware of Su-

zanne Delage, though my mother often mentioned hers; in
high school, as I indicated, though I was in much closer
proximity to the girl herself, this was hardly altered. I
heard of her vaguely, in connection perhaps with some
friend of a friend. I must surely have seen her in the cor-
ridors hundreds of times—if one can be said to see, in a
crowd, people one does not know. I must sometimes have
shared classrooms with her, and certainly we were together at assembly and in the vast study hall. She would
have attended many of the same dances I did, and it is
even possible that I danced with her—but I do not really
believe that, and if, indeed, it happened, the years have
so effectively sponged the event from my mind that no
slightest trace remains.

And in fact I think I would never have recalled the
name of Suzanne Delage at all, as I lay in bed last night
listening to the creaking of this empty house in the au-
tumn wind and searching the recesses of my memory for
some extraordinary incident with which to attest the author's thesis, if it had not been for something that took
place a few days ago.

I had been shopping, and happened to meet, on the
sidewalk in front of one of the larger stores, a woman of
my own age whom I have known all my life and who is
now the wife of a friend. We stood chatting for a moment
—she, after the usual half teasing reproaches about my
(supposed) gay bachelor life, gossiping about her husband
and children. As she turned to leave a girl of fifteen or so
came out of the store and, smiling but intent upon her
own concerns, walked quickly past us and down the street.
Her hair was of a lustrous black, and her complexion as
pure as milk; but it was not these that for a moment en-
chanted me, nor the virginal breasts half afraid to press
the soft angora of her sweater, nor the little waist I might
have circled with my two hands. Rather it was an air, at
once insouciant and shy, of vivacity coupled with an innocence and intelligence that were hers alone. To the woman
beside me I said: "What a charming child. Who is she?"

"Her name?" My friend's wife frowned and snapped
her fingers. "I can't think of it. But of course you know
whose she is, don't you? She's the very image of her
mother at that age—Suzanne Delage."

Naomi Mitchison, a native of Edinburgh, has a lifetime of deeds and accomplishments that beggars description. Among other distinctions, she was a Labour candidate in England, and was tribal advisor to the Bakgatla of southeast Botswana (and is in Africa as this note is being written). She has had published approximately fifty books, including several about Africa, and a novel called *Memoirs of a Spacewoman*—feminist science fiction, two decades ahead of its time, and never yet properly appreciated though often reprinted.

Here, however, she deals with ... magic.

The Finger

BY NAOMI MITCHISON

Kobedi had a mother but no father. When he was old enough to understand such things someone said that his father was the Good Man. By that they meant the Bad Man, because, so often, words, once they are fully known, have meanings other or opposite to their first appearance. Kobedi, however, hoped that his father was the fat man at the store. Sometimes his mother went there and brought back many things, not only the needful meal and oil, but tea and sugar and beautiful tins with pictures, and almost always sweets for himself. Once, when he was a quite little boy, he had asked his mother where she kept the money for this and she answered "Between my legs." So, when she had drunk too much beer and was asleep on her back and snoring, he lifted her dress to see if he could find this money and take a little. But there was

99

nothing there except a smell which he did not like. He had two small sisters, both fat and flat-nosed like the man at the store. But his own nose was thin, and the Good Man also had a thin nose as though he could cut with it.

Kobedi went to school and he thought he now understood what his mother had meant though he did not wish to think of it; at least she paid the school fees, though she grumbled about them. He was in Standard Three and there were pictures on the wall which he liked; now he wrote sentences in his jotter and they were ticked in red because they were correct. That was good. But in a while he became aware that things were happening around him which were not good. First it was the way his mother looked at him, and sometimes felt his arms and legs, and some of her friends who came and whispered. Then came the time he woke in the blackest of the night, for there was a smell which made him feel sick and the Good Man was there, sitting on the stuffed and partly torn sofa under the framed picture of white Baby Jesus. He was wearing skins of animals over his trousers, and his toes, which had large nails, clutched and burrowed in the rag rug Kobedi's mother had made. The Good Man saw that Kobedi was awake because his eyes were open and staring; he pointed one finger at him. That was the more frightening because his other hand was under the skirt of a young girl who was sitting next to him, snuggling. The pointing finger twitched and beckoned and slowly Kobedi unrolled himself from his blanket and came over naked and shaking.

The Good Man now withdrew his other hand and his dampish fingers crawled over Kobedi. He took out two sinews from a bundle, rubbing them in the sweat of his own skin until they became thin and hard and twisted and dipped them into a reddish medicine powder he had and spat on them and he pointed the finger again and Kobedi slunk back and pulled the blanket over his head.

The next day the tied-on sinews began to make his skin itch. He tried to pull them off but his mother slapped him, saying they were strong medicine and he must keep them on. He could not do any arithmetic that day. The numbers had lost their meaning and his teacher beat him.

The next time he became aware of that smell in the night he carefully did not move nor open his eyes, but pulled the blanket slowly from his ears so that he could

hear the whispering. Again it was the Good Man and his
mother and perhaps another woman or even two women.
They were speaking of a place and a time, and at that
place and time, a happening. The words were so dressed
as to mean something else, as when speaking of a knife
they called it a little twig, when they spoke of the heart
it was the cooking pot, when they spoke of the liver it
was the red blanket, and when they spoke of the fat it
was the beer froth. And it became clear to Kobedi that
when they spoke of the meal sack it was of himself they
were speaking. Death, death, the whispers said, and the
itching under the sinews grew worse.

The next morning all was as always. The little sisters
toddled and played and their mother pounded meal for
the porridge and called morning greetings to her neigh-
bors across the walls of the lapa. Then she said to him:
"After the school is finished you are to go to the store
and get me one packet tea. Perhaps he will give you
sweets. Here is money for tea."

It was not much money, but it was a little and he knew
he had to go and fast. He passed by the school and did
not heed the school bell calling to him and he walked to
the next village and on to the big road. He waited among
people for a truck and fear began to catch upon him; by
now he was hungry and he bought fatty cakes for five
cents. Then he climbed in at the back of the truck with
the rest of the people. Off went the truck, north, south, he
did not know. Only there was a piece of metal in the
bottom of the truck, some kind of rasp, and he worked
with this until he had got the sinew off his ankle and he
dropped it over the side so that it would be run over by
many other trucks. It was harder to get at the arm one
and he only managed to scrape his own skin before the
truck stopped in a big town.

Now it must be said that Kobedi was lucky; after a
short time of hunger and fear he got a job sweeping out a
small shop and going with heavy parcels. He was also
allowed to sleep on a pile of sacks under the counter,
though he must be careful to let nobody know, especially
not the police. But under the sacks was a loose board
and below it he had a tin, and into this he put money out
of his wages, a few cents at a time. He heard about a
school that was held in the evenings after work; he did
not speak to anyone about it, and indeed he had no friends

in the big town because it seemed to him that friends meant losing one's little money at playing dice games or taking one's turn to buy a coke; and still his arm itched.

When he had enough money he went one evening to the school and said he had been in Standard Three and he wanted to go on with education and had money to buy it. The white man who was the head teacher asked him where he came from. He said from Talane, which was by no means the name of his village, and also that his father was dead and there was no money to pay for school. The truth is too precious and dangerous to be thrown anywhere. So the man was sorry for him and said well, he could sit with the others and try how he did.

At this time Kobedi worked all day and went to classes in the evening and still he was careful not to become too friendly, in case the friend was an enemy. There was a knife in the shop, but it was blunt, and though he sawed at the sinew on his arm he could not get it off. Sometimes he dreamed about whispering in the night and woke frozen. Sometime he thought his mother would come suddenly through the door of the shop and claim him. If she did, could the night school help him?

One of the Motswana teachers took notice of him and let him come to his room to do homework, since this was not possible in the shop. There were some books in the teacher's room and a photograph of himself with others at the T.T.C.; after a while Kobedi began to like this teacher, Mr. Tshele, and half thought that one day he would tell him what his fears were. But not yet. There came an evening when he was writing out sentences in English, at one side of the table where the lamp stood. Mr. Tshele had a friend with him; they were drinking beer. He heard the cans being opened and smelled the fizzing beer. At a certain moment he began to listen because Mr. Tshele was teasing his friend, who was hoping for a post in the civil service and had been to a doctor to get a charm to help him. "You believe in that!" said Mr. Tshele. "You are not modern. You should go to a cattle post and not to the civil service!"

"Everyone does the same," said his friend, "perhaps it helps, perhaps not. I do not want to take risks. It is my life."

"Well, it is certainly your money. What did he charge you?" The friend giggled and did not answer; the beer cans chinked again. "I am asking you another thing," said Mr. Tshele, "This you have done at least brings no harm. But what about sorcery? Do you believe?"

The friend hesitated. "I have heard dreadful things," he said, "What they do. Perhaps they are mad. Perhaps it no longer happens. Not in Botswana. Only perhaps— well, perhaps in Lesotho. Who knows? In the mountains."

Mr. Tshele leaned back in his chair. Kobedi ducked his head over his paper and pencil and pretended to be busy writing. "There is a case coming up in the High Court," said Mr. Tshele. "My cousin who is a lawyer told me. A man is accused of medicine murder. The trial will be next week. They are looking for witnesses, but people are afraid to come forward."

"But they must have found—something?"

"Yes, a dead child. Cut in a certain way. Pieces taken out. Perhaps even while the child was alive and screaming for help."

"This is most dreadful," said the friend, "and most certainly the man I went to about my civil service interview would never do such a thing!"

"Maybe not," said Mr. Tshele, "not if he can get your money a safer way! Mind you, I myself went to a doctor who was a registered herbalist when I had those headaches, and he threw the *ditaola* and all that, but most certainly he did not murder."

"Did he cure your headaches?"

"Yes, yes, and it was cheaper than going to the chemist's shop. He rubbed the back of my neck and also gave me a powder to drink. Two things. It was a treatment, a medical treatment, not just a charm. I suppose you also go for love charms?"

Again the friend giggled, and Kobedi was afraid they would now only speak about girls. He wanted to know more, more, about the man who had cut out the heart— and the liver—and stripped off the fat for rubbing, as he remembered the whispering in the night. But they came back to it. "This man, the one you spoke of who is to be tried, he is from where?" the friend asked. And Mr. Tshele carelessly gave the name of the village. His village. The name, the shock, the knowledge, for it must indeed and in truth be the Good Man. Kobedi could not speak, could not move. He stared at the lamp and the light blurred and pulsed with the strong terrible feeling he had in him like the vomiting of the soul.

He did not speak that evening. Nor the next. He wondered if the Good Man was in a strong jail, but if so surely he could escape, taking some form, a vulture, a great crow? And his mother? And the other women, the whisperers? But the evening after that, in the middle of a dusty open space near the school where nobody could be hiding to listen, he touched Mr. Tshele's coat and looked up at him, for he did not yet come to a man's shoulder height. Mr. Tshele bent down, thinking this was some school trouble. It was then that Kobedi whispered the name of his village and when Mr. Tshele did not immediately understand: "Where *that one* who is to be tried comes from. I know him."

"You? How?" said Mr. Tshele and then Kobedi began to tell him everything and the dust blew round them and he began to cry and Mr. Tshele wiped his dusty tears away and took him to a shop at the far side of the open space and gave him an ice lolly on a stick. He had seen boys sucking them, but for him it was the first time and great pleasure.

Then Mr. Tshele said, "Come with me," and took him by the hand and they went together to the house of his cousin the lawyer, which was set in a garden with fruit trees and tomato plants and flowers and a thing which whirled water. Inside it was as light as a shop and Kobedi's bare feet felt a soft and delicious carpet under them. "Here is your witness in the big case!" said Mr. Tshele, and then to Kobedi: "Tell him!" But Kobedi could not speak of it again.

But they gave him a drink that stung a little on the tongue and was warm in the stomach, and in a while Kobedi was able to say again what he had said to his teacher and it came more easily. "Good," said the cousin who was a lawyer. "Now, little one, will you be able to say this in the Court? If you can do it you will destroy a great evil. Modimo will be glad of you." Kobedi nodded and then he whispered to Mr. Tshele, "It will come better if you take this off me," and he showed them the sinew with the medicine. The two men looked at one another and the lawyer fetched a strong pair of scissors and cut through the sinew; then he took it into the kitchen, and before Kobedi's eyes he put it with his own hand into the stove and poked the wood into a blaze so that it was consumed altogether. After that Kobedi told the lawyer the shop where he worked. "So now," said the lawyer, "no word to any other person. This is between us three. *Khudu Thamaga.*"

That night Kobedi slept quickly without dreaming. Two days later a big car stopped at the shop where he was sweeping out the papers and dirt and spittle of the customers. The lawyer came to the door and called him: "You have not spoken? Good. But in Court you will speak." Then the lawyer gave some money to the man at the shop to make up for taking his servant, and when they were in the car he explained to Kobedi how it would be. The accused here, the witness there. "I will ask you questions," he said, "and you will answer and it will be only the truth. Look at the Judge in the high seat behind the table where men write. Do not look at the accused man. Never look at him. Do you understand?" Kobedi nodded. The lawyer went on, "Speak in Setswana when I question you, even if you know some English words which my cousin says you have learnt. These things of which you will tell cannot be spoken in English. But show also that you know a little. You can say to the Judge, 'I greet you, Your Honour.' Repeat that. Yes, that is right. Your Honour is the English name for a Judge and this is a most important Judge."

So in a while the car stopped and Kobedi was put into a room and given milk and sandwiches with meat in them and he waited. The time came when he was called into the Court and a man helped him and told him not to be afraid. He kept his eyes down and saw nothing, but the man touched his shoulder and said, "There is His Honour the Judge." So Kobedi looked up bravely and greeted the Judge, who smiled at him and asked if he knew the meaning of an oath. At all times there was an interpreter in the Court and there seemed to be very many people, who sometimes made a rustling sound like dry leaves of mealies, but Kobedi carefully looked only at the Judge. So he took his oath; there was a Bible, such as he had seen at his first school. And then the lawyer began to ask him questions and he answered, so that the story grew like a tree in front of the Judge.

Now it came to the whisperers in the midnight room and what they had shown him of their purpose; the lawyer asked him who there were besides the accused. Kobedi answered that one was his mother. And as he did so there was a scream and it came from his mother herself. "Wicked one, liar, runaway, oh how I will beat you!" she yelled at him until a policewoman took her away. But he had turned towards her, and suddenly he had become dreadfully unhappy. And in his unhappiness he looked too far and in a kind of wooden box half a grown person's height, he saw the Good Man.

Before he could take his eyes away the Good Man suddenly shot out his finger over the top of the box and it was as though a rod of fire passed between him and Kobedi. "It is all lies," shouted the Good Man. "Tell them you have lied, lied, lied!" And a dreadful need came onto Kobedi to say just this thing and he took a shuffling step towards the Good Man, for what had passed between them was *kgogela,* sorcery, and it had trapped him. But there was a great noise from all round and he heard the lawyer's voice and the Judge's voice and other voices and he felt a sharp pain in the side of his stomach.

Now after this Kobedi was not clear what was happening, only he shut his eyes tight, and then it seemed to him that he still wore those sinews which the Good Man had fastened onto him. And the pain in his stomach seemed to grow. But the *kgogela* had been broken and he did not need to undo his words and he was able to open his eyes and look at the Judge and to answer three more questions from his friend the lawyer. Then he was guided back to the room where one waited and he did not speak of the pain, for he hoped it might go.

But it was still there. After a time his friend the lawyer came in and said he had done well. But somehow Kobedi no longer cared. When he was in the car beside the lawyer he had to ask for it to stop so that he could get out and vomit into a bush, for he could not dirty such a shining car. On the way to the Court he had watched the little clocks and jumping numbers in the front of the car, but now they did not speak to him. He had become tired all over and yet if he shut his eyes he saw the finger pointing. "I will take you to Mr. Tshele," said the lawyer and stopped to buy milk and bread and sausage; but Kobedi was only a little pleased and he began less and less to be able not to speak of his pain.

After a time of voices and whirling and doctors, he began to wake up and he was in a white bed and there was a hospital smell. A nurse came and he felt pain, but not of the same deep kind, nor so bad. Then a doctor came and said all was well and Mr. Tshele came and told Kobedi that now he was going to live with him and go properly to school in the daytime and have new clothes and shoes. He and the lawyer would become, as it were, Kobedi's uncles. "But," said Kobedi, "tell me—the one—the one who did these things?"

"The Judge has spoken," said Mr. Tshele. "That man will die and all will be wiped out."

"And—the woman?" For he could not now say mother.

"She will be put away until the evil is out of her." Kobedi wondered a little about the small sisters, but they were no longer in his life so he could forget them and forget the house and forget his village forever. He lay back in the white bed.

After a while a young nurse came in and gave him a pill to swallow. Kobedi began to question her about what happened, for he knew by now that the doctors had cut the pain out of his stomach. The young nurse looked round and whispered: "They took out a thing like a small crocodile, but dead," she said.

"That was the sorcery," said Kobedi. Now he knew and was happy that it was entirely gone.

The young nurse said, "We are not allowed to believe in sorcery."

"I do not believe in it any longer," said Kobedi, "because it is finished. But that was what it was."

Among the trees in the academic groves,
there *is* a Lowry Pei. He was observed a
couple of years back running a Writing Program at the University of California in San
Diego, was next sighted in the purlieus of
Princeton, and is presently receiving mail in
the environs of Cambridge. Since this *rara
avis* changes his roost every year (and never
answers his phone) it is not easy to pin Pei
down for the usual bio. One would have
liked to ask him some searching questions,
if only because—

This is a haunting story.

Barranca, King of
the Tree Streets

BY LOWRY PEI

My friends lived on Chestnut Street, and when I was
looking for a place to live they said, "Go see Barranca,
up at the barber shop, he owns half the tree streets."
  "Tree streets?"
  "Chestnut, Maple, Spruce—right around here."
  "Oh."

In the grocery store (if I remember right) I saw a
young woman who looked like a girl I was in love with in
college. They were called girls, twenty years ago. She
said "hi" to me in the checkout line and also later, on
Chestnut Street, as if I looked like someone she knew,
too. I noticed the unselfconsciously arrogant way she held
a twenty-dollar bill between two fingers as the clerk
bagged her groceries. Outside the store, I passed a couple

of other young women and caught a whiff of some perfume, like an odor of sanctity, that went right into me
and hit the mark.

Chestnut Street was lined with pin oaks, sugar maples,
lindens, and scarlet oaks—the ones whose leaves tell you
their name because there is a "C" cut out of the leaf and
their Latin name is *Quercus coccinea*. There was a Chinese Redbud that I looked up in the *Atlas of Woody
Landscape Plants,* and it said "barely survives in central
Indiana." It was doing fine in northern New Jersey.
  "Hi," she said.

I thought of the voice of a singer, long ago: "It's late
September and I really should be back in school." I had
trouble remembering where I was staying while I looked
for a place.

I went into the barber shop; a bell clicked and dinged
over the door.
  "Yes?"
  "I'd like to speak to Mr. Barranca."
  "He's busy right now."
  "Well, do you know when he'll be back?"
  "What would you like to see him about?"
  "I'm looking for an apartment and I heard that—"
  "You come back later."

I described the man I had spoken to—graying, gaunt-
faced, short, kneading his cheek as he stood looking out
the barbershop window, one foot up on a chair. "That
was Barranca," said my friend.
  Every day there were more and brighter leaves on the
sidewalk. "The maidens taste, and stray impassioned . . ."

I bought a new corduroy jacket like one I had had in
college, such as I had been promising myself for years,
but somehow I forgot to take it with me. I also forgot that
I had bought it, until the next day, when I remembered,
because I had it on.

That same day I met the same young woman at the corner of Chestnut Street. She said "hi" again, and since

we were both going down the hill, I asked her if it would be all right to walk together. "Sure," she said, smiling, and the coldness left her face for a moment, leaving her almost shy. I found out her name was Caroline, which was all right—not the same as the other. I told her something about plants, especially the ones on the street. She was a student, as I thought, and asked if I taught a class. When we reached the bottom of the hill, she turned to the left and I did not have the courage to follow her. "Maybe we'll meet at the corner again," she said, smiling once more. She wore a beige trench coat and carried a square leather bag with a shoulder strap; her hair was a splotch of red-gold against the grey blotter of the afternoon. From behind she looked exactly as I remembered her. I watched her for a long time, afraid that she would look back and see me watching. At one point a couple of blocks away she suddenly seemed to grow very tall; then she returned to normal size.

"Mr. Barranca?"

"Mr. Barranca is not in right now," he said, moodily watching the sidewalk. I didn't know what to say.

"Perhaps you remember I was here the other day, asking about apartments. Did you speak to him about it, by any chance?"

"No, I . . ." He seemed to lose interest in the conversation. After a while he said, "He doesn't have anything right now."

"Well, thank you." I turned to go.

"What were you interested in?" he said as my hand touched the doorknob.

"Something right around here—you know, the tree streets—nothing elaborate, just for me."

"You got pets?"

"No. Well, I might have a cat," I said, surprised at this piece of information. "Some friends of mine are keeping him for me." I couldn't remember their names, but I recalled the cat perfectly now.

"You let them keep him, huh?"

"Do you think it would help me," I said, looking at him as directly as I could, "you know, with Mr. Barranca?"

He glanced at me briefly. "Yes."

I began devising ways to show up at the corner of Chest-

nut Street ten times in an afternoon without simply hanging around. On the third day I met Caroline there, and
we walked down the hill together again. At the bottom,
where I expected her to turn, we both kept straight on,
past the music school, until we reached a frame house
where she said she lived. She invited me in for a cup of
tea; my heart pounded, not bcause of the stairs. It turned
out she lived in one large white room at the top of the
house. There were few furnishings—a big square table
of unstained oak, a mattress on the floor with an antique
quilt over it, some bentwood chairs. It was impeccably
clean. I put down her groceries and reached up to pull
the string that hung down from the overhead light, but
she said, "No, that makes everything ugly," and turned
on a lamp by the table.

As she made tea she talked to me about the anthropol-
ogy she was studying and how curious people were. I
thought that I might have been content to sit in silence,
watching it grow dark, without a light in the room except
her breathing and my own. The tea steeped in a heavy
brown stoneware pot, white-flecked in the glaze. I told her
how beautiful it was, how beautiful her room was, but she
did not reply.

I tried to tell her a few things about myself, my life,
but could manage only stumbling phrases, and I found
the subject of no interest.

She was silent for a long time, looking at a picture on
the wall (I thought). I did not get up to make sure what
it was. When I began to speak she shushed me.

Finally I became convinced she was not going to speak
again. I got up and moved toward her with the intention of
saying goodnight. Awkwardly, I stood in front of her,
offering my hand; she looked up. "Why did it take you so
long to come back?" she said. I bent down, putting my
hand on her neck, to kiss her; at the last moment she
turned her cheek to my lips with half a smile. "My name
isn't Caroline," she said, now that I was unable to speak.
Her hand touched mine gently, moving it away.

I went to wherever it was I went at night and slept and
slept.

Click, ding.

"Mr. Barranca," I said, taking all my courage in hand,
"I must have a place to live."

"Mr. Barranca is not in," he said tiredly, perfunctorily. "So, you must, eh?"

"Yes."

"Whereabouts do you want to live?"

"The tree streets. Chestnut Street."

He sighed profoundly, turned the sign on the door from "Open" to "Back in Ten Minutes," put on his jacket, and showed me out.

We walked down the hill, scuffling red leaves, in silence.

"Anyone you know live here?" he said.

"Yes—a couple of friends, in one of these houses here," I said, indicating vaguely.

"Anyone else?"

His questioning annoyed me, and I did not answer.

We continued down the hill to the bottom, straight on, past the music school, to a frame house with a large white room at the top. Her furniture was gone. I could see holes where picture hangers had been driven into the walls. One seemed to be in the spot I remembered. He turned on the overhead light.

"Previous tenant just moved out."

"But—"

"You say you must have a place, nothing elaborate, here is a place."

"Yes."

"Well?" He seemed very old, his eyes hooded; he did not look at me.

"Yes, I'll take it."

We walked back up to the barber shop so that I could sign the rental agreement, under the pin oaks, the sugar maples, the scarlet oaks with a "C" cut out of their leaves. When I had completed the papers and paid, he said, "And now you will have a haircut. On me. This apartment-hunting has been hard on you." He gestured me toward a chair.

"Oh, no, I couldn't think of—"

"Yes, I insist, it is my trade after all, and you will know that I am glad to have you for a tenant."

"So you are Mr. Barranca, then," I said triumphantly, expecting some acknowledgement, but he impassively motioned me to sit back in the chair.

"And a manicure," he said, as if I had not spoken.

From the side of my field of vision, a woman took my hand in professional fingers. I looked over.

"I haven't seen you in an age," she said. "It's wonderful, the people I meet in this shop."

"Hello, Alison," I said, closing my eyes. Nothing else, but still the red-gold hair.

George P. Elliott died untimely at the age
of sixty-one on the 3rd of May 1980. He
had been Professor of English at Syracuse
University for seventeen years. He is best
known for his novels: *Parktilden Village,
David Knudson, In the World* and *Muriel;*
he had several volumes of short stories,
poems and essays to his credit; and, within
the genre, his story, "Among the Dangs," is
well-remembered from its first appearance
in *F&SF*.

In Yahvestan, when the choice is whether
to be a wolf among wolves or a hog among
swine . . .

Thomas in Yahvestan

BY GEORGE P. ELLIOTT

Thomas awoke to an ache in his broken tooth, and all
day the pain, which he did not mention to any of the
caravaners, made him reflect gloomily on his follies and
errors. Why had he ever left home? Childbirth kills
women no deader in Illyria than anywhere else. And that
solitude he had been hankering after? There was plenty
of it five miles from his native town. And at least the
people of Illyria didn't talk wrong, dress wrong, look at
you wrong. As for the China this caravan was headed
for, his urge to go there had not survived the first week
with the caravan; now, the only reason he could think
of for going to China was to tell the people at home about
it, and home was what he was running from. This mountain range they had been winding up and down and
among for twelve days, so bleak it didn't even have a

name, though some of the men said they'd heard of some country called Yahvestan in these parts somewhere and though Wry Neck said he came from there—even the animals were wrong hereabouts, griffons, people said, werewolves, birds with teeth. While the others were eating the evening meal, Thomas sat on a mound well apart from men and camels, chin in hand. He'd gone over the edge of the world as he'd promised himself to do, he deserved to be punished, he had no right to complain.

But the moment Wry Neck sought him out and asked why he was not eating, Thomas complained.

Wry Neck shrugged, and looked solicitous. His hand reached into an inner pocket and fetched out a dried leaf; his fingers twiddled it. "This is a cure for pain. I'll seethe this for a while in camel's milk, and at least you'll be able to sleep tonight."

It was a good thing he used only the one leaf of dried lanthan; the drugged milk was so formidable a potion that Thomas' toothache vanished after he had drunk a cup of it. However, so far from straightway falling to sleep he bounced into an amiable, silly delirium, swinging like the clapper of a tinkle-bell: first he would giggle to be feeling so good; then he would remember how painfully his tooth had been throbbing just a little while ago, and his lower lip would tremble, he'd blubber. Wry Neck, for the sake of his longed-for slavery, had to talk Thomas back into some semblance of masterfulness; but he could not think what to say. He had resolved not to mention the priestess of the love-rites, the Tuma, till they were already in Yahvestan, reasoning that a man as fastidious as Thomas would not be able to endure the very thought of such a lewd navel-licking woman—though once Thomas was a member of a wedding, the lanthan would trick him into mindless desire. But here and now, with Thomas insufferably silly from the lanthan, Wry Neck could not think how better to restore him to dignity than by giving him something to look down on, the Tuma. He told Thomas about Yahvestan and her.

When Thomas had stood at Maria's winter graveside, fists clenched and eyes dry, the thud of the first shovelful of earth hitting the coffin made his heart pound to join her, and by the time the grave was filled he had vowed eternal fidelity and chastity; but that had been a plain and several mountains and two wide seas ago, and his loins had not been consulted in the matter. Now, susceptible and incautious, at Wry Neck's mentioning a priestess of pleasure, Thomas' mind filled with images so lascivious that he grinned for more. Wry Neck, greatly relieved, chattered on, assuring Thomas that the lewder the images the holier they were in the Tuma's eyes, though nothing was holier than navel-licking. "Ah?" said Thomas and frowned solemnly at his navel. After a while, he wobbled to his feet and informed Wry Neck he was ready to set off for Yahvestan then and there. Wry Neck persuaded him to lie down first and rest. Thomas fell asleep as soon as he stretched out.

By midnight he had slept off the giddiness but not the images. They were more vivid than the stars above him in the moonless sky. 'Shame,' his heart reproached him, 'are you not ashamed of such base thoughts?' 'It's not that I want to, but the flesh is strong and besides these God-forsaken regions are given over to devils.' 'Faithless, inconstant husband.' 'No! I love Maria and only her and I always will.' 'To the whores with you.' 'I can't help it.'

Hearing Thomas groan, Wry Neck came awake, poked up the fire, and watched him gnaw his lip.

"Human Beings," Wry Neck said, "like to be married by the Tuma as often as they can, except the Sinseekers, of course."

"You ever marry?"

Wry Neck sniggered, and spat. "Usually people marry themselves along with nine other couples."

"How often?"

"Every new moon. The dark of the moon unmarries them. Mostly they remarry each other, but there are always some who are looking around. Young women especially."

"Well," said Thomas, "every month?"

"Tonight's the night for us to take off and go there. Shall we?"

"Why not?" Thomas thought, hunching down further.

"The wolves," said Wry Neck, "were howling around last night, and I told the others that werewolves run in the dark of the moon."

"Do they?"

Wry Neck winked.

"Blch," said Thomas and spat through the hole made by his broken tooth.

The country into which Thomas was about to disappear was triply sequestered from the world: by its poverty, by mountains behind and desert before, and by its religion. The few Outsiders who had ever come this way had had many strange gods, wheras Human Beings (as the people of Yahvestan, or God's Country, called themselves) had had only one god and furthermore had always claimed that he was the oldest and strongest god, more attentive to his people's welfare than other gods were to theirs. Furthermore, so they used to say, in order that time might begin he had come down through a hole in the sky and entered a high, cone-shaped mountain in the center of Yahvestan; they called him Mountain, though of course he only lived there. But then, a few generations back, he had gone away. Thereafter, Human Beings were shunned even by the few traders who had used to come every few years. What had Human Beings done that their god would punish them so cruelly as to abandon them? To that question no one, including the Human Beings themselves, could conceive an answer. Outsiders ceased to mention Yahvestan, wanted to not-know what abominations had been committed there lest such knowledge inflame their imaginations, tempting them to do likewise.

When Mountain had belched flame, and a river of molten rock poured from his lip, and bottomless cracks appeared in the earth, and ash settled on all Yahvestan, the Human Beings had been stunned. Cowering, they thought to appease his wrath by muttering the prayer for mercy; he was not appeased. After the days of his roaring, Mountain suddenly died: obviously the fountain of fire had burned a hole in the sky, and he had gone up through it. The priests set about to discover what prayers, rituals, sacrifices, would win him back. Some Human Beings thought this was a waste of time: wherever he was, he was surely so far away that the sound of their voices could no longer reach his ears or the smoke of their sacrifices please his nostrils. Most, however, lords, commoners, and slaves alike, agreed it would be a good idea to maintain the ancient ways so as to be worthy of him when he returned: a rite might chance to snare him long enough for them to pray him back into the mountain, where they would glut him with sacrifices forever after. But in fact most Human Beings were too occupied getting along in a world without god to bother worshipping him on the off-chance; the job was delegated to a priest, God's Remembrancer, and a handful of priestesses, Custodians of Tradition, who lived on the side of Mountain, sequestered from all other Human Beings; and in Yahvestan generally religion etiolated for lack of fresh blood, most of which was pumping into arguing about the foundations of justice, authority, and love.

These arguments never ceased. What they lost in vigor over the years they gained in ingenuity.

It was obvious that without god's justice, ultimate and infallible, Human Beings must construct their own justice, winnow all the grievances, lay all the blame, do all the punishing. The never-resolved question was: how to lay a foundation on which so great a palace may safely be erected? The only consensus by way of answer to this question was negative: neither might nor exceptional ability could be the foundation to Human justice. But without god to sanction the authority of Human Beings, how shall they prevent brute force from triumphing? Only by treating each other as equals. But how can they do that, since they are not in fact equal? No, but authority can be distributed more or less equally, not much for anyone, a little for everyone. The many who neither want to nor are competent to handle authority were quelled by the following argument: who but god dispersed authority all over Human Beings by abandoning his people to fend for themselves? It took the idea a couple of generations to establish itself, so shocking was it, but finally it was generally accepted: god had sinned. By abdication, god made each responsible for all and all for each; if you don't like this state of affairs, blame god; the sin is his. (There was some talk of changing the name of God's Country, but the name was kept: his sin stayed fresh on people's tongues.)

Justice and authority: in common to these was governing. Who should rule? (It occurred to some Human Beings that all government should be abolished, but they were dismissed as harmless madmen.) How better to make responsibility universal than to have everybody at once own another and be owned by another? There must be no rulers, no leaders, but only judges: a Council of Twenty judges was elected annually by all Human Beings; the twenty elected from among themselves the year's Settler (so called since, as the final court of appeal, he settled

grievances once and for all); then the Council publicly
criticized and cast doubt on, though seldom negated, almost every decision the Settler made, even as the popu-
lace at large unfailingly complained about the Council's
decisions as well as the Settler's. The result of this dense
reticulation of mutual distrust was that Human Beings
milled and drifted like a shepherdless flock of sheep and
watchdogs all tethered together, complacent in their freedom and equality: the group free to wander, all the mem-
bers equally constrained.

In order to endure the justice they had bound themselves with, Human Beings had to satisfy their acute need
for personal freedom of some sort. Practically, where
could most of them find it better than in love?

Once god was no longer there to sanction sexual love,
Human Beings felt free to make it all themselves. But
how free, and especially how free from politics? At first,
they liberated love even from marriage; but the consequence of this was that every act of love, whatever
else it did, also surreptitiously sloganized *I am free*, and
this assertion tainted love's pleasures with the anxiety
to prove it true: I *am* free. Human Beings came to fear
the very love they had to have. So, in monthly form, they
reinstated marriage: better to resent the restraints on
your love than to fear the love itself. Also, they instituted
the ceremonial use of a long-forbidden drug; it weakened
the will dangerously, but they decided this was worth
the risk, for the drug also released desire until not even
satiety's "I want no more" stopped it, but only capacity's
"I can not." The combination of weakened will and in-
genious lust freed love even from politics, at least during
the monthly nuptials.

It was this drug, lanthan, which Wry Neck adminis-
tered to Thomas.

"If we leave tonight," said Wry Neck, "you will have
a month to get ready for the next love feast."

"Pthluh," said Thomas and licked the roof of his
mouth. But then a Fatima with kohl-grey eyelids and a
ruby in her navel began loosening for this never-hermit
the veils of her lounging, and his biceps twitched. 'I can
go on with this miserable caravan and be a wolf among
wolves, or go off with him and be a hog among swine.'
He hit his forehead with the heels of both hands, straightened up, took a deep breath, and gave Wry Neck a bil-

ious look. "But I only know a few words of your language."

"I'll teach you all you will need to know at first," said
Wry Neck. "You will be a simpleton for a while and
not need to say much. You learn fast."

"I do," said Thomas, and the Fatima twitched for him.

Wry Neck had been exiled for insubordination: no
man would have him for a slave, because he demanded
more mastery than Human Beings were capable of any
longer. His immediate problem was to get Thomas to
the wedding without either of them being caught by a
Sinseeker, and both of them were visibly so different
from ordinary Human Beings that the risk was great. If
only the Tuma would make tall, flat-bellied, handsome
Thomas a Human Being, then Wry Neck could be
Thomas' slave and all would be well.

When asked where he came from, Thomas would only
say "from the west." He never hinted at what he was
fleeing or even that he was in flight, but his imprecations
and sullenness had to do with kings and captains, rich
men, the powerful, and his oaths had a Christian ring
to them. It took Wry Neck weeks to believe that this was
not some sort of pose on Thomas' part, for Wry Neck
had fallen into the role of Thomas' inferior so naturally,
with such grateful consciousness, that when Thomas offhandedly exercised command over him Wry Neck assumed without even thinking about it that Thomas knew
what he was doing; however, after weeks of Thomas'
attacks on the hierarchies of power, finally Wry Neck
had to conclude that Thomas was not aware of his own
natural lordliness. This only heightened his value in Wry
Neck's eyes, for now he would shine forth all the more
brightly in Yahvestan. There, hierarchy had been razed
flat and privilege mangled to a pulp three generations
earlier; Human Beings had forgotten what a lord looked
like, and Wry Neck was sure that many of them yearned,
as he did, to have one.

He taught Thomas how to greet any Human Beings
they might come upon and how to behave when he came
into the presence of the Tuma.

Wry Neck pointed down into a valley at three baked-
earth houses huddled together at the edge of a river, and

he told Thomas the time had come for him to see how he made out alone with strangers.

"Why don't you come with me?" said Thomas.

"I've been here before, Sinseekers live there, I'll be recognized, and then . . ." He made a chop at his throat. "I've returned to Yahvestan without permission, and I have no master. I'll be safe in the Valley of the Tuma, Sinseekers don't go there."

"Where will we meet?"

"Go where they direct you, towards the City. Don't worry, I'll find you soon enough and we'll go on the way we've been going."

Well before Thomas reached the houses, he came on three little girls playing on the bank of the river. They ran shrieking towards a thicket, from behind which there marched a chunky little woman who planted herself in front of him, squinting up at him and chewing her lips.

"What are you doing here, Outsider?"

He knew her for a Sinseeker by the black mark on her forehead the size of a thumbnail. "Sister," he began, "fellow Human Being," but her glower halted him. "We are all twins," he said deferentially.

"You're no twin of mine." Her voice was flat and raspy.

"God's Remembrancer sends me to the City, and I have lost my way. I need help to uncover my sin."

"That's more like it. You're going to the right place." She barked a laugh without ceasing to glower. "I know what there is to know about sinseeking." She held up her arms; her left hand had been cut off. "I got that for praying to Mountain in my sleep. Three different husbands testified against me. I haven't done it since."

Involuntarily Thomas started to cross himself but stopped before he had done more than touch his forehead with his right thumb. Without his knowing it, this gesture melted her suspicions of him: it meant he wanted to be a Sinseeker too. She told him there was no point in his hurrying to the City because the Council of Twenty would not be meeting till the full of the moon. Why didn't he stay here? The next love feast was the day after tomorrow, and she hadn't had a new husband for over a year. He lacked words to answer her with; he just smiled and shook his head mournfully. "Oh, it's one of those?"

she said. "Well, come back after you have found your punishment."

As he was walking in the direction she pointed out to him, he heard one of the little girls say, "What will they do to him for being so good to look at?"

"Slit his nose, I expect," said the mother.

"And he's so tall."

"If he's done something bad enough, they'll cut him off at the knees. I hope they don't have to because then he couldn't come back and marry me."

A burly guard admitted Thomas into the audience-chamber, which was also the chamber of love. An incense-heavy room with an earthen floor, twice as long as it was wide. A divan on a bearskin near the back wall. Who was this woman of bangles and bulges, with a pot over her head, that he must cringe before her?

Sitting motionless on the divan, cross-legged and bare-footed, the Tuma watched Thomas approach upright on his knees.

Closer, he saw she was not really wearing a pot. A kind of cap woven of many-colored beads sat on the crown of her head; out from it stood a circlet of brass, and on wires from the edge of this circlet dangled frilly perforated copper discs; this fringe hung to her chin, and the discs in front rustled with her breathing.

She did not like the coldness in his eyes, and his obeisances were clumsy. She was about to gesture the guard to take Thomas away, when some subtle shift towards deference in his manner stayed her hand.

He had got close enough to smell garlic on her breath —during the dark of the moon the Tuma sucked garlic to fend off werewolves. His knees forgot their soreness: he could not stand up to a woman with garlic on her breath, because in Illyria it was the custom for a mother to chew garlic before she beat her child, and Thomas' mother had been fond of garlic.

When he was within touching distance of the divan, he sat back on his heels, as Wry Neck had instructed him to do, neck curved, hands on knees, and addressed the Tuma respectfully in a low voice.

"Lady, I memorized flattery for you, but now that the time is here, my tongue cannot find the words. For I feel such emanations from your presence as wither every calculation and falseness from my heart." It was a good thing neither of them knew these emanations were garlic fumes. "I was told to remember that, even though you are the priestess of love, you are only a Human Being. My mind remembers, but my heart does not believe. You must be a higher order of being, Human yet more than Human. My mind asks: how can you be a priestess of yourself?"

"If you proceed one more word in that direction," she also spoke in a low caressing voice, "I shall have your tongue cut out." Slowly, somewhat grandly, her right hand slid under the chemise. "I am only a Human Being."

"As you will," he said and bowed till his forehead touched the bearskin.

"But," she said, "you have not been enlightened, so what can you know? If you were a Human Being I would think of marrying you. But, no." He breathed hard with relief, but she interpreted it as a sigh of regret. "Arlu," she called to the guard, "my crown."

Arlu took hold of the brass circlet with careful fingers, and slowly lifted the headdress straight up so that none of the discs touched her.

Thomas was prepared to be dazzled by beauty or shocked by deformity; instead, he saw another pudding-faced, middle-aged woman, distinguishable from others chiefly by reason of the fact that her head was shaved, even the eyebrows. She rolled her head around a few times and waggled her shoulders, and he watched intently, as though she were doing something more than just loosening up after sitting rigid a long time.

"You wonder why the Tuma is bald," she said, and Thomas nodded dumbly. "It is ugly, no?" One shake of his head was as much untruth of this sort as he was capable of at the moment. "Yes, it is ugly," she said with a slight preen to her voice. "Otherwise the Tuma's husband would die of sorrow when his month is up. Now then." She flounced, and parted her chemise so that her belly was exposed.

Thomas stared as though paralyzed at the absolutely ordinary indentation in the middle of that considerable mound.

"You may do what no Outsider has ever done," she said graciously. "You may lick the navel of the Tuma."

"No!" he cried, and his ears told him there was too much anguish in his voice.

She blinked at him.

Arlu squatted behind him, and Thomas felt the point of a dagger at his left kidney.

"Lady," he said, his voice trembling, "have pity on me, a miserable Outsider. You have been gracious beyond my merit even to grant me this audience. But you are the Tuma, and I am not even a Human Being."

"Not yet, no." Her right hand reached inside his shirt on the left side and fondled the pectorals. "But I think the time is not far off when you shall become one." She leaned back and held the sides of her belly with both hands. "Now."

He could not oppose her. He knew only, with incipient panic, that he had to escape before she commanded him to marry her. "I am not worthy," he said fervently, and licked.

She smiled, and sat up straight. "Tonight I shall marry Arlu again; it's been over two years since I married him last; and you shall guard the door in his place. A month without love in the chamber of love—we shall see how worthy you are."

Thomas backed away on hands and knees—he could not have stood, for dizziness.

When he had withdrawn a suitable distance, she nodded, and he stopped, squatting on his heels. She spat out the clove of garlic, rinsed her mouth with water, and took a nibble on a lanthan leaf; then, lying on her side, she assumed the Sleeping Dog position and within a minute had entered a trance, eyes rolled up so that only a slit of white showed. Her nose was running a little.

'Christ in heaven.' Thomas groaned inaudibly. 'The priestess of herself—what was I thinking of when I said that? On my knees to that sow. What am I doing here at all?'

Another prod of dagger over the kidney reminded him he was not going anywhere.

The wedding that evening began with a dignity he was surprised to find Human Beings capable of, and it mounted with an intensity that took him along.

In the center of the room, on a round dais lighted by a score of candles, stood the Tuma; Arlu was just behind her but facing the other way. The twenty-eight brides, standing about a foot apart, made a circle facing her, behind each of them a groom as close as he could stand without touching, also facing in. Everyone but the Tuma, men and women alike, wore a straw-colored sleeveless hempen shift that was clasped tight about the throat and fell straight to the ankles; the Tuma's shift was pink, the color of love, but was otherwise the same as theirs, and her head was in the pot-crown she'd had on when Thomas had first seen her. Throughout the long opening part of the ceremony, during which she was standing, she slowly revolved, Arlu careful to keep back to back with her.

The Tuma would chant a sentence; the rest, led by Arlu, would respond with a single word, alternately *love* and *freedom*, on *love* stamping with their right foot, on *freedom* with their left.

"Once: the mountain was God."

"Love."

"The mountain is the center: of the world."

"Freedom."

"In the center of the mountain: a hole."

"Love."

"In the center of every Human Being: the same hole."

"Freedom."

"My navel reminds: my mother."

"Love."

"My father is gone: forever I fear."

"Freedom."

"Bearers of the womb: mothers."

"Love."

"Open your wombs: to the desolate sons."

"Freedom."

"Let them become: unborn again."

"Love."

"Sons: bearers of the connection."

"Freedom."

"Fill the wombs: of the desolate mothers."

"Love."

"The cord of the again-unborn: reminds me of my sinful father."

"Freedom."

After a great deal more of responsory chanting, of the couples half-dancing and circling about one another, suddenly the Tuma raised her arms, and everyone fell still. She spoke forcefully, but without shouting.

"The world is reasonable. We must always rub hands with each other."

When she had proclaimed this in each of the four directions, she solemnly rubbed hands with Arlu. Then he took off her wig, pulled her shift over her head, and laid it out on the dais—she had on a pink bodice and trousers. He knelt at the end of the cloth, when she lay down on the shift on her back, he rested her nude head on his thighs. Her knees lifted and spread, and her hands held her ankles so that the soles of her feet clapped—the Silent Wind position.

Meanwhile, the twenty-eight couples had been doing an intricate prancing serpentine, without music but with much smiling and humming, during the course of which everybody rubbed hands with everybody else several times.

At a lull, the Tuma called in a hollow voice, "Holy of holies, the time has come. Will is the obstruction of love. Weaken it."

Each woman produced a lanthan leaf, took a nibble, and gave her man the rest to chew. The room filled with a moaning hum, everyone swaying. The Tuma, now standing, held out her hand towards Arlu and began to chant "Come come come." He took off his shift and laid it out on top of hers—he was left in a loincloth of the same pink as her bodice and trousers—and followed her, step by step as she backed toward the door behind the divan. Meanwhile, the couples helped each other off with their shifts, and now, all fifty-six entirely naked, they stretched their shifts out carefully, men's on women's, in a wheel about the dais. Then they sang in unison, women falsetto, men growling, a hymn of which Thomas could make out only the first words but which inflamed his lust: "Come let us enter the forest of copulation."

As soon as the door to the bedroom closed on the Tuma and Arlu, the men's "Freedom" chorused with the women's "Love," and they all lay down on their shifts, feet towards the dais, and copulated.

After a period of general stillness when nobody moved, half a dozen couples stirred, took up their clothes, dressed

with their backs to the circle, and departed, slipping by
Thomas at the door without looking at him—he shrank
from them. But during all this, their decorum was pelted
by hoots and jeers; only this bullying kept a good many
waverers from leaving, too. What tipped the balance in
favor of the insatiety the scoffers were after was a dark-
haired woman's yelling "There's too much light in here"
and darting around the dais blowing out candles. The
ceremonial circle dissolved, and the flickering shadows
from the fireplace began to pullulate with restlessness:
squeal of false enticement and chuckle of false capture,
the curlicues and switches of lubricity, the large broken
gestures of rampaging langour. Thomas' nausea turned
into muscular distress: he stood rigid at the door, mace
in hand, wanting nothing so much as an opportunity to
use it on some of those hot turnips.

When the dark-haired woman's man sprawled by
the way, she roamed the floor for better, but none endured.
Presently she stood, hands on hips, mouth a rictus, ap-
praising Thomas. He looked murder at her. She did not
approach him until she had recruited a couple of other
gorged hungerers. The three heavy-bellied dust-stained
young women paused just beyond sniffing range of him.

"Look at the scowl on him," said the dark-haired one.

"And the grab he's got on that ax-handle," said the
fat one.

"Will," said the one with breasts of different sizes, "It's
all over him."

"He needs some lanthan," said the dark-haired one.

"We're not supposed to give any to *her* guard," said
the lopsided one, "you know that."

"I know a lot of things we're not supposed to do,"
said the dark-haired one, licking her lips.

"Let me alone," said Thomas through clenched teeth
and he hefted the mace a time or two.

The lopsided one took a step back, ready to run off, but
the other two sneered.

"I wonder," said the fat one, "if he needs lanthan."

"What do you mean?" said the lopsided one, nervously
taking a step closer to him. "Look how tight with will
he is. Of course he needs it."

The dark-haired one had been prowling. Suddenly,
she leaped onto him from the side, hugged him, began
nuzzling.

If she had given any sort of warning, he would have knocked her down at the least, preferably have cleft her head; but the press of her flesh, viscid and funky, surprised the lust he had not known was still in him, flushed it out into the open, so aggravated it that, as her grip around her body tightened, his grip loosened on the mace, which fell back against the wall.

"No," she taunted, peering at his averted face, "he doesn't need any lanthan."

"Let's make a Human Being of him," said the fat one, rubbing against him on the other side.

"How?" said the lopsided one.

"He's Human enough for me already," said the dark-haired one.

"No!" cried the lopsided one. "He's not free. He's got to be free to choose."

"And love," said the fat one, "don't forget love. We've got to make him Human."

"All right," said the dark-haired one, "but let's hurry."

They rounded up seven other women, and the ten of them stripped Thomas of his clothes and made him stand with his hands behind his back; then, one after the other they licked his navel, laughing hilariously at the flatness of his belly, and all rubbed hands with him and one another, chanting "Now you are a Human Being."

"He was my idea," said the dark-haired one, "so I get him first."

"It was my idea," said the fat one, "to make him a Human Being. I get him."

"Choose!" cried the others. "Go ahead, man, choose."

The diffident one, covering her lopsided breasts, looked as though she were about to cry. He took her, partly in the hope her gratitude would temper the baseness of rut, but mostly out of malice towards the other two. The pain in the fat one's snarl and the thrashing fury of the dark-haired woman, whom the rest of them had to drag away, gratified his malice immediately, and the lopsided one was grateful, all right. As soon as his boil of lust was lanced, he blanked out of turbid consciousness into sleep.

He came to at dawn, the hall empty and cold. He wished he had chewed lanthan; maybe it would have prevented the images that were now soiling his memory, or, if they had to come, maybe it would at least have made them seem pleasant. There was nothing for it but to get out of this *freedomlove* he was chained to.

More painful than any image, there rang in his mind's ear the whisper of the woman with whom he had copulated: "I'll come back next month and marry you, now you're a Human Being. I already love you." He knew he would marry her if only to fend off the Tuma, and he despised himself. He thought of honest whores with nostalgia, of Maria not at all.

'O Lord, love is yours to give as you will, it is you. I have done the things of love and made not love but a rancid travesty of love. Love is not for us to make. It is for us to incarnate for little whiles, when you please to allow us to do so.'

"Then I'm a Christian?" he said aloud and clutched his head. "O my God, I'm still a Christian? No! I will not be!"

Yet he had to pray, and the only prayer he could recall at the moment was the Lord's Prayer. He meant its words. Who had led him into the temptation to which he had just yielded but God to punish him for backsliding? Who but God would deliver him from this evil?

Yet within a month he had convinced himself that he must change his ways to conform to theirs. They were right: we Human Beings belong to one another, we are part of one another, in each other we find ourselves; we are not ruled by the privileged but rule each other and ourselves, we are all privileged equally; I am my brother's keeper; love must be free. He allowed himself to become a Human Being and marry, to take Wry Neck as his slave every Fairday and be another man's slave the other six days of the week.

For over a year he told himself his repulsion for this country was wrong. Only here was privilege seen as wickedness and hedged about with justice which is equality, so he must be wrong. He willed consent to mutual enslavement and free love. But in doing this, he so benumbed himself against the seething confusion of his feelings that it took a violent shock to get him out of Yahvestan intact.

One Fairday when Thomas took the knout off its chimney hook, he thought he saw not dread but a glint of expectation in Wry Neck's eye, and it was not many weeks till it seemed to Thomas that his hatred of Wry Neck had become unreal. Wry Neck corrupted the beatings by translating Thomas' blows into something like caresses, so that Thomas could derive no satisfaction from these punishments. Instead, he got the unreal satisfaction of withholding punishment: 'I ought to beat you, but I shall not because you want me to.'

Even his hatred of slavery was turning unreal. Some kinds of slavery came to seem to him better than the rancorous freedom Human Beings had worked out for themselves.

Clay was real, and his hatred of digging the slimy stuff and lugging it to the potters' shed was real, tangible, direct. In need of some uncrooked hating, he did much more than his share of digging and carrying.

And there was his lopsided wife, his "remedy for concupiscence." At first he took her "I worship you" and "I am all yours" to be trite hyperboles. It had never occurred to him to kneel in adoration of Maria, and she for her part had been more disposed to tease him than pray to him; consequently it took him several months to realize how wrong he was about the worship of this woman whom he could barely endure.

One night he was awakened by her thrashing about in her sleep and muttering "Mountain" in a yearning voice. He shushed her and said her name, whereupon she crouched beside him and did what people still did when —and only when—they visited God's Remembrancer on the mountain: she clasped her hands behind her neck and bowed three times, saying successively, "God have mercy on me, God accept my adoration, God forgive me." But it was Thomas she was bowing towards, not the mountain. And when she murmured with the breathlessness of passion, "Oh how I love you god," Thomas was petrified. To his great relief, she presently sank into sleep. Maybe if that commotion went unmentioned it would not mean anything.

He wanted to escape then and there. But she was pregnant and he could not in all conscience stop remarrying her every new moon. He would wait till she had the baby to look after, and the roots of that poison tree her love would have someone else to twist into for nourishment.

He volunteered to dig and carry all the potter's clay

from then on, thereby perplexing his master and making himself an object almost of awe to other slaves. He did it to keep his mind ox-dulled with fatigue and also to keep at least some of his hatred steady—and any man must hate this heavy drudgery. Otherwise he might follow the example of Wry Neck and come to love the loathly.

He dreamt of the nine tiers of angels, each of them higher than the next, caroling their joy in celestial hierarchy, and when he awoke with that song fading in his ears, a terrible sadness settled on him to reenter this joyless life. He told himself that his detestation must be wrong and shunted it aside as best he could, but he could not prevent the heavy sadness coming.

Yahvestan had given Thomas the solitude and the level justice he had thought he wanted when he fled from Illyria. That is, his connections with Human Beings were unreal, and privilege had been pretty well smashed flat here. But Yahvestan was off the map. He wondered sometimes in his sadness if he would ever see a Christian land again, where hierarchy was in the nature not only of divine justice and love but of men's too. Not that he was Christian, not really, but the map seemed to be.

Mother and child died in childbirth, and Thomas made Wry Neck dig the grave.

Because Wry Neck had never been able to exercise the innate authority he had always known was his, because his chin was held from assuming the cock it wanted, he had pushed his masters one after another towards a strength of rule they not only were incapable of but shied from. Hence he had been overjoyed to have found Thomas, who seemed to him naturally superior to other Human Beings in every way that counted, and to have got Thomas to take him as slave. But Thomas, his melancholy increasing, had become negligent in his mastership, and at the graveside Wry Neck mistook Thomas' sodden silence for conjugal sorrow, a domestic sentiment which he thought unworthy of an exemplary master.

He taunted Thomas with having been a curse to both his wives. This was enough to provoke Thomas to make the ultimate threat. But he delivered the threat curtly, almost offhandedly—"Say that again and I'll kill you"— with little of the haughtiness and none of the conscious complacence Wry Neck desired. In open transgression,

Wry Neck drove the taunt in to the hilt: "Eh, you're a
woman-killer." Thomas killed him.

Under extreme circumstances, a master had the right
to punish his slave's disobedience with death, and Wry
Neck was well known to be intractable. But there had
been no witnesses to this punishment, and Thomas' behavior for some time had been incurring suspicion: he
was the only master who had been able to govern Wry
Neck, he was by far the hardest-working slave anyone
had ever heard of, and he had never given his own master
occasion to beat him.

No killing, justified or not, went unpunished by at least
an ear. The Settler, who had formerly been a butcher,
sliced off Thomas' left ear and threw him into prison to
await trial by the Council of Twenty.

Thomas accepted all this with unclear resentment. He
knew he had not disobeyed the law; moreover, he had
taken oath that he believed the laws of this land were
just. Doubtless, justice would be done. But the wound on
his head was very close to his soul. His dreams were
ferocious.

A white-haired, pink-skinned youth with weak eyes was
assigned to instruct Thomas in chanting the rites of sup-
plication, confession, and resolve. (No Human Being was
found "innocent" but only at most "not guilty as charged";
nothing was more Human than to feel vaguely guilty all
the time, though not necessarily of anything in particular.)
As a child, White had had to squint to see, and the other
children tormented him on the sly; but since it became
clear at an early age that he could sing beautifully, he was
protected, the only Human Beings allowed to excel with
impunity being singers. Thomas, having no qualms about
excelling, memorized the rote chants very fast, with the
result that White, whose happiness was to sing, spent all
the time he could in singing songs of every sort.

Listening to these songs with little substance, no more
Human than Christian, carefree, delightful, Thomas realized he had not been free of himself for over a year, even
for little whiles. But after six days of repeating into nonsense such rote as this, "I am no one unless I am my
brother's keeper and he is no one unless he is my keeper
but I alone am responsible for every sin I commit,"

Thomas found White's singing too gentle any longer to give much relief.

Late in the afternoon of the sixth day, White, feeling Thomas' mood, closed his eyes and tilted his face, and, in a delicate wail, sang a new song. Thomas listened, his thoughts going every which way like fish in a pool; but something about the last line made all his thoughts dart to it.

> Come, Love,
> Come grace my groin, my tongue, my hand,
> Till the flow of letting all I am.

Thomas did not know what those last words meant, but he knew they meant something.

White told him, in a low voice, that this song survived from the days before god had sinned and if *they* knew what it meant they would not allow it to be sung. When Thomas asked what it did mean, White trembled; yet there was something strange in his trembling. He begged Thomas not to tell anyone what he had just said, and as he was fumbling among words, "God's Remembrancer" dropped out. He hurried off, hand over mouth, eyes wide, and did not lock the door behind him.

It took Thomas several minutes of staring at the unlocked door to realize that White had given him a chance to escape and a hint of where to go first. Even then, Thomas did not move but considered whether it was worth the risk to waylay the Settler first and kill him for having cut off his ear. Thomas knew this impulse was foolish, but he could not dislodge it—till White's song came back to him. It called for Love to come help you be yourself body and soul—"till all I am." Not Human sexual love, but the god Love. Yes. The rigid urge to kill melted away. How could he take revenge on these whose real sin was being what they were? He fled to the mountain and those who remembered god.

Of the five widows, Custodians of Tradition, spinning and weaving under the arbor, none was beautiful and only one was as young as Thomas, but all were clean, their hair was long and loose, and they greeted him with a simplicity of gaze and friendliness of gesture he had not encountered in Yahvestan before. The oldest shapeless little woman of forty or so, her smile open, her grey eyes unclouded by suspiciousness, rose, held out her right hand, and told him in a low, merry voice that he was welcome. When he stammered, she laughed with the same quiet merriment and said, "Don't bother, friend, it's different here." Then she led him by the hand to a bench, gave him a piece of bread "for Mountain's sake," told him to make himself easy for a few minutes, and went off towards the nearby mouth of the cave. The other four smiled at him and continued with their work, one of them whistling quietly through her teeth.

God's Remembrancer was much the tallest Human Being Thomas had seen, half a head taller than Thomas himself; he wore a full beard, in a land where Thomas had not seen so much as a mustache; and, though he was fat, he was solid inside his fat, and his movements were as confident as were the inflections of his resonant voice.

'Ah,' thought Thomas, 'it is even better here than I had hoped.' He had come prepared to dance through a ceremony of rote questions and rote answers. Instead, this manly fellow in the prime of life sized him up man to man rather than priest to suppliant and greeted him with the natural question *what brings you here?* rather than the ceremonial probe *when last did you visit the high places?* Thomas' body swiveled just a little, his eyes flashed, and his voice rang out more happily than at any time since he had left Illyria, the words equally his and the ritual's.

"I come to find out how to cleanse my soul of the blood on it."

The sigh of pity thrummed the women.

"Ah?" said God's Remembrancer. "I have been hearing about you, Thomas, and I have been waiting for you many months. But I did not expect you to come for this reason. Whose blood stains you?"

"My Fairday slave's. He taunted me."

"This mountain was god, and there," the priest gestured towards the cave, "in god's pocket one says differently. When you have prepared, we shall go into god's pocket." But he did not move.

"I have only this pheasant to offer you, god's man." Thomas pointed at the small body on the ground beside him. "When the hunter is hunted, any is all."

"Roast it," the big man ordered the women. "We shall eat it as soon as it is well charred. Then, Thomas, we shall go inside god's pocket." He turned towards the cone of the mountain and intoned, "God have mercy on me." Thomas joined him. "God accept my adoration. God forgive me. God remember me."

The priest turned towards the women by the fire. "O Custodians of Tradition," he sang in a liturgical drone, "behold this Human Being."

Thomas recognized his cue, and fell into the rote. "I have not forgotten god," he droned in response.

The priest turned, and looked at him. "Behold this Human Being."

The women responded, "We behold him. Let him speak."

"I come in uncertainty," said Thomas.

"I am myself," said God's Remembrancer. "I am not you. Are you yourself?"

"Not yet," said Thomas, and he lost track, thinking 'what does it mean to say that?'

God's Remembrancer frowned at him. "Disarray," he prompted.

Thomas nodded. "Not yet, for I am still in disarray, the disarray of unclear sin."

They raised their arms and sang the words with which the rite concluded: "God forgive us. God forgive us sinners all."

Thomas had no idea what would come next.

"Come here," called the priest to the youngest of the women. "Minister to him for an hour, beloved, then we shall feast on the offering he brings us." He squinted at the sun; it was still high but starting down the westward arc. "He and I will not leave until tomorrow."

"You are going away with him?" she said.

"He must seek his sin elsewhere, for he is too tall to live with Human Beings without being taken down for it. Therefore, I must go with him and protect him from the Sinseekers till he is safely out of God's Country. Now take him to the font, beloved." He put Thomas' hand in hers.

She squeezed it friendlily and said to Thomas in a tender voice, "I serve God's Remembrancer in all things." She led him in silence along a mountainpath.

This young woman was not so turnipy as most and walked with a light swing to her hips; her eyes sparkled; her voice lilted. God's Remembrancer and she were the first persons he had met in Yahvestan whom he simply liked.

They came to a small natural amphitheater in the center of which was a pool so still that its surface mirrored the cliff-face above it. She knelt on a patch of moss full in the sun and dipped her cupped hands into the water.

"You too," she murmured, and Thomas joined her.

She lifted her dripping hands towards the cone above, and said, "As I wash my face, so do I wash away my sins." Then she splashed the water on her face and rubbed. Thomas did likewise.

"First I must wash you," she said, "I am your slave for an hour. Let us love one another while we can."

They took off their clothes. She led him into the cold water and washed him clean of dust and blood. They lay on the warm moss till they were dry; then with a teasing laugh, she licked his navel.

"Come," she crooned, and he joined her in the nuptial song.

Come let us enter
the forest of copulation.
Where is the clearing?
No way is the way.

Not to hurry. Not to loiter.
Each way is first where
touch leaves touch.
Let go. Let go,

that we may join to plunge
into that halo
nothing to be.
That way all ways.

It was not stranger's love they made, and after they were done, Thomas lay on his back, his head turned toward her, and she on her side facing him, one arm doubled under her head.

"I see in your eyes," she said, "or I think I do, that you will never become so reasonable as to forget god."

"When I was a Christian, I ate God's body and drank his blood. How could I forget part of myself?"

A veil he had not realized was there vanished from her eyes, and her lips were purely sensual.

"Yes," she said, "of course, and you are the most beautiful Human Being who ever lived."

"Will you come with me?" he said. "I could love you."

Her forefinger tapped his lips. "I am a Custodian. I serve whoever would remember god."

"I am afraid," he said. "I need you. Come with me."

"Shh." She was weeping, but without sobs, smiling. "No more talk. Let us make love again before my hour is gone. That is all there is."

Thomas grunted himself up, *no, no,* in the middle of the night and struggled to get out of the mud-pit of sleep into which he had fallen. Out in the open air it was still; he stared about blindly. Then he shook his head free of clogging dreams and knew exactly and vividly what that *no* had been addressed to: the girl had said "that is all there is."

'That is not all!'

He had been lying watching her put her clothes on, practical and graceful, and he extended his open hand toward her. She half-smiled, touched his fingertips with hers, and in a voice as serene as her face said for a second time: "That is all there is." He thought she was just saying something vague and agreeable, meaning *how good love makes me feel,* and he smiled responsively. But when she said, no less serenely, "I must go back now," and left, with the small smile still on her lips, a sadness rose like mist from his contentment, obscuring it, a sadness which had not come from the poignance of parting but from the empty sorrow of *that is all.*

'That is not all. It is only pleasure.'

A question rang in his mind's ear, and he crouched as tense as though he had heard a growl in the underbrush, though in fact there had been no sound. Then he noticed the words of that ringing, *where are the angels?*, and the memory pounced on him of God's Remembrancer asking him if he knew the angels.

So far as he could see, angels did not matter much one

way or the other. God's Remembrancer had said, "When god abandoned Human Beings the angels went with him. They brought us mercy, and grace, and communion. They taught us to rejoice. Now they are gone, and we Human Beings are forgetting what they taught us."

And later, Thomas remembered having refused to answer his question about the Christian God. "What have I to tell you? You have lived well enough without god for a long time."

Smiling, the big man bent down, almost whispering in his ear—they were in god's pocket. "The secret is this: behave as you would if you knew god was spying on you, and then you'll be as comfortable as you would be if he really is. That's the goal, to be comfortable with yourself. Where god is has nothing to do with it, only how you address him."

Now, out in the dark under the stars, alone, the others asleep in god's pocket, Thomas knew why there had been such melancholy in the voice of the smiling priest, and his leg muscles twitched with the impulse to run from this comfort without angels.

For lack of the angel of love, Human Beings had only pleasure. For lack of the angel of merciful justice, they became Sinseekers demanding impossible equality. The things they constructed were untouched by the angel of beauty. What were the words in which their wedding song culminated? *Nothing to be.* For lack of the angel of grace, they aspired to be nothing, rejoiced at being nothing, asked no more than to be comfortable with themselves.

Thomas resolved to escape before this horror wore off, to go without the help God's Remembrancer had offered, to sneak away without even saying goodbye to the woman who had ministered to him so sweetly. He liked them too much; God's Remembrancer might ask him if he wished to stay a while before fleeing, and if she joined her voice to his, Thomas might forget how terrible their lack and stay with them. No! He had not the charity to love them clearly; love of them would turn into a stew, as his feelings for Wry Neck and for his recent wife had done. Better to risk having the Sinseekers catch him and cut him off at the knees for being handsome, tall, various, than to love these who, in deprivation of angels, wanted to be nothing.

He had fled long enough. He had come to Yahvestan not knowing what it was; he had fled from, not to; if he fled any further he would fall off the edge of the world entirely. He must go back in the direction from which he had come, though it would no longer be home when he got there. He would have to make it his home again if he could.

He squatted with his back to the mountain and dozed. He would be ready at the first crack of dawn.

Thomas M. Disch is the quintessential New
Yorker in that he is a true cosmopolitan—
at home everywhere, with the possible exception of Minnesota. Recently he has taken
up painting. Among his other accomplishments: exquisitely crafted short stories (*Getting Into Death, Fun With Your New Head*),
widely various poetry (*The Right Way to
Figure Plumbing* and the forthcoming
ABCDEFG HIJKLM NPOQRST UVWXYZ
(sic)), and the consummate novel (*Camp Concentration, 334, On Wings of Song*).

He moves on familiar terms with the gods.

The Vengeance of Hera
or, Monogamy Triumphant

BY THOMAS M. DISCH

Hera's attendants were drying her after a ritual bath at
the spring of Canathus when her friend Iris arrived with
the Sunday edition of *The Times*. Wrapping her hair in
a towel, Hera settled down beside the pool to weed out the
sections of the paper she had no use for. At last, with
a grateful sigh, she found her way to the Social Announcements.

LYN LORD PLANS MAY BRIDAL, *The Times*
announced under a Bachrach portrait of the bride-to-be.
Hera nodded her approval. Lyn was the youngest
daughter of Mr. and Mrs. Julius Lord of Bayside, Queens,
a family with a particular reverence for the goddess of
marriage and the family. Their eldest daughter Marjorie
was already, at age twenty-six, the mother of five children, and Hera intended in the fullness of time to make

Marjorie's descendants a major force in Bayside politics and throughout the borough of Queens. Lyn, unhappily, could not hope to become a great matriarch, for she'd come to marriage tardily and was destined by the Fates to die only two years later in an accident on the Major Deegan Expressway. Alas for all poor mortals—but still how fresh and engaging she looked with her loose-flowing hair and the double strand of pearls. Hera wished her well.

Turning to the next page, the goddess was pleased to note that Mary Kemp Ross had married Ensign Theodore Tyler of the United States Navy in a ceremony at the Barrington Congregational Church. Two months ago that outcome had still been very doubtful. Also, Melinda Edwards was affianced to an assistant vice president of a prominent supermarket chain. And here was a surprise: Dr. Caroline Rhodes planned to wed one of her colleagues at Duke University! Hera had never heard of the bridegroom, but she couldn't imagine Caroline Rhodes making any but a prudent choice.

She turned to the last page where the very least of announcements declared that Bonnie Malvin of Amityville had married Jack Fleetwood.

Hera's large eyes widened with disbelief. "Iris! Look!" She tapped the offending paragraph with a well-manicured nail. "Jack Fleetwood—married! Again!"

Iris arched a sympathetic brow. "Isn't it disgraceful?"

"Can it be the *same* Jack Fleetwood?"

The announcement left little room for doubt. The bridegroom's parents resided in California and Kuwait. His father was an Aramco executive. No mention was made of the schools he'd attended (and been asked to leave). Could there be two such Jack Fleetwoods?

"I shall not allow it!" Hera declared, flinging down the paper.

"It's too late, my dear," said Iris. "The harm's been done."

"Were they wed in a church?" Hera demanded.

"The First Presbyterian. There was a photographer, a four-tiered cake, limousines, a honeymoon in Bermuda —no rites were omitted. Her mother was a Quigley, of the Amagansett Quigleys. Very traditional people."

"And this girl—Bonnie? I have no recollection of her."

"She's not exactly been one of your votaries. There

was an earlier marriage, in California, in somebody's
back yard, one of those do-it-yourself ceremonies. Even
then she was not a virgin. The marriage lasted a year and
four months."

"Children?" Hera inquired.

Iris shook her head. "On the pill."

A gleam came into Hera's eye. "And is she still?"

"Oh yes. From the first Jack's been insistent as to not
wanting children."

"Then pray tell me, why did he marry?" Hera asked
rhetorically. "Only to make a mockery of *me?* He shall
learn, Iris, that Hera—and the Institution of Marriage—
are not to be mocked. He has done so once with impunity.
Admittedly his first marriage was the thinnest of legal
fictions. An offense to my nostrils, naturally, but there
are not enough hours in Eternity for me to chastise all
such infractions as they deserve. I was wrong, however—
I should have exacted my revenge then. Where is she
now, this new bride of his?"

Iris closed her eyes and concentrated. A vision formed,
on the rippled surface of the pool, of Bonnie Fleetwood,
née Malvin, seated in the sunken living room of her new
home in White Plains, watching *Sesame Street* as she
brushed her long, lightly tinted hair.

Hera knew at a glance how the bored young matron
was to be dealt with. "Go to her," she bade Iris with
the calm, terrible authority that only the gods can command. "Enflame her with philoprogenitive desire. Make
her my minion. Jack Fleetwood shall not wriggle free of
the bonds of matrimony a second time."

Shortly after *Sesame Street* but before Mike Douglas
had properly begun, Iris, in the mortal form of Bonnie's
old friend Sharon Salomon, appeared before the fieldstone-
trimmed facade of 1282 Exeter Road. In her right arm
she bore a sleeping infant. Another child peered out,
Janus-like, from the canvas carrier strapped to her back.
She rang the bell and waited. Within, the nagging voice
of Margaret Hamilton advertising Maxwell House coffee
was silenced in mid-imperative.

Bonnie answered the door, regarded the goddess with
a frown of curiosity, and then exploded into welcomes.
"Sharon! Sharon Salomon!"

"Sharon Wunderlich now," said Iris with a smile that begged for approval as candidly as any puppy.

Immediately their relation was re-established on its old, unequal footing. "Of course." She leaned forward and kissed one of the goddess's freckle-constellated cheeks. "How good to see you!" She kissed the other cheek. "Come in, come in."

After only the briefest synopses of their marriages, the two women soon had settled down to the more comfortable (for Bonnie) subject of Mount Holyoke where they'd both majored in English Lit. With delicate enthusiasm, as one might unwrap china long stored unused, they invoked the memories of Cora Barnham; of Professor Harrison and her odd ways; of the night of the dormitory fire drill; of their Sunday morning dozens of Dunkin' Donuts. All the while they reminisced, little Marietta slumbered on beatifically in her mother's lap and Jason flailed quietly on the sofa beside her, gazing at the furnishings of the Fleetwood living room with a wandering, wonderstruck attention that put Bonnie distinctly in mind of her 9 A.M. class in Romantic Poetry. ("There was a time when meadow, grove, and stream, the earth, and every common sight, to me did seem apparelled in Celestial light, the glory and the freshness of a dream," etc.) What a lovely child. And how radiantly energetic dear old Sharon seemed, how altered. How much happier than Bonnie felt herself.

Marietta woke and asked with low gurgles to be nursed. Iris peeled away half her bodice and offered her breast to the smiling infant. Iris's bushy red hair, back-lighted by the picture window, formed an aureole expressive of maternal fulfillment.

"Tell me," said Bonnie, already caught in the toils of Hera's devising, "about your babies. They're both such . . ."

". . . inexpressible darlings—aren't they? What can I say? I guess the most incredible thing about them, the thing I least expected, has been the *energy* I get from them. Like now, with Marietta nursing, I can feel a kind of . . . like a lightning bolt I've trapped inside my spine."

Bonnie tried to preserve a rational skepticism. "I've always thought they'd be a drain. Especially the first few months."

Marietta unclenched a tiny fist, pressed her fingers

against her mother's resilient breast, and cooed bubbles of milk.

"Oh, there's that side of it, too," Iris admitted. "But they *replenish* much more than they ever drain. The other thing, or maybe it's the same thing from another angle, is the way they connect me to Reality. I mean, before Jason I was avoiding Reality."

"I wish you'd tell me how to do *that*," said Bonnie with a nervous laugh.

"I mean, staying around the house and never going out or seeing anyone. Just watching TV and combing my hair. Like that."

Bonnie winced.

"And I felt so *empty* all the time. But now, with the children, the whole world seems different. More solid. Coming over here today is an example. Before Jason I might have thought, 'Wouldn't it be nice to drive over to White Plains and see Bonnie?' But I never got round to doing it. No oomph."

"Don't apologize. I'm just the same."

"But that's my point, Bonnie—I'm *not* the same, any more."

Bonnie looked at her transformed friend, then at Marietta, then at Jason, and saw herself mirrored in them. A premonitory tingle tingled in the small of her back. Not a lightning bolt yet, just the merest hint of what she now knew to be her preordained and necessary fulfillment. How could she ever have been so blindly selfish as to have agreed with Jack, that afternoon in Bermuda as they downed rum swizzles, that theirs should be a childless marriage? She remembered how passionately as a girl she had mothered her little family of dolls—Selma and Baby Susan, Whiffles and Wanda, Lily and Rose; how she'd never allowed them to grow up and become self-mirroring Barbie dolls but kept them always in the livery of infancy, pink and baby blue; how, until Jack had announced his allergy to cat fur, she'd cuddled and coddled and cared for those two beautiful Persians from the animal shelter. All these signposts pointed to a single destination, which she could see now as clearly as a spire rising from the plain: Motherhood.

Iris, having accomplished Hera's purpose, announced that it was time to return home and start the pot roast. On the way out the door she admired the macrame pot hanger cascading stringily down from the ceiling of the breakfast nook. Bonnie insisted on giving it to her as a present, languishing ivy, ceramic pot and all.

"No, really," Iris protested. "It's much too nice."

"Not at all. It will give me a chance to make another."

"You made it *yourself?*" the goddess marveled.

"It's easy once you get the knack. Like tying shoelaces all day."

"I'm sure this is nicer than most of the ones I see in shops. You could make it a business."

Bonnie laughed in self-deprecation. "That's what Jack said yesterday. I think he's afraid my mind will rot, sitting around all day with nothing to do. And I think he may be right."

Iris scooped up Jason from the couch and popped him into the carrier, then slid the straps over her shoulders. "I can tell you *my* solution to that problem."

She did not need to say more. Bonnie's eyes were brimming. Her hands strayed, unconscious, to cup the shallow convexity of her still unquickened womb. Her soul hungered.

That night as her fingers exercised their almost lost facility on lengths of coarse twine, Bonnie began the slow work of bending her husband's will toward her new-formed purpose. It wasn't hard to manipulate Jack. Having no guiding principles beyond serendipity and his own caprice, he had little staying power against a will sturdier than his own. This pliancy accounted for a large part of Jack's charm. His photographs had the same quality of careless accommodation to prevailing winds.

Not that Jack any longer considered himself a serious photographer. For the past three years he had photographed little but beds: beds with sheets, with blankets, with spreads, with comforters. These photographs appeared in magazine advertisements and in department store and mail order catalogues. That it was possible to make nearly forty thousand a year photographing beds always struck Jack as an astonishing testimony to the colossal size of the world he lived in. To think that there could be so many people who needed to proclaim the merits of their particular sheets and pillowcases that a man's entire life could be directed to that single purpose!

This matter of purpose proved to be his Waterloo in

the discussions with Bonnie. What was the purpose, she
wanted to know, of their marriage? It could not be the
furtherance of his career, since Jack was prepared to admit that his career amounted to little more than a joke.
But then he asked no more. Bonnie would not accept this.
There had to be more. There had to be a purpose. What
was the point of living in her parents' two-and-a-half-
bedroom ranchhouse instead of in the city, where at
least you could go out to a movie sometimes?

What but a baby?

Jack was certain he would not enjoy a steady diet of
parenthood, but he had to admit that this theory had not
been put to the test of experience. Bonnie was just as
certain that fate had decreed her to be a mother, and her
certainty had the force of a faith behind it. By the time
the last half-hitch had been snugged into place on the
new macrame pot hanger Bonnie was pregnant.

Four weeks after the birth of his daughter, Joy-Ann, Jack
Fleetwood moved out of his suburban home on Exeter
Road and into his photography studio in a still very raw
loft on West 26th Street in the city. Since earliest youth
Jack had been able to solve the successive crises of his
life by the simple expedient of running the other way.
When he was twelve he had refused point-blank to cope
with the decimal system, and after only a little while his
parents had transferred him to a progressive school. The
invention of the pocket calculator confirmed Jack in this
first grand refusal, and those that followed all seemed to
endorse the same moral—that a problem resolutely
ignored was a problem solved. While other young men anguished over the trials and errors of young love, Jack
sipped the nectar from each flower that invited and flut-
tered on to the next. While others elbowed and shoved
their way into the elevator of success, Jack took a job on
the ground floor. Far from deteriorating, his character
took on the agreeable, hard-rubbed patina of a vintage
car that has spent all its existence in a museum. At the
age of thirty-two Jack still retained the ideal fecklessness
of his pampered childhood. Not for him, therefore, the
colicky nights and pails of diapers of responsible parenthood; not for him the pretense that Joy-Ann's birdlike
noises and muscular spasms were objects of perpetual
proud fascination. As a fetus she'd never represented

more to him than a disfiguring growth in Bonnie's no longer smoothly functioning body. As an infant squalling in a crib or being suckled at his wife's engorged and drooping breast she was unendurable, and accordingly Jack did not endure her.

There were allied considerations. The house on Exeter Road, which had been dangled, prior to the wedding, as a carrot was still, two years later, the property of Bonnie's father, a professional son-of-a-bitch, who continued to dangle it at the end of an ever-receding stick. Meanwhile it had become evident, living in the dump, that the reason he'd enticed them with this particular property was that its divers liabilities (electric heat, a cellar prone to flooding, and the threat of a highway that was to be their new view from the back windows) made it all but unsaleable. (It had been their intention to sell it as soon as it legally belonged to them.) Bonnie was livid over her father's treachery, but Jack's temperament was as little given to outrage as to long-suffering. However, since the promise of the dower-house had been a decisive factor in their decision to undergo matrimony, it seemed reasonable to Jack, though not to Bonnie, that Mr. Malvin's failure to deliver the goods released them from their side of the bargain. Jack didn't care to argue about it (arguing never accomplished anything) but when he did pack his bags and sort out his records from Bonnie's it was without any pang of guilt for having been derelict in his duty. As for the Diaper Monster, that had been Bonnie's initiative from the first: so bye baby bunting, Daddy's gone a-hunting.

Bonnie, wholly given over to the passion of motherhood, expressed but one regret—that with Jack away from home she could not have more children without incurring the guilt of adultery. Jack, half-jokingly, suggested artificial insemination, and Bonnie half-seriously considered it but decided at last that adoption would be a more wholesome possibility. She actually started filling out reams of application blanks sent to her by the various agencies that supply orphans, but the only one that did not seem to take exception to her status as a still undivorced single parent was an agency in Seattle that arranged the adoption of children born in a large Korean leper colony (guaranteed not to be lepers themselves). Even these orphans might not be made available for another year, so

Bonnie was obliged to lavish all her affection on her solitaire jewel, Joy-Ann.

Jack, among the model beds of his studio, experienced no difficulty readjusting to the zippier rhythms of inner-city life. In the day he shot sheets and pillowcases; by night he disported upon these same percale plains of Cherry Blossom, Royal Blue, Terra Cotta, Cream, and Carnival. The young women who shared his pleasures were always offered, as a keepsake, a complete change of bedding from among the ever-replenished stock. If his meals were not so regular as they had been on Exeter Road they were certainly more exquisite and less starchy. Soon his waist was a born-again thirty-one inches. He had never looked better or felt healthier, and his conscience seemed as trouble-free as the engine of his new Jaguar XJ6L.

Meanwhile on Mount Olympus Hera could not believe that he had so easily evaded the lesson she'd meant to teach him. Her fury waxed. She determined to use the utmost of her power against him. If in doing so she should also exact a long-delayed vengeance against Min-Tsing Bullard, so much the better!

It had been Jack's earlier marriage to Min-Tsing, ten years ago, that had first alerted Hera to his impiety. Min-Tsing was the daughter of an aide to the Indonesian delegation to the United Nations and a fellow student with Jack at Pratt Institute. They knew each other through weekends of marathon bridge at the apartment of a mutual friend. When her father was recalled to Djakarta, Jack had been the first U.S. male citizen she'd approached with an offer of matrimony. Her object in marriage was to escape being deported when her student visa expired. At eighteen Min-Tsing was interested in sex only insofar as it related to photography. She'd approached Jack before anyone else because she sincerely admired his bridge game and his black-and-white studies of second-story windows along Sixth Avenue. Jack dropped out of Pratt as soon as the marriage contract was signed and Min-Tsing's father had paid out the stipulated fee of $5,000. He continued to see his wife over the bridge table on such weekends as he was not otherwise engaged in squandering his windfall, but through all the time they were wed to each other he made no attempt against her chastity.

The benefits to be reaped from this arrangement didn't cease with the first lump sum. When she was twenty-one

Min-Tsing fell in love with, and was ravished by, Jerome Bullard, a highly successful photographer's rep. By the time Min-Tsing had divorced and remarried, Jack was settled into his new life-work. Bullard, though ordinarily an Othello of jealousy, had compelling proofs of Jack's honorable conduct toward Min-Tsing, and he was made to share her enthusiasm for Jack's talent as well. Bullard exercised his influence with a number of department stores and mail-order houses, and in little more than a year Jack had established himself as America's foremost photographer of bed linens, confirming his often-expressed opinion that success depends not on what you know but who you know. Bullard, as rep, got a symbiotic third of all Jack's fees and shared with him the distinction of being known, in the industry, as the Lord of the White Sale.

That Jack should prosper so undeservedly had been a source of aggravation to the goddess of marriage, but this was compensated to a degree by the unhappiness of Min-Tsing in her life as Mrs. Bullard. Bullard was a bully, sexually, socially, and in the conduct of his business. He alternated between long, morose sulks and spells of witless, cocaine-inspired garrulity. He grew fat, and then grew still fatter. He philandered, disappearing for days at a stretch with frowzy teenagers he obtained from agencies supplying office temporaries. The charming, intense, knowledgeable Bullard whom Min-Tsing had fallen in love with vanished before her eyes, and gradually she resumed her earlier attitude towards the realm of the erotic, which was simply to have nothing to do with it. From separate beds she and her husband evolved to a condition of separate bedrooms and then of separate apartments, albeit in the same building (which he owned). She continued, nevertheless, to work for him, since no one else could manage the complicated duplicities of their system of bookkeeping.

This had been their status quo for many years when Hera determined to use Min-Tsing as the instrument of her fuller revenge. Summoning young Eros from his mother's side, she instructed him to inspire Jack with a passion for Mrs. Bullard, and her with a passion for him. No need here to chronicle the delights and afflictions of the lovers: any program of popular music will relate Love's universal truths (albeit only a select few). Jack wanted her love, he needed her love, and, this feeling being mutual, he

got her love. For six months they lived as though in a
heaven of fleecy, flesh-supporting clouds, and then the
teeth of Hera's trap snapped shut about their unsus-
pecting limbs. Min-Tsing was pregnant. (The pill, needless
to say, is no precaution against the power of Hera.) Since
Min-Tsing's moral principles did not allow her to think of
abortion, she was soon unable to conceal her condition
from her husband-and-employer. Nor did she require
much persuasion to name the father of her unborn child.
Can Love ever hesitate to pronounce the beloved's name,
if it is truly Love? In any case, she could not have palmed
the baby off on Bullard as his own: there had been no
sexual congress between them for nearly a year.

   Min-Tsing had misjudged the effect her candor would
have, expecting Bullard, after his first annoyance, to take
her infidelity in the same civil, uncensorious spirit in which
she took his. Instead, he reverted to his Othello manner.
He denounced the lovers. He threatened physical violence
to Jack—if ever they should meet. He revelled in horror,
outrage, and self-pity. And he vowed to bring Jack Fleetwood's career down about his ears. Jack's dealing with the
merchants he worked for had mainly been conducted
through Bullard, who had set the fees and arranged the
kickbacks—and so was able now to call the tune. Jack's
work was suddenly not in demand. He was billed for immense inventories of bedding that had been consigned to
him in the clear understanding that they were to be his,
and when he indignantly refused to pay, he was threatened with legal action. Most painfully, because most un-
justly, Bullard simply withheld money owed to Jack for
work he'd already done. Within a month Jack was con-
fronting the clear prospect of bankruptcy.

   All the while Jack foundered, Min-Tsing would telephone with the news of her latest moods, which succeeded
each other with such whirligig impetuosity that Cleopatra
herself would have acknowledged her as an equal. Giggles
alternated with despair. She pitied Bullard from on high,
then wanted to kill him, or at least confront him and have
a proper shouting match. More than once she set off to
her old office (she of course had been fired) to have it
out, but Jack was always able to stop her. Then she urged
Jack to take her home to Djakarta. There Jack would
marry her and open a photography studio. She described
life in Indonesia in lyrical superlatives, and became angry

when Jack refused to be tempted. She discovered drunkenness and the heady pleasures of public hysteria. The barb of Eros was still lodged securely in her flesh.

Jack was not so fortunate. At the first axstroke of ill fortune, Love disintegrated into a welter of practical anxieties. It happened suddenly, like a slide being changed, snick-snack, by a slide-changer. Yet he could not, even so, have recourse to his usual solution, flight, if only because he still hoped Bullard could be made eventually to come round to a more accommodating attitude. This hope, however, could be realized only on condition that Min-Tsing were made to comprehend Love's last universal truth, that it dies. Much, therefore, as he'd have liked to simplify his existence by taking off on his own for Las Vegas or Miami, he remained at Min-Tsing's beck and call, hoping that by gradually weaning her from his already cooler embraces he might yet escape complete destitution. Besides, it is always delightful to be loved so thoroughly; more delightful perhaps, in an epicurean way, when the transaction is *not* reciprocal, for then the beloved will have the presence of mind to marvel at the sweetness of so much unmerited fond attention, instead of vibrating in blissfully unconscious resonance.

Time passed. Min-Tsing, far from tapering off, became clingingly dependent and still more wildly erratic. The studio had to be sold, and most of its equipment. Jack was reduced to looking for jobs at the very studios whose business he'd stolen during the years of his ascent, but Bullard had been before him, offering the old plums back and blackening Jack's name, and so his abjection was of no practical value. Another photographers' rep, whom he went to with his portfolio, told him he was unemployable without a good reference from either Bullard or a previous employer. The whole city seemed to be in a conspiracy against him.

Then one half-soused night when he was watching an old musical with Min-Tsing in her new and so much grottier apartment, a walk-up on West 19th, the phone rang and dumped a load of new worries in his lap. It was Bonnie, wondering where his last three child-support checks had gone to and asking, as though in passing, for a divorce. Jack felt as the captain of the *Titanic* must have when it became known that his ship lacked lifeboats. Bon-

nie had been his ace in the hole—Bonnie and her son-of-
a-bitch father, whom Jack had made no serious effort to
exploit since the debacle over the house on Exeter Road.
Jack told Bonnie to stay home, he'd be right there to discuss the matter seriously. Then, ignoring Min-Tsing's
threats of suicide (which she did not carry out), he set
off in his Regency Red Jaguar for White Plains and a last
bid to keep from going to the bottom.

Five miles from the entrance to the Major Deegan Expressway his Jaguar collided with a yellow Toyota
driven by Mrs. Lyn Balch, née Lord. As Hera had fore-
known two years ago, young Mrs. Balch died instantly.
Jack, however, survived, though not without severe and
permanent impairment to his vision as well as lesser
fractures and abrasions that time could be expected to
mend.

The vengeance of Hera was complete. Jack pleaded
guilty to a reduced charge of second-degree manslaughter
(you can't argue with the testimony of a breathalyzer)
and was given a twelve-year suspended sentence to be
spent in his wife's custody. The judge said he was being
unusually lenient because Jack had already been punished
most terribly by the loss of his eyesight.

While Jack stayed at home on Exeter Road, looking
after his daughters by Bonnie and Min-Tsing and the
three Korean orphans (ages eight, nine and twelve) whom
Bonnie had adopted in the meantime, Mrs. Fleetwood
studied to become, and then became, a real estate agent
like her father and grandfather before her. Jack was morose at first, unable to meet the demands of his new role
in life, but at Bonnie's urging, and with her patient tute-
lage, he turned to macrame, discovering creative talents
that he'd never known himself to possess.

Hera did not begrudge Jack his small fulfillment. The
gods, after all, are only human, and once their rage has
been placated they are perfectly capable of acts of mercy
and grace.

Raylyn Moore, resident in California for
many years, was born in Ohio, worked as a
newspaperwoman on the Prescott, Arizona
Evening Courier and the Salt Lake City,
Utah *Deseret News & Telegram;* as an editor
in the New York office of *The Executive
Housekeeper* (a trade journal); and has since
taught journalism and English at Monterey
Peninsula College. She has had published a
contemporary novel (*Mock Orange*), a
literary-critical biographical study of L.
Frank Baum (*Wonderful Wizard, Marvelous
Land*) and the science fiction novel, *What
Happened to Emily Goode After the Great
Exhibition.*

She writes here of that event which must
mobilize all one's faculties, the moment as
to which Chicken Little issued the clarion
call so long ago. The sky is—

Falling

BY RAYLYN MOORE

Jillis and her children and husband, and old Nana who
was believed to have come with the house, and the dogs
and cats and the monkey had all lived under the tower
for something like ten years.

Others in the town had lived under the tower much
longer, some probably even dating their residency back to
the long-ago time when the tower first appeared (or was
built).

But Jillis felt especially involved with the tower because
her house, a well preserved pile of gingerbread and lattice-
work with a spectacular stained-glass window at the stair
turning, was closest of all. The enormous concrete footings
on which the huge metal silo rested rose practically out of
Jillis's maple-shaded backyard, affording an incongruity of
landscape that never failed to amaze her.

The children, one by one as they grew strong enough and sufficiently coordinated, learned to climb up onto that rough, unyielding bulwark, skinning their knees, at the top drawing near enough to the tower itself to touch its black-painted flanks, tipping back their heads to stare dizzily up toward where the top of the tower disappeared into the clouds.

Naturally the monkey could do better. By standing on the head of one of the taller children he could leap and grab the bottom rung of a narrow black metal ladder that spiraled up the sides of the tower.

He would scamper up and around and up and around, but not to the top. At a certain place he always stopped and cast a worried look back over his shoulder. Then, dazed by fear or overcome by caution, he would return, rappelling as judiciously as any telephone company line-man.

Of course the children were warned early and often never to try this. Their mother could never be absolutely sure they obeyed at all times, but at least she had never caught them on the ladder.

On cloudless days, Jillis had noticed, one could either see or imagine the top of the tower in full view. Either way it was too far for details to be discerned, though at times it appeared that a picket fence, of iron as black as the body of the tower itself, ran in a drunken circle around the top edge of the structure.

Jillis spent a lot of time wondering about the tower. And even when she wasn't actually looking at it, she was aware of being in its presence.

But this was bound to be an effect produced by anything that large, that overwhelming and subtly threatening. Like a local god it posed certain mysteries and demanded propitiation, but all this in a way so ambiguous that Jillis could never organize her feelings about it into conscious thought.

And there were the obvious riddles which she also failed to understand. Why, for instance, no matter which side of the tower she stood on, and no matter which way the clouds were moving, when she was right up beside it, looking up, did the thing always appear to be slowly, slowly, very slowly falling in her direction? Falling over on her? None of the children seemed to notice this, or if they did they didn't mention it.

Meanwhile, her life went on. There was a succession of sunrises. Seasons replaced one another. The children—there were three of them, and then four—eventually made some headway toward growing up after having lived through enough of these seasons (though Jillis had never seriously believed they would ever grow up and the ten years seemed to her more like a century). Jillis's husband John went on commuting six days a week by car to the city fifteen miles away. Groceries had to be brought home once a week and put away. The moon doggedly went through its phases in order to repeat them. The PTA met fortnightly. The mailman arrived every morning and the bills every thirty days.

Then finally, Jillis observed, things seemed to be coming to the point at long last after all this aimless cycling.

One of the dogs, who for years had been given contraceptives in her food, whelped a litter of mongrels.

And one Sunday morning very early the family was awakened by a strange, relentless thudding coming from the foot of the backstairs. Jillis struggled up out of deep sleep and went to discover that old Nana had had a stroke and fallen downstairs. She had to be rushed to the hospital, and then after a week or so brought home again and put to bed and nursed.

The emergency brought up again the never really resolved question of where Nana had come from in the first place. At the time Jillis was married, she had supposed Nana was an elderly retainer from John's family who had retired and was expecting to be taken care of in return for her years of faithful service. But John swore he had never seen her until after the honeymoon, when they moved into the house by the tower. He said if she wasn't someone Jillis knew, then she must have been left over from the family that occupied the house before them.

Whoever she was, she hadn't ever really been assimilated into the present menage. Though Jillis tried, especially at first, to be friendly and supportive, Nana—who might have been any age from seventy to a hundred-and-fifty—remained suspicious, uncommunicative, even furtive. She spent her days in the third-floor room she claimed for herself, doing crewelwork, slipping down the backstairs in the early mornings to make herself a pot of strong tea.

Something of the same kind of enduring obscurity hung over the urn of ashes on the parlor mantel. At least the urn's contents were presumed to be ashes, and human ashes at that. The urn, which had a sealed top, was the kind that comes from a mortuary, with a somber dark blue glaze and no decoration to speak of. Both Jillis and John believed the urn had been there on the mantel over the fireplace the day they moved in.

Through all the years Jillis dusted around it—though she was not the driven sort of housekeeper who dusts often—thinking vaguely that whoever it belonged to might some day call to pick it up.

Sometimes now Jillis saw herself, with almost bitter amusement, as curator to a vast collection of useless objects, beginning with the eight puppies, which couldn't be given away because no one wanted them, and extending through all sorts of unfunctional gimcracks, to Nana and the urn of ashes. Depending on her mood, Jillis did or did not include the children in the list.

Then, at midmorning on a day of no particular distinction, Jillis noticed the monkey was missing. She could not recall having seen him since dawn, when he had scampered across the bed, waking her and putting John into a foul humor. She remembered now that he had not been on hand when she fed the other pets. Nor was he in a habit of going off alone. On the contrary, he was extremely gregarious and always underfoot.

For herself Jillis didn't particularly care if she never saw the animal again. But out of consideration for the children, who claimed to be fond of him, she began searching the house, calling and looking under beds, standing on chairs to see all the way to the back of high shelves. And though there was evidence he had been around fairly recently—he was a spider monkey and could not be housebroken—she satisfied herself that he must now be somewhere outside.

She thought of the tower, then discounted it because the three children tall enough to assist the monkey into position for his favorite trick were all in school. But after she had checked out the front yard there wasn't anywhere else to look. She went to see if he could be playing alone on the concrete. He was not.

Even though she had already decided the monkey couldn't have reached it, she looked at the spiral ladder anyway. Walking slowly around the tower to follow its upward course with her eye, she became aware of something wrong much higher up. At the very top of the tower it looked as if a huge chunk of iron picket fence had become detached and was falling straight toward the house.

Reacting instinctively, Jillis curled herself into a ball to protect her vital organs and rolled like a windfall apple down off the footing and in under the maple trees, with her arms wrapped around her head and face.

In the backyard she picked herself up and started for the house, telling herself that the important thing now was not to give way to panic.

If her home were going to be crushed, obviously she must vacate it, but in an orderly fashion. Taking along what?

As she passed through the enclosed back porch, she snatched a pillowcase out of the dirty laundry and went from room to room loading it with indispensable items, half a jar of pickle relish from the refrigerator, a broken retractable tape measure from the table in the hall, an overdue library book from the coffee table in the parlor, a blouse she had never particularly liked but which happened to be the first thing she saw when she opened her bedroom closet.

After awhile she came to herself and set down the bag of valuables. She went to the telephone and dialed the operator and asked for the police.

"Something's falling from the top of the tower," she said with admirable calm to the dispatcher. "I'm afraid it's going to crush my house."

"Give your full name and address, ma'am."

"Oh, for heaven's sake! This is an emergency. Oh, all right. I'm Jillis Carver. Mrs. John Carver. We live at five-oh-five Summit Drive in the house beside the tower. We're about to be wiped out. Something that heavy falling all that distance—"

"Has anything actually happened there, Mrs. Carver?"

"Not yet, but any minute now—"

"We can't deal with an emergency before it's happened. Let us know when—"

Jillis hung up the telephone and rummaged through a desk drawer for the pamphlet called THIS IS YOUR COMMUNITY DISASTER PLAN. Surprisingly, she found it.

"Save this plan," a line of flame-orange type directed

brightly on the front of the brochure, "and it can save your life."

She riffled through. There were sections on fire, flood, air pollution, nuclear attack, and earthquake. Nothing seemed quite applicable, but the act of sitting at the desk forcing herself to examine the pages of information in novelty typefaces had a calming effect.

She was able now to remember Nana in her room upstairs and the dogs and cats all over the place, particularly the eight pups in a basket in the basement. Her youngest child would also soon be home in the car pool from the preschool he attended three mornings a week.

Clearly she would have to make arrangements for getting them all safely out of the house.

But she had delayed so long already that she saw no harm in delaying a second or so more while she examined the new plan for flaws.

Right away she found one. Or rather, in that second or so she happened to recall a story she had read in a high-school literature class about an avalanche in—was it the Alps? A family living in a mountain cottage had heard the rumbling several miles away and had all run out of their house to presumed safety. But at a crucial moment the avalanche struck some barrier which caused it to divide just above the cottage. So afterward there stood the house, safe, while the people, who would have done better to remain unperturbed around their hearth, had all perished.

Of course it was only a fiction, perhaps or perhaps not based on reality, yet the fortuitous memory of it served to feed her natural hesitancy, her reluctance to do a wrong thing in haste. Jillis decided for the present to leave well enough alone inside the house, while she went outside again to see how bad things really were. There was always the chance she had misjudged the situation before, perhaps even imagined at least part of it.

But as soon as she got to the backyard, she saw that if anything she had underestimated the seriousness of the problem.

The falling piece of iron fence was much nearer now, so near she could see its jagged, raw pickets, like a phalanx of fixed bayonets seemingly aimed right toward where she stood looking up, shielding her eyes.

Still, this could be a trick of the light, an optical misconstruction. Surely the thing was still too far to judge exactly where it would land. If she could make herself believe this, she would be free to fix her attention upon the further complication. For behind the fence she saw that another, far larger object was hurtling downward. A massive hunk of black iron siding with a curve in it, a fragment which must be part of the tower wall itself. Did that mean the whole structure was beginning to collapse?

If a good many such pieces began falling, some were sure to strike the house and some the yard. So neither place could be counted perfectly safe, or even half safe.

That settled it then. She would have to go on with her original plan of evacuating the house and fleeing the neighborhood of the tower, getting her brood out of the way altogether, including the invalid Nana, the helpless puppies, her youngest child when he arrived home, the monkey if he could be found, though this seemed less and less likely. (Had some extrasensory warning alerted him early? Had he already saved himself then?) And yes, she really should take along whatever family valuables could be gotten together without too much trouble. The older dogs and cats could fend for themselves.

Yet even as she was plotting all this so decisively, calling up all her inner resources for the effort she knew would be needed, she was again struck with an exactly contradictory notion.

Why, for ten whole years they had all been safe in this house. In all that time nothing really bad had happened (if she discounted Nana's stroke). In ten years one can accumulate a very comfortable supply of complacency if nothing interferes. So why assume the worst now? Why couldn't she just go on as usual, say nothing, forget what she had seen in the backyard, meet the car pool as always and bring the baby in and give him lunch, take Nana up her tray, and then lie down herself for an hour before the older children came in from school?

It was by far the most tempting of the plans she'd thought of, and who was to say it might not be as good as any?

After all, it was only by sheerest chance she knew about the fragments falling from the tower. If she hadn't gone out searching for the monkey she would never have looked up, and there would now be no occasion for concern.

Most of her life, she reflected, she had been lucky, and she had done nothing now to deserve to have her luck change.

When she was eighteen, during the summer between high school and college—she still thought of it this way though as it turned out she never went to college—her remarkably enlightened parents had sent her to Europe with a bicycle and enough money to last several months. They wanted her to discover herself, they said. To get to know herself. To decide what she really wanted to do with her life before she settled down.

What Jillis discovered about herself was that she had no particular occupational ambition or bent. The person she really got to know was not herself but John Carver, a vacationing compatriot poised between college and an enviable job offer from a firm back home. They were wed practically as soon as they had cleared customs on their return.

She had never been consciously sorry. The Carvers had deliberately had their family while they were young. That had been more or less John's idea as she recalled it, "To get it over with so Jill will have plenty of time later to do whatever she wants."

John was handsome, generous, considerate, and not a bore. The children were handsome, bright, socially adjusted, and not sickly. When it occurred to her to do so from time to time, Jillis congratulated herself on the direction her life had taken even though she really hadn't ever done anything on her own to shape its course. Nor had she the faintest clue what she might do when that time came that John had promised her. When she could do whatever she chose.

Jillis Carver was in fact a drifter. Not the lonely kind who has no certain home and drinks wine by the pint out of a paper bag. Not the frightened kind who goes from love-partner to love-partner seeking the perfect alliance. But a drifter all the same, a secret drifter of a kind far more numerous than is imagined by the compilers of data on this and that. It was as if she was becalmed in a backwater hidden from the view of the mainstream.

Not that she was unaware of the alarms and stresses of the times. She certainly did not approve of the oppression of the meek or the exploitation of the unfortunate by the fortunate. Yet she had never felt personally affected. Perhaps she would feel so later.

To the well-worn argument that if one didn't come to grips with things now there might not be any "later," she had long since replied, "Well, but people have always said that, haven't they? And things have always come out all right."

It was exactly this kind of optimism that suffused her in the face of the threat from the tower.

She went out once more to the backyard to reassess her situation.

As if to underscore the essential rightness of this latest impression that everything might yet work out well if she did nothing, the descending fence fragment, although even closer now than when she had looked earlier, seemed to have slowed considerably, as if its rate of fall were steadily diminishing the nearer it came to earth.

True, near the top of the tower a third fragment, much, much bigger than the fence, even bigger than the piece of curved siding which immediately preceded it, seemed to have broken free and be on its way down too. But this monster piece of debris was still so far away that it looked far smaller than it really was. And that was a comfort.

A blessing as well that, the way things were going, it too could be counted upon to diminish in speed as it neared.

Wasn't there something she had once heard about a train which, if its speed were decreased by half, and that speed by half, and that by half again, would never reach the terminal? Or did she have this thoroughly confused with something else?

There was no one now that she could call on the telephone to talk things over. As it happened John was on a business trip for the rest of the week and wouldn't be driving home from the city that night. Nor did she, at the moment, know how he could be reached. He was probably still on the plane. And her best friend Kathy, who lived in the neighborhood, was on a camping vacation in Canada with her own husband and children.

Because the car pool was late Jillis took the time to slip up the backstairs to Nana's room, not with any idea of alarming the old lady, just to see how she was getting on. Usually at this time of day Nana was alert and waiting for her lunch. Now she was napping, her calm, ven-

erable face full of wrinkled dignity against the unwrinkled
(no-iron) percale pillowslip.

Jillis went to the basement to look in on the dogs. On
the way down she discovered yet another complication.
In a storage niche on the stairwell were a new family
of four kittens and their mother, a strange female that
Jillis was quite certain did not belong to the household. Or
at least had not until now. The mother cat stared out
at Jillis from the dimness of the niche, beaming a green
gaze of fatuous pride and fearlessness.

That pretty well settled matters then, if they had
not been settled already. None of the things in her charge
was portable. She didn't even think she could bring herself to pack up and carry away the ashes from the mantel
after they had been allowed to remain where they were
all through the years. It wouldn't be right.

Once more arriving in the backyard, she looked up at
the descending particles. The jagged fence was so near
it was almost piercing the roof, and above it the sky was
blotted out by vast pieces of metal torn loose and descending.

But slowly.

Luis Urrea comes from Mexico and lives in San Diego, California. With his left hand he writes stories (and, it is rumored, a novel), with his right he draws indescribable pictures, and with other hands he does something in films and something in rock music. Currently, he is on the staff of San Diego Mesa College, running a bilingual literary contest.

"Things that do and do not exist pass by, one after one."

Father Returns from the Mountain

BY LUIS URREA

Us, and them
And after all we're only ordinary men
Me, and you
God only knows it's not what we would choose to do
—Roger Waters

The car is red. It has a sun-baked and peeling black top. Little flakes of fake leather blow away in the wind. The roof is crushed. Windows are shattered. The front end is crumpled. The axles are split and the tires slant crookedly. Dry blood on the hood. The steering wheel is twisted. Details of violence. An American Motors Rambler 440, 1966. Slivers of glass are stuck in the carpets. Dust settles on the stains. A photograph of my father and me is caught under the seat, fluttering like a flag, like a wounded bird trapped in the wind. There is a dime in the broken driver's seat. Blood where the radio should be./ This is the truth. The truth is a diamond or at least a broken mirror. There are many reflective surfaces and we observe the ones that we choose. We see what we can./ The car is red. It stands in a dusty compound among

163

other crushed machines. A note to my father blows out of the glove compartment. It says "Dear Alberto" a hundred times as it spins away. There is a chain-link fence that rattles in a breeze that smells of dogs and perfume on women's bellies. A yellow sticker is pasted to the hood. Children scare each other by touching the crusty patches of my father's blood. "He'll come back and eat you!" The dead man, the dead man./ A Mexican cop slides down the slope. He squints in the early morning sun. He can hardly see my father in the wreckage. He runs back up and calls for help. The blue light atop his car flashes, flashes, casting marching shadows over the rocks. Pink urine spreads across my father's clothing. The pain is a sound that hums inside his guts, that pierces his skull. Darkness. Sleep./ The telephone feels warm. I look out the window at a Monday sky. "Hello," he says, "this is Jaime. Do you remember me?" Morning sunlight reaches through the trees. "Of course I remember you. What's up?" His silence buzzes for a moment. When he speaks he speaks carefully. "Your father . . . has had an accident." "Is he hurt?" "Yes." "Badly?" "Yes." I lean forward. I think of my father being hurt. I think of him in pain. The tiny agony of tears pinches the corners of my eyes./ We are on a balcony in Puerto Vallarta. My father's hand on my shoulder, lightning bombarding the hilltops. Rain undermines the streets and floods the river that eats great rifts in the jungle. We spend the entire night in each other's confidence./ My father is severely damaged. His eyes are open but will not function. They scrape open and shut but do not break the thick coats of darkness that cover them. He cannot move. His mouth is a thickened traitor that will not function. It fills slowly with liquid. When it reaches his lips there is a slow, endless snail of red slipping down his cheek and hiding in his ear. I am sitting in my room listening to music./ "How bad?" I ask, a little afraid, a little unwilling, a little unready. "Very bad. He seems to have had a stroke while driving. He hit a mountain in San Luis Rio Colorado." "He was almost home." "Not close enough." I feel small. "He is paralyzed. He can't see or speak. He has head and internal injuries. The family has started out." The sun is bright./ The police compound is quiet. A scrawny cat licks the speedometer./ The police lift him into the ambulance. He tries to talk he tries to see. He is a slab of meat and it makes him angry. The pain makes him angry. The cuts on his face sting. He is taken to a hospital where they strip him naked decide that he will be dead soon, and shoot him with morphine. They put him in a room at eight A.M. where he struggles alone for eight hours. He is given no aid. My cousin finds him struggling to talk. "Calm down tio," he says, "we're here with you. Don't be afraid." The blood has made his throat black./ I sit alone in the funeral home. There is little sound from without, even downtown Tijuana rests at three A.M. I open the coffin lid and look at him. He is broken. His chin is a black openness, little grey whiskers have pushed their heads through the wound. His shirt is stained. I put my face on the side of the box and I stare and stare. I watch for a flicker, a twitch. I wait for a microscopic flare of the nostrils. The sealed eyelids seem ready to pop, to rise and lower. I want, in terror, to see him lick his lips so that I can break the sealing glass, pull him up, save him, embrace him. There is no movement. There is no sound./ I found a photograph just yesterday. In it my father stands with the president, with generals, senators. His captain's uniform looks as crisp as a salad. At times I shuffle through his official papers and look at his federal police badge. His smiles look like mine. We are connected by the lips, the grin is our chain./ I lie on the floor beneath the coffin. I close my eyes to sleep, my last night beside him. I am a poet at that instant. A shadow passes over my face. I jump up, thinking that someone is approaching. There is nothing. Again the shadow. Again nothing. Again and again. I imagine him waving farewell. As I slip into sleep I hold on to a vision of a puffy hand stiffly reaching over the edge./ The dreams have come in a series. They are diamonds, they are broken mirrors. In the first I am run over by a truck. I pull at people's legs from the black street./ Death is here. I am aware of that now. Perhaps innocence is not knowing that it is grinning at you from the corner. It has pressed its face against the windows, it has stalked in with the fog and awaits its turn./ At eight P.M. he tried to open his eyes. His straining produced no results. He had been waiting for the Mexicans to bring an ambulance to take him to Yuma, Arizona. The Mexicans did not respond. An American ambulance crew waited for an hour at the border. My father was born in Rosario, a little town in the south of

Sinaloa. He died in San Luis Rio Colorado, a small town in the north of Sonora. I can imagine his grey hair against the dirty pillow. His lips, white, rolling slowly back. His abdomen searing red hot then tingling pink as he passed through to the new side. Possibly music, a fragment of a tune wafting through the haze. I hope he heard music. "This is Jaime again." "Tell me." "His condition deteriorated for several hours." "And?" "And your señor . . . rested." "Dead?" "Dead." "Just now?" "Yes. Your family didn't want to call you." "Thank you." "Are you all right?" "Thank you."/ No one comes to the funeral home to get me. I have watched the corpse for seven hours. I have closed the coffin lid. I think of Rosario again. He died returning from his birthplace. The stupidity of it makes me angry. I have not eaten since the day before. "I hate waiting," I say to myself. "I know, son, I always did. It's boring." I spin around, but the lid remains closed. "Do you hear me, papa?" I ask. "Yes," he replies. "I love you," I say. "I know," he says./ Mexicans love the dead. They are a lovely treat with which to terrify each other. People passing on the street push open the door to try to see the dead man. "What are you looking for, you vampires?" I yell at them. "El muerto," they whisper, "El muerto."/ We carry the coffin to the graveside. I have to go to the bathroom. Dogs are running on the graves. Whores are working downtown. People are eating and defecating and laughing and sweating and my father is dead. The world has not even hesitated. Nobody has noticed. The hard part is watching the box go down. Watching it being pushed into the black mouth, knowing that his flesh is being hid from you, and if you should search for a touch of it again you will find dusty corruption. The body goes. I walk away from the weeping. White clouds in the distance. I keep my back to the crowd. Tijuana looks nice from a distance. I was born there./ My friends and I bring his organ to the house. He spent hours with it daily. I put my fingers on the keyboard. Cold hands grow up the insides of my arms and put fingers inside my chest. They surround my heart and squeeze. I retreat, a coward before pain./ I sit in my house alone, working on a book. I hear a car in the driveway. When I open the door I see my dead father leaning on the steering wheel. His hair in disorder, his eyes uncertain. I lead him inside. His hand is very cool.

"What happened?" he asks. I look into his face. Maybe I should remain silent, perhaps I can fool him and in doing so, keep him alive. It is impossible. "Papa, you were killed in an auto accident." Shock spreads over his face. "No," he says, "it can't be." I am afraid of hurting him, but I must. "Go away, you're dead." "I can't be," he insists, frustration and pain mixing on his face./ As a child I would stand beside him as he drove, holding tight to his shoulder./ I kneel at his feet and take his pant-legs in my hands. "Papa, go away, you can't be here. You're dead!" He shakes his head sadly. I weep like his little boy wept, with my head on his knees. "You're dead, you're dead, you're dead."/ His fingerprints are still on the organ keyboard. Late at night I think of licking them from the ivory. It would be a kind of communion with him. I need him and he is gone./ A stonemason gets into the grave and pours concrete over the coffin. We don't have enough money for a headstone. Maybe a tree will grow here, or something. Other mourners file in to feed the hole beside my father./ The car is red. The cold desert wind moans in it at night. There is a scar on the mountain where it was hit by the car. It flipped and rolled six times. It is rumored that my father went out the windshield as it rolled. His glasses bend the moonlight between the crumbling rocks./ I hear his car again. He looks much better. "Get in," he says. I get in. He takes me through miles of dream lands. Things that do and do not exist pass by, one after one. We are free to go wherever he chooses. We go to Rosario. "Did it hurt to die?" I finally ask. "Well," he says, "it hurt before I died." "Were you afraid?" "Of course. I listened for you, but you never came." My stomach tightens. "I wanted to be there. I couldn't get to you. Don't you think it hurt me to let you die?" He smiles. "I know," he says. We pass the ruins of a railyard. "Your grandfather is proud of you," he says. I look at him. The tears come, I try to stop them, but they force their way out anyway. "I don't want to be without you," I blurt. He looks at me for a long while, then taps me on the knee. "You've got to stop all this crying. You sound like a little girl." Then; "You aren't without me. Remember that." His eyes are clear. "Where are your glasses?" I ask. "They're still on the side of the road," he says. "But that's all right, I won't be needing them now." "Were you cognizant in the hospital?" I ask. "Yes," he says with disgust in his voice. "I was stuck inside of that damned dead body. I hated that." "I'm sorry, papa," I tell him. He looks at me. "Don't be sorry. You waste time that you need." I nod. "I closed the coffin," I say. "Thank you, I didn't want to be on display." I touch his arm. "Papa, did you, did you see God?" He smiles at me and turns on the radio./ When I was fourteen my father and I spent hours laughing in the night about nothing, nothing at all./ The car is red. The driver's seat is torn. There is a bee-hive inside it. Bees fly where his eyes used to be. They fly through the air that used to touch his lips. They walk on the bent wheel that cracked his ribs. They sit where he used to sit. A slow, warm cascade of honey spreads over the traces of demolition. It is gold. It catches the sunlight and reflects the clouds that move in its depths, minute and sparkling white. Droplets reflect the blue of the sky. They hint at the smile in my father's eyes.

> Rosario, my earth
> little town in which I learned to love
> I dream of you, I miss you
> thinking that one day I should return

> Life took me from you,
> but I never, never forgot you
> my grandest illusion
> is to be able to return to you
> in the years of my nightfall

> Alberto Urrea
> June 2, 1915—January 10,
> 1977

M. J. Engh, the author of 1976's stunning
novel of world conquest, *Arslan* (about the
general, all the particulars) ... was born
and raised in a small town in southern
Illinois; attended the Universities of Chicago
and Illinois to receive an undergraduate
degree with a major in "history, the queen
of subjects"; has lived since college in Chicago,
the Philippines, Japan, Illinois (again), followed by a long stretch in Oklahoma, and
has now taken up permanent residence in the
state of Washington.

Engh writes "trying to work out questions
... bothering me. . . . It helps to clarify
thinking. . . . I did not arrive at good answers, but I understand the questions better."

The Oracle

BY M. J. ENGH

CHAPTER 1

Several people stood watching a slender woman who
sat, or more nearly crouched, on the edge of an ornate
chair. She had been speaking, trying to explain something to them. Now she bowed her head deeply, thrusting
forward against some invisible obstacle, making strange
motions with her hands, of swimming or fending off. They
could not know why. To her it seemed as if her head
were garnished with a densely ramifying growth, like
the tendril-curled staghorns of Scythian art, a growth
that arched downward and outward from her forehead,

169

dragging her down, dragonward, out. Seemed as if; because she knew it for an idiom of the mind, not a physical monstrosity. Yet it was real, in its way, and she intended to force a course clear, to master this weight and tangle, shake it back like a mane of not untidy hair. The watchers saw her as a woman crushed down and abject with pain; but within herself her feelings were not abject. The pain that was killing her seemed to her somewhat irrelevant.

Philippe Montoya laid his hand on her back, the thumb curling a little possessively over the ridge of her shoulder. He waited, rather like a magician displaying one of his more casual tricks. The woman straightened gradually. She laid her hands in her lap. They trembled; her face was flushed as if with embarrassment. Montoya gave instructions, and those who were servants went about their business. The doctor shook his head testily. This case had annoyed him from the beginning.

"It will be all right," the woman said, anxious to reassure them. "The only danger is . . ." But it was exactly in trying to explain that danger that she had come to grief, and she felt still the shadow of horns over her brow and shoulders.

A woman servant, shriveled and grandmotherly, with a perpetual stoop, stooped farther to take her elbow and lift her gently. Montoya's hand released her, sliding lightly down her back as she rose. The servant guided her out of the room. In this house, everyone treated her solicitously, fondly. At times she suspected that this was a function of the house itself, that just beyond its doors waited the ravenous bruising maelstrom that had slammed her once almost to the rock bottom of existence. But Philippe Montoya had been gentle to her from the first.

"What do you think, Doctor?" As he might have asked an auto mechanic. "What do you think?"—and reserving, as in that case, the right to disagree.

The doctor repeated his headshake. "I can't tell you anything I haven't already told you, Mr. Montoya. Her physical condition is improving well enough. If you think she should have psychological help, you should consult a practitioner in that field—as I've said before. I can't help you there. Of course," he added irritably, "her eyesight is not very good. No doubt you know that."

Montoya, whose organs were all eminently sound,

was surprised. It had not occurred to him that she might have a constitutional defect.

The moist heat came with the sun. Even in the earliest morning, when things were just becoming distinguishable by color, the least exertion would leave a dew of sweat standing on her skin. It was pleasant then, a soft warmth that was like peace made tangible; but there were a few hours at midday when she was always sick, physically ill with the ballooning pressure of the heat. That was the siesta time. Often she slept. Often she lay awake, listening to the sounds of the house that sustained her—the soft steps of the servants, the chattering of the birds, the clocks' ticking—and, outside, as from beyond a layer of insulation, voices and traffic, going their own ways, busy with their own purposes, wonderfully unaware of her, of her here safe in their ignorance.

"The only danger is that I might not die." That was how she framed it to herself. What she was struggling with was very strong; it seemed hardly possible that she could master it and live. Either it would destroy her in battle, or she would die in the act of victory. Neither, to her way of thinking, would be a loss. The only danger was that she might not die; that she might adjust, adapt, learn to live with it unmastered; that she might learn to say, "My son is dead," before she knew what dying meant.

At night, it was almost cool—quite cool, sometimes. At night, when she had come to the end of her excuses, with a small sigh she committed her body to the bed. Delicate sheets of a cotton like the fabric of a cloud covered her. White draperies of the mosquito net surrounded her. Outside, the night hummed. She lay waiting with open eyes.

They had been caught in one of those anti-government, anti-foreign riots that had begun the abortive revolution. Her son, with the simplicity of adolescent manhood, had tried to defend her, and she had watched him beaten to death, after which her own circumstances had ceased to concern her very actively. This was fortunate. On the basis of her American passport she had been identified as an enemy of the people, and detained, with other enemies, for interrogation. She was the only American in the little group; the rest were Europeans. She was, eventually, the only woman, the other having died under something less than the treatment she survived. One or two of the prisoners actually had some connection with foreign governments. All of them, with her exception, promptly or eventually cooperated as well as they could, revealing or inventing any information they were asked for, making pro-revolutionary statements for publication. It was not a situation for which any of them had been prepared. One night there had been an unusual commotion, with gunfire very close and strange splashes in the sea. (They were being held at the time on one of the tiny coastal islands.) Even before she understood certainly that this was rescue, she had a fierce surge of life. When Philippe Montoya burst in, giving orders very concisely—"Run!" in three or four languages, with a pointed flashlight to indicate direction—she contrived to be on her feet, and even to run most of the way. Someone, not Montoya, caught and helped her roughly through the last yards and into the boat, so that she was preoccupied for some time with the pain of her body. But it was Montoya who examined her briefly in the darkness and carried her to a bunk in a tiny cabin. A little later he came back, turned on an electric light, and bent over her. For the first time she saw Philippe Montoya as something more than a powerful moving shadow—a smooth Oriental face, distant and alien like a mask, even his eyes still, opaque as ebony. At that moment her condition had altered somehow. Months later, almost a year, she was still puzzling over what had happened—whether at that moment she had decided to accept whatever was coming, or whether, on the contrary, it was only from that moment that she had resisted or withdrawn.

Someone had brought water and other things. Montoya proceeded methodically to clean her and apply first aid to her wounds—sketchily, but gently and businesslike as a good nurse. Later, that night and often through the next days, he returned to sit beside her on the bunk and hold a one-sided conversation, telling her how the weather went and of the other prisoners (all, he said, had been saved unhurt, though one of his own men was badly wounded and might yet die), answering unselfconsciously the questions she might have asked if speech had not been too great a burden. "My headquarters are in the Philippines, but I do business anywhere I can make money. I do a lot of business in Indonesia." When he talked, his face was not masklike. "I heard there were Europeans being held on that island, and I thought, 'It's not their war. They don't belong there.' So . . ." He shrugged. "It was on my way."

He thought at the time that she was a European too. He had tried several languages on her, and fancied that she showed some response to French, so that he went on speaking French to her thereafter. She was glad of that—passively glad—because it made it easier to ignore most of what he was saying. But in due time she began to answer him—at first hesitantly in French, later, in a horrible gush, in English. From this he learned how her son had died, and incidentally her nationality. But whenever he asked her name, or how to contact her family or friends, she would take refuge again in the unassailable helpessness of shock.

His plan had been simply to deliver his refugees to their respective consulates in Manila. He was well enough known in official Philippine circles, and would not be bothered further. But this woman was unexpected.

The last morning of the voyage, he walked her out onto the half-deck, where a bed of matting had been prepared for her in the shade of a sailcloth awning. To Montoya, the sea was a healing, revivifying thing, and he felt dumbly that it should have the same effect on her. Now she saw for the first time what sort of vessel she was on, though she did not know how to identify it. It was a motorized sailing craft, light and long, with a great low-slung sail. Lying there, a few hours later, she saw Montoya strike one of the men he had rescued, a square-jawed Dutchman of sixty, whose wife had died beside her in a smell of filth. Montoya's open hand cracked against the side of the Dutchman's head, a sudden, contemptuous blow. The Dutchman sprawled. She watched with large, gloomy eyes. Montoya jabbed his foot into the man's side, a token kick, and turned away. The Dutchman lay gasping. In a few minutes, one of the sailors helped him up casually. They were Malay-looking, these sailors, their faces shaped in broad planes, lit sometimes by swift and brilliant grins.

They came to land in an inlet south of Manila, to avoid the red tape of the harbor, and lay there overnight. As always, Montoya slept on the floor of the cabin, beside the bunk where she lay. It was the only cabin on the vessel, and it was his. At dawn he stood looking down at her. Everything visible was soft with the faint blurring of twilight. "Where do you want to go?" His voice was impatient. It was a question he was tired of asking her.

She moved her head a little on the pillowless mattress, not so much in sign of negation as in hopeless restlessness. "Nowhere," she said at last.

He did not answer her, except with a small nod that she did not notice. Much later she understood that this had been the last real question he was to ask her.

A vehicle was waiting for them on the dirt track that came almost down to the water—a jeep remade into a species of open-air mini-bus, with narrow benches down the sides of the canopied bed. She rode wedged upright between Montoya and the driver, the Europeans disposed uncomfortably on the benches behind. Their route at first was circuitous; with so many unidentified passengers, Montoya thought it well to bypass the checkpoint on the main road. The first stop was at a private medical clinic, where it appeared that Montoya was known. She sat in the waiting room while he argued with the receptionist. The ride had been deliriously painful; consciousness of externals was returning to her in scraps. "Dr. Aguilar," the receptionist asserted, "arrives at nine o'clock, and other patients are already waiting."

"Give me your phone." He helped himself to it. Eventually he handed it to the receptionist, who listened with compressed lips that opened to say disapprovingly, "Very well, Dr. Aguilar." Then she hung up, pulled out a pad of forms, and addressed Montoya, with a scant glance toward the woman he had brought. "What is the lady's name?"

He did not bother with a glance. "Renée Delisle," he said.

So, for the record, she had received a name.

On shipboard, as during her captivity, the difference between sleeping and waking had been unclear. She had slept, no doubt, by fits and starts, whenever pain had relaxed for an instant. But perhaps beds had much to do with it. As a prisoner, she had not seen a bed, or even a substitute for one. On Montoya's vessel, she had been always in bed. Nowhere had there been a clear distinction between sleeping time and waking time. But that day she had spent several exhausting hours, first in the jeepney, then at the clinic, where she was examined, sterilized, medicated, splinted, bandaged. He was waiting for her not with a jeepney this time, but with a big American car. The drive was short. Two men ran to open a gate for them, and they pulled into the driveway of a house that sat like a Chinese mandarin, ornate and bellied. And here, at last, was a bed, a true bed, soft, broad, pillowed and canopied, and in that richness, clean at last, dressed in a long cotton gown that quiet women had slipped over her shoulders, she fell asleep.

He let her sleep. He would have liked to let her heal for a few weeks undisturbed. But he had business to attend to; and it was better, he thought, to have things clear from the beginning. So, a little before sunrise, when there was light enough to see by and darkness enough for modesty, he woke her, gently, saying, "I'll try not to hurt you." She was not surprised.

All this was long ago. It was, in a way, the beginning of recorded history. She was an excellent student. Every day, sometimes several times in a day, she went over it all, repeating every detail she remembered and sometimes discovering new ones, reviewing the whole to see if her perspective had changed. She had become so expert that she could run the whole sequence through at high speed, many times faster than it had happened. At such a rate it was almost painless, like a dentist's high-speed drill.

But all this was merely the preliminary, the warm-up for her real work. For she worked hard, in that house where to the uninitiated observer she seemed to do nothing serious, to drift idly from dressing and make-up to wandering in the garden to whistling at the birds in their cages to nibbling and toying with the cook's intricate productions to playing carelessly with the children— long days and evenings of baths and siestas and dinner parties with feather-light banter.

The dragon at the bottom of the world . . . Montoya would have told her—would have told her gladly—that dragons are really not like that; but Montoya knew nothing of the fantasies that tormented her. The closest he had come to a glimpse was on one of her bad nights

when, writhing in his arms—whether to get closer or
farther away, he could not tell—she had gasped out, chok-
ing with nausea, "It smells—it smells!" But he had thought
she meant the hovel where she had been tortured.

In Philippe Montoya's experience, people to whom hideous things had happened reacted simply in one of two
ways. If the trauma had been too great or had lasted too
long, they remained crippled—malfunctioning, paranoid,
unreliable to do business with. If it had been briefer, or
less essentially crushing, they recovered—often very
quickly, and always in the same way: they would pack the
hideousness into a separate mental compartment and
leave it there. It was a normal, practical solution; it let
you go on living your life on the basis you had already
constructed, without wasting time on the contradictions
in the compartment.

But this woman was abnormal. In Montoya's opinion,
what she had suffered was not so very bad—not bad
enough, certainly, to cripple a healthy mind. But she
was not recovering. In some ways, she was getting worse.
For a time he had been puzzled and concerned. Now he
stood in a kind of exasperated awe, for he understood, in
essence, what she was doing. She was trying to absorb
the contradictions; she was trying to integrate what she
had learned in the riot and the torture chamber with what
she already knew of life. Montoya esteemed clear-
headedness. He was very ready to admire this sort of
endeavor, however troublesome the process might be, because it aimed at clarity of understanding and freedom of
action, and because it demanded determination. He himself had come a long way by determination.

So that it was really unnecessary for her to explain it
to Montoya, as she had tried to do that day in the doctor's
presence, when the fleshy antlers had first sprung from
her bursting forehead; Montoya understood the principle
very well, though the details escaped him. But she did not
know that.

The dragon at the bottom of the world . . . The stench
in which that monstrosity coiled was so thick that it was
tangible, almost ponderous—a soupy fog that you could
scoop up and pour from hand to hand, while thinner
fumes of it rose visibly like steam. It left your fingers im-

pregnated with a stink of rot that neither soaking nor scrubbing removed, a stink that sank into the flesh and spread, so that in time your whole body seemed gangrened. But there was a cure. She was totally, speechlessly grateful, with a gratitude so unexpressible that it left her limp and motionless—grateful that there was a cure so often and easily available to her. For Philippe Montoya's touch was healing.

The house had been built and furnished by a Chinese businessman, the proprietor, among other enterprises, of an ice cream plant. His heirs had not wanted to maintain the house—he had had other houses—and Montoya had been able to buy it outright, as part of an arrangement in which mutual concessions were made elsewhere. Montoya, too, had his other house—on Palawan, a practical measure, since his maritime operations were centered there—but he had not yet achieved a summer home on the cool heights of Baguio.

The birds had come with the house. Along one side of a narrow courtyard, an aviary replaced the wall. Two stories high, twenty feet wide, but scarcely more than a yard deep, it formed the outside wall of a sitting room on the first floor as of the bedroom where she slept on the second. Bushes and a small tree grew in it. Here the birds quarreled, fed, and nested. They were finches, for the most part, both native and imported: bright, sprightly little birds, tuneful and sociable. All this was under the care of an old man, who had also come with the house, and to whom Montoya was merely a part-time resident and a disburser of funds. It was due to the old man, whose name was Cheng, that there were other birds in the house, whose cages he moved from room to room in accordance with the movements of sun and wind—singles and pairs of birds newly purchased or being specially fed or nursed. This old man seldom spoke to her, or to anyone else; but from the beginning he had exchanged nods and smiles with her when she talked to the birds, his broad pleased grin to her uncertain smile.

She found a pencil. It was odd, perhaps, that in this house where everything was provided, she had never seen a pencil before. (Montoya had always a couple of pens in his pocket, and no doubt there were other writing im-

plements at his desk in the upstairs room where he often
worked; but she had never seen his desk.) She had not
asked for a pencil—she asked for nothing—but when she
found it, a little blunt stub, probably a discard of Montoya's intended to be thrown out, she cherished it in her
hands and held it to her breast like a parody of a baby.
Then she wandered about the house, seeking unobtru-
sively. In the kitchen she found a bit of rice paper in
which some coconut confection had been wrapped. She
smoothed it out on a table, sticky side down, and began.

Hours later she was still at it, now on a linen handker-
chief she had tacked flat on one of the broad window-
sills. Montoya bent to kiss her; she was so busy, she
barely turned up the side of her head for him. "What are
you doing?" he asked, intrigued. She showed him.

He thought at first that it would be her son's face. But
at a second, longer look, it was not so very young. It
would be her husband, then, or her lover. He did not
know if she had a husband living somewhere, or an ex-
husband. There had been no ring on her finger when he
found her; but any rings would have been taken by her
captors. "Who is it?" he asked. She shook her head.

That day he had drawing pencils, sketch pads, pens
and ink, and a small easel bought for her. Her hand
shook sometimes, so that she spoiled many sketches;
otherwise she drew well, though slowly. The same head,
in different aspects, hairless, bearded, young, old; then,
abortively, trees and landscapes that were very unsuc-
cessful; then birds; two or three formless swirls that she
destroyed with a violence he had not seen in her before.
After a few weeks, he asked her, "Do you want some
paints?" She nodded and wept. Gratefully, helplessly;
he was appalled and touched. "If you want something,
tell me." She looked at him with big eyes. "If you want
something, you must tell me," she said firmly, understanding that an absolute order was required. She pressed her
drenched face against him, limp with peace. But she had
not known she wanted anything.

What had attracted him to her in the beginning was her
explanation of why she had not capitulated like the
other prisoners. Lying very flat on his bunk, she had
said in her small, cool voice, "It's not my war." That
voice had seemed to him tiny and childlike in the quiet

cabin, where the sounds of the sea and the boat were to him like silence, or like an infant's breathing to its mother. "I don't know which side right is on," she had said. "Probably neither. Probably it doesn't matter. If they had asked me politely, I would have told them anything I knew. But they didn't ask." She had lifted the broken reed of her left arm, her fingers at odd, stiff angles above the rough bandage with which he had bound ripped flesh to splintered bone. Her lips formed a little hard pout, almost humorous. "It made me mad," she said.

He had liked her very much for that show of spirit, at once quiet and full of panache. Since then she had often confused and disappointed him, though never enough to counteract the first impression.

The other rescued prisoners had praised her courage grudgingly. Some of them had complained that her unbending stubbornness had brought worse mistreatment on all of them. In fact, she was a reproach to them, and the most sensitive felt it most keenly. The stubby Dutchman was the worst. The last day on the boat before they reached Manila, he had exasperated Montoya to the point of anger, by blaming her outright for his wife's death. Even so, Montoya had struck him only once. It was his habit to be gentle with old people.

CHAPTER 2

Philippe Montoya was troubled. He had to make a business decision that would affect his whole future, and present circumstances made it awkward. He was, in a word, considering marriage. This was an option he had reserved for the most profitable opportunity. He was thirty-five years old now, and the opportunity seemed to have arisen. The daughter of a senator, twenty-three, pretty and Catholic, had been offered him. It meant a contract that was worth a hundred thousand pesos to him at once, and contacts that should be worth millions, directly and indirectly, in time. His position in the Philippines was still precarious in some ways, though he had been in business here for six years, and a citizen for more than three; this would regularize everything. The senator was on the correct side in Philippine politics; he was a winner; his family was extensive. The girl, too, was agreeable company, and her mother was in good figure and good temper at fifty, a promising omen. Still, he had certain reservations about these Filipina women. To his taste, they were inclined to be a little strident and grasping, and even physically coarse. This was, of course, unfair; but Montoya's esthetics, like his business sense, had been shaped in Indochina.

Whenever an event took place, major or minor—the death of a bird, the fall of a government—she would consult the oracle who lived in her mind: and he would answer, with his pale smile, "I knew it would happen."

"But why?" Her question was always an anxious "why?" Yet that was not necessarily what she wanted to learn from him. The secret that he held for her was not the *why* of any particular event; it was the secret of knowing, itself. For he *knew*, knew truly—not only the events that would happen to him, but how he would feel, what he would think; as if he remembered his future with a perfect recall. Everything he would ever know, he knew now. And yet he was alive, and conscious, and even sane. It was this that made him miraculous and valuable; it was for this that she drew and painted his face, again and again, trying to wrest that secret from its contours.

The first typhoon of the season brushed them with its wet, vast wing. All day the rain flamed down, meeting walls headlong, licking along gutters and under the low eaves. Everything shuddered; in the distance, metal roofs boomed under the wind. Torn fronds like seaweed flowed past the windows in the running rain. Inside, the house was filled with a changing underwater dusk, punctured by the irregular glow of oil lamps; the electricity, like the telephone, had failed.

In the garden, as the rain penetrated the baked soil between the potted flowers, subterranean clods stirred, extended feet, and shoveled to the surface. They were toads that had slept like stones for months, waiting for the tempest that would soak them back to life. Now, in the lulls of the wind, the garden rang with their wet cries, as if the landscape were rejoicing.

In intervals between successive waves of storm (for

after the first plunging flood it came in long pulses, slowly dying) the household drifted out onto the porches, watching the sky. Masses of grey cloud sped silently across it; in the gaps, an evening star showed once and again, golden yellow. The toads chorused. From among the great curving leaves of a banana tree, split and frayed by the wind into the likeness of palm fronds, a butterfly rose, tilting upward in slow spirals, stately, higher and higher, unaccountable in this drenched and ravaged world, until she lost it somewhere in the high grey air.

Philippe Montoya had idiosyncrasies that people noticed with surprise after they had known him for some time. He smoked only a little, and drank very little indeed. It was possible to attend a number of hard-drinking occasions with him before you realized that he never had more than two or three drinks, and often less. Perhaps it was his hands. In such gatherings, most people's hands are noticeably empty unless they are grasping something —a glass, a cigarette, another person. They look superfluous, embarrassing. But Montoya's hands, even quiet— and they could be very quiet sometimes—never looked unoccupied.

"I knew it would happen," said the oracle.

She strove to feel his feeling; that was all, since it was not possible to know his knowledge. But he existed—he existed, because she could see and hear him—and therefore it was possible for a human mind to have total knowledge and yet not be destroyed. He was young, much younger than she; his memory of the past must be short. But he would live to be old, she thought, for his face showed the track of old memories, and they could only be memories of a long future. "Will you live to be old?" she asked him.

But a twitch of amusement, like a single switch of a cat's tail, furrowed his calm oval countenance. "That," he said precisely, "depends on what you mean by 'old.' And don't assume," he added, "that that implies I shall be old in any *obvious* sense. Or even live."

She was disappointed. "But you do know?"

"Yes."

"Then why don't you tell me?"

"I don't know."

"I thought you knew everything."

"I know what, not why. I knew you would ask me these questions, and I knew I would give you these answers."

"Then can't you change them? Couldn't you give different answers?"

"Of course. But the point is, these are the answers I choose to give."

"Why?"

"I don't know why. I only know what." He was laughing, gentle and delighted, as you might laugh at a child's questions. "I know that I won't tell you. I knew I would say these words, and now I am saying them. I could say any other words, any words I choose, but I knew I would choose these. Do you understand?" His mouth, a little supercilious always, softened toward her. "But keep on asking. You *will* keep on asking. And sometimes I will answer your questions."

Raging, ranging, its long legs sweeping with tireless strokes. Her body humped in spasms of distress. Thuds, thuds of rifle ends into flesh. One man swung by the butt, another by the barrel, as if they were amateurs, their methods not yet standardized. Flesh was not separate from self, it was self that the rifle blows were smashing, however much you might twist and turn, fleeing in, in, into the labyrinth of mind, crying, "There is no connection!" For mind is contained in flesh. Voice is made by flesh—by windpipe and vocal cords and broken mouth, by dying lungs that the booted heels crush in—there is one with boots, why is there always one with boots? And when voice is gone, the residue of self breaks, breaks, in the broken flesh. And then? Then there is night. You lie wiped out, like a ceased shudder. The dragon lurched, sinking, into the center. She gazed unblinking into the dark, asking, without the impossible effort of words, "Why am I not dead?"

"You will die," the oracle said soothingly. "You will die."

Since it was necessary for her to have a nationality, and since he had given her a French name, Montoya made her a French citizen. He was a French citizen himself. All his life he had been a citizen of at least two nations—

not always the same two—and he was deeply convinced of the value of foreign citizenship. It was a lifeline connecting you to somewhere else—no matter where; and you never knew when you might need a lifeline. It would have been easier, in some ways, to forge a Philippine citizenship for her; but that alone, in Montoya's opinion, would have been worse than no citizenship at all. It would be to lock her in the prison of a single nation's laws and regulations. As for confirming her American citizenship, that was a possibility to be rejected out of hand. Evidently she did not want to bring her past to the surface; therefore Montoya, for his part, would make no motion that might stir it up.

To the Chinese and Filipino servants he had acquired with the house, Montoya had added two or three who had come from Indochina with him—among these the old woman who functioned as nurse and governess for the little girl whom Montoya believed to be his child. At any rate, he had known the mother, and she had elected to leave the baby literally on his doorstep, though that might have been a compliment as much to his prospects as to his paternity. To clinch the matter, Montoya had legally adopted the little girl. Marie-Ange was the name he had given her. She was seven years old now, a luminously beautiful child, quiet but utterly un-shy, who played with the other children not as a leader but always as an active, observant second.

For the house was as full of children as of birds. The oldest were children only by courtesy, or rather by the technicality that they were not yet independently employed. These had shared Montoya's spectacular flight from Vietnam some nine years earlier, when in one wild night he and his household had bulldozed and burned two hundred hectares of rubber trees before decamping over the border—an act of flagrant illegality, since he had just accepted a rather substantial sum of money from the Provisional Revolutionary Government for that very acreage. Other children had accumulated around him (it was an almost chemical process, like precipitation in a supersaturated solution) during his short career as a businessman in Cambodia, where also his putative daughter had been born. So far in the Philippines he had acquired only two more, a boy toddler and a girl about the daughter's age.

All these young people received remarkably little thought and attention from Philippe Montoya. He gave them food and shelter, a degree of legal protection, and a casual but total acceptance. For the rest, they were informally adopted by various of the servants, who dressed and fed them, taught them and disciplined them, as they saw fit. Sometime in their teens, if they had stayed with him that long, he would hire them into one of his operations or find them a job elsewhere. In return, the best and worst alike of the children adored Montoya, and stood ready to burn whole forests with him, wherever the shooting star of his chosen destiny might lead.

To this conglomerate, many-tongued menage, in which no one seemed responsible for more than a tiny fraction of what went on, Montoya had added two Negrito guards as a finishing (or at least the latest) touch. They were tiny, well-knit men, armed with bolos and with automatic pistols that looked huge in their hands. Their function was deterrence; Negritos had, here, a reputation for ferocity and loyalty. Montoya persisted in thinking of them as if they were identical with the montagnards he had known in Indochina, and this made their communication difficult, as if they were shaking hands with long poles; still, it sufficed.

She always rose early, so that her nights were as short as possible. She had somehow managed to convey her need—or perhaps Montoya had conveyed it—to the old nurse, who came always to wake her, gently but persistently, at first dawn. She would have her coffee beside a wide window, where she could watch the light reborn, the world reborn under the light, each petal and blade assuming shape and color, shuddering (it seemed to her) just imperceptibly with resurgent life as it crowded back again into itself. She would be strong enough, she thought patiently, for another day.

CHAPTER 3

In fact, Montoya did not see enough of her to realize to what an extent she *had* gotten better. It was a mark of how spasmodic and agonized their communication had been that he knew how her son had died, but not his name. This death in itself made a difficulty between them of which she was not aware.

The boy had been beaten to death with rifles. Montoya knew where those rifles had come from. Of all the commodities in which he dealt, guns had proved one of the most profitable; and Indonesia had been a fruitful market. What it came to was that the same expedition that had saved her life had killed her son—had indeed, in a sense, put her to the torture. Montoya thought best not to bring this to her attention. She must, he supposed, know it as a possibility. But he was afraid of hurting her. She looked very fragile to him.

To herself she seemed wiped out—no longer a person, but a desolate battleground where only the ram and thunder of moving forces lived. Outsiders, of course, had a different perspective. "That little Frenchie of Montoya's is quite a character" was how one of the Americans expressed it. The little Frenchie had slapped a man for saying something that displeased her. The victim, who was drunk, had never grasped what the to-do was about—he had been trying to compliment her—and even Montoya had misunderstood. When the drunken American referred to the lucky chance that had brought her there, Montoya's simple thought was that the imbecile should have known better; all the guests had heard at least one version of Madame Delisle's short history. But it was not "lucky" to which she objected in that description; it was "chance."

But how was anyone to know? She had delivered her slap with cold, sudden fury, and turned without transition to Montoya, who had gone, as it were, into an invisible crouch. "Tell him it's nothing personal," she said, and walked away to find another drink. Her tall, slight figure moved with a certain hauteur.

Montoya laughed and patted the man's shoulder. "Nothing personal, Joe."

"Yeah," said the American, blinking, and added as an afterthought, "My name is Freddie."

"It doesn't matter to her," said Montoya.

All else was trivial, irrelevant. It amused her—all other daylight feelings gone, she could still be amused—to notice that the population of this dream world, from Montoya to the toddler sucking sugarcane in the kitchen, felt that what they did was of consequence. This was what made her laugh.

For she did laugh, a cascade of merriment that delighted Montoya and his household, and sometimes puzzled his guests. There was no malice in it. She was like a child laughing at dead leaves lifted and blown by the wind. They seemed as unreal to her, these people, compared to the reality inside her darkness, as the leaves to the child; real in some limited way, no doubt, but only marginally relevant. It was absurd that sometimes these leaves, blown into her face by sudden gusts, should try to touch her, should invite her to join them, to become a wind-tossed leaf. It was absurd—except that there were the children.

She could not look at the oldest ones. They came too near her son; she could not endure their young male bodies, their voices. Full of their own things, they were happy to ignore her. To them, she was like a large, exotic pet, in which they took a certain family pride. She strove, even, not to know their names. When Montoya said, "I'm taking Nguyen to Palawan; he can make himself useful on Pagbo," she looked at him as blankly as if he had spoken an unknown language. She did not even notice that this was Nguyen's certificate of majority; he would have a job to do on Pagbo, he would no longer be a child, with his smooth golden-brown chest and slender arms and swift jeering smile.

It was different with the younger children. In the kitchen, she sucked sugarcane gravely with the toddler, exchanging choice pieces, gazing wordlessly over the stalks, big eyes to big eyes, until the child melted into gurgles of laughter. Marie-Ange brought her worms, insects, spiders; this exquisite child had a taste for all small things that moved. They hovered together at the mesh of the aviary, cooing and chirping to the birds. A finch perched inches from their faces, settling and rearranging himself with flippant movements. They exchanged a look of arcane delight, fellow initiates. A thick, wet cloud ran steadily across the sky, bumping and dragging small cloud cushions around its edges. The child's eyes sparkled; she opened her small fist slowly. A creature stood upon her palm, sedately waving its antennae. Its lacquery green sides glinted with spots of brilliant gold, as if molten drops of the actual metal had lodged and hardened there. *"Je le donne au Philippe,"* she confided, a husky whisper. It was by this quaint denomination that all the children referred to Montoya—*le Philippe,* as if the addition of the definite article changed his name into a title, at once respectful and familiar.

She bent low, her forehead almost to the child's. *"Au diner,"* she suggested conspiratorially. *"Dans sa verre."* They tilted their faces upright to grin at each other, savoring the idea of Montoya discovering this jewel-like beast in his glass at dinner. They laughed together. The small hand closed like a flower. The child danced away with sidewise skips, uttering sweet, high-pitched yips to which the birds replied.

She could come that close to the child—to any of the children. But when she would have gone farther, when her arms were opening, her shoulders dipping to lift that warm mite and cuddle it against her breasts, something as physical as an iron brace suddenly held her rigid. Her heart folded coldly like a closing triptych, and she said behind her eyes, *Goodbye.*

She drew portraits of the guests on their napkins—Freddie as a mole, Dr. Aguilar as a little cat—catching her bottom lip between her teeth, her head tilted like a child's intent on play. Montoya spread his arms wide in mock despair. "No wonder I'm going broke—new napkins every time somebody comes for dinner!" He tucked the mole into Freddie's shirt pocket. "Why don't you wear a barong tagalog like the rest of us? Never mind, any man who wears a shirt and tie in Manila deserves to be hot."

"Here, Renée, do mine!" "Do mine!" They drifted like schooling fish from the dining room onto the patio, lit by Chinese lanterns. But she clapped her hands and turned back, saying to one of the servant girls, "Is the table

cleared yet? Don't take the cloth away." A minute later
they were all leaning over the dining table again, vying to
hold the cloth flat for her flying pencil, stretching to recognize the fish as she traced their faces. "There you are,
Peterson! Hey, who's that?" She could sketch very quickly
for an exercise like this.

It was a society without a past, moving as instinctively as
the fishes. No one asked, "Where did you come from?"
"How did you get here?" "What were you before?" People
with pasts they wanted to keep did not come here.

It was very different, of course, for those whose past itself was here. In the society at whose threshold Montoya
stood now, the present was merely the necessary link between the past and the future. If money could replace
family for some purposes, it was only because both were
durable goods. Personal character, like personality, was
temporary, and hardly entered into consideration.

CHAPTER 4

Within her memory, Josepha Sandoval had never been
frightened by anything, and it did not occur to her to be
frightened of Philippe Montoya. He did, though, give her
a strange feeling, of venturing into the unknown, somewhat like leaving home for the first time to attend a distant college. She realized now that the young men she had
known had been too absorbed in their youth to have
much time for anything else; and men of Montoya's age
or older had bothered to notice her, if at all, only as a desirable but unavailable instrument for masturbation. Montoya, however, noticed her seriously, and he seemed to
her a serious man, though all their conversation so far had
been very light. His history, as she knew it, was exotic
and adventurous, and yet his present position must be stable and comfortable—otherwise her father would not
be considering him as a son-in-law. Then, too, he was
handsome—strikingly so, with his Chinese eyes—and he
carried an unobtrusive but distinguishable air of cosmopolitan ease. He did not look like the businessmen and poli-
ticians to whom she was accustomed, still less like the rest

of mankind whom she lumped as "peasants." With his smooth piratical face and his masterful way of moving, he looked perhaps like a sea captain.

She knew about Madame Delisle—everyone knew about Madame Delisle—but only as an added piquancy, which seemed to have no relevance to her own life. Montoya's world was full of mysteries. When—if—the time came, Madame Delisle would be brushed back into the shadowy reaches that stretched away from him.

The dragon at the bottom of the world . . . There was no refuge, none; and she sought no refuge. That deep battle was all her business. Still she was grateful for the house that protected her from extraneous horrors. No one who entered here would hurt her. It made her very unself-conscious. She moved among these people, servants and guests alike, as if she fancied herself personally invisible, like a scientist among objects of study. It was as if she no longer believed that anyone could take any interest in her unless to hurt her; since no one in this house would hurt her, ipso facto they were not interested in her, and therefore what she said and did was of no significance to anyone but herself. It gave all her behavior a strange quality —impish, sleepwalkerly—that male guests, especially, found unsettling and charming. The servants had promptly categorized her with the children—one more difficult, injured waif. She was surprised, and momentarily frightened, whenever she met someone's eyes.

"I knew it would happen," said the oracle.

She held the body in one hand, it was so small. "Why?" she asked achingly.

"All that lives must die," the oracle said. "That's Shakespeare."

She nodded; because it was true, and because she accepted his mockery as a sort of corrosive kindness, eating at her ignorance. "Yes."

"Shakespeare died, too," he added.

When Montoya was not there—and Montoya often was not there—her nights were precarious. She would lie down painstakingly, extending her slight body on the bed in a position that seemed to her appropriate for death. Beneath her, the fragile crust of the world lay quiescent. In the

dark, her first steps were always faltering. She touched her
son's thick hair, and heard his voice, bantering and ag-
gressive, a young man's voice, or a boy feeling his manhood. She could bear this, though her hand burned at the
contact; in less than a year's time she had learned to look
at her son and say, "He will die like that." They stood together on a street of Djakarta in their ignorance, and all
around them, behind the façades of buildings and faces,
the mucky whirlpool of a revolution was stirring, turning;
so that when it suddenly tightened, wheeling, spinning, it
was inevitable that they must be sucked down. And at the
bottom of the world a filthy mouth had taken them with a
yawn. But she shied away, dancing sideways with quick
small serious steps. She was not ready to think of that yet;
before she came to battle, there were affairs to settle.

(And Montoya was not there. And her bones ached
with tiredness, tears not of grief or pain but of tiredness
welled in her eyes, and it was not that she would evade
the battle, but only postpone it a little while.)

All the things, she thought, that added together had
brought them within that whirlpool's circumference—
all the accidents and decisions that looked like chance or
choice—they had been inevitable, too. Now in the darkness she went over them carefully, all those distant events,
verifying the silent necessities that had seemed possibilities then, mere possibilities among other possibilities. But
it was inevitable, she thought; those other possibilities
had been only illusions. Beyond the door, in the warm,
breathing house, servants slept lightly, ready to wake
and tend her. In the cages the birds slept, silent, crouched,
their long toes locked around twigs or perches. This, now,
was the critical time. The crust of the world lay still, and
she too would sleep. Sometimes she would sleep. But
sometimes a piece of the crust would tilt up before her
like a hinged lid opening, and she would be facing the
great gape of the dragon's mouth. She made a sick noise,
a groaning whine of unwillingness, and sank in a wet
heap. Its breath seared her. She rose, to match the poor
heat of her anger against the breath of hell. The dragon
laughed; spurts of soiled raw flame squirted between
its teeth. Waves of stench assaulted her. She stood and
drew great breaths, eyes blind with effort. Hell opened
wider. Twists, thrusts; some gross dry object rammed

between her legs. This she could bear. This, she thought bitterly, she could bear.

Philippe Montoya could not easily have said what his Renée was to him; he did not very clearly know. She was now, of course, a convenience and a decoration; but it was not for that that he had brought her here and been moved by her. In part, it was no different from the recurrent impulse that had filled his house with children. This was not charity. The waifs and orphans he had picked from the turbulent life of the gutter were not the most helpless—no more than they were, by most people's standards, the most appealing. It was more nearly the impulse of fellowship, a sense of the brotherhood of loners. Nothing had ever summed up better what he loved and admired than that bleak, humorous, hopeless, wry and resigned bravado, "It made me mad." But he did not understand her battles in the dark. He thought they were only bad dreams.

Sometimes she reneged—she turned away from the dark. Those were the dangerous times, as she rated danger. For she could really have done it, really have fallen into the easy drift of the days, content to be Montoya's woman, aging and a little mad, with nights no more real than other people's nights; could have drifted, perhaps, until some prosaic chance or choice cast her back on the shores of her past life, simply a woman who had lost a son and had an adventure, cast her among people who would say "My goodness" and "How horrible"; and have drifted on among them, knowing no more than they knew, no more than she had known. But she hated those times and was ashamed.

Most often, she faced it out. It was not really so hard —she had, after all, nothing to lose—there was always just a sick moment at the beginning when she thought that this time, this particular time, she could not bear it. But if she did draw back, the sick feeling stayed with her, even in the depth of her relief. And the next night she would think, "If I had gone on, last night, I would be that much closer to the end," and despise the cowardice that had set her back by twenty-four hours.

For these struggles in the dark were not fruitless. She

progressed; darkness by darkness she moved closer to knowledge.

"Why do you want to know this?" the oracle demanded. His eyes burned with resentful envy.

Yes, why? Billions had suffered as much, she knew, and asked nothing better than to forget. What was important, surely, was to live, to leave the past, to close the wound. "No," she said strongly. For it was wrong, wrong, those billions had been wrong. "Because," she told the oracle, "if the wound closes before it is probed, it festers inside." But suddenly metaphors seemed to her cheap, deceitful. "Because," she said angrily, "if people don't *know* what happens to them when they make mistakes, they go on making the same mistakes over and over again."

The oracle smiled knowingly. His voice was a hateful purr. "Then why do you say it was all inevitable? If it's inevitable, what difference does it make how much you know?"

Her fingers clenched on her pencil. She would draw him now, now, while she hated him.

She held the child's arm between her hands, the child's face with her eyes. There was not a line, not a surface, that was not soft and clean. "Is she his child?"

"How should I know?" replied the oracle. The child escaped her, casually.

"I think she is," she said. "Or I think it doesn't matter, which is the same thing. I think the mother left him the baby because he ought to have it. You can tell. You can tell," she explained earnestly. "I think he must make love with other women the same way he does with me. Which is *with*, not *to*. Do you understand what I mean?"

"No," said the oracle.

"*With*, not *to*—how else can I say it? 'Make love' isn't the right phrase, though. It doesn't have anything to do with love. 'Have intercourse' is very, very accurate, if you can hear what the words say and forget how awkward the phrase has always sounded. We have intercourse with each other. And I think that's normal for him; he doesn't fuck women, he has intercourse with them. Of course, there are special circumstances sometimes—but he doesn't enjoy it much that way, it doesn't seem normal to him. That's what I think," she finished a little hesitantly.

The oracle smiled—a mute, tormenting smile that stung her, and she cried eagerly, "Will he—Will we—"; but before she could frame her question, the triptych closed; she did not want to know her future with Montoya. It would be suicidal, and she was not ready for suicide. She had to live to finish her battle; and it was exactly the unadulterated present with Montoya that preserved her, the present untouched by past or future.

"Philippe Montoya," Josepha said playfully. "With a name like that, you *had* to come to the Philippines someday. It's destiny."

"And all this time I thought it was good business," Montoya responded good-humoredly.

"Well, think of it! This is the only Christian democracy in the hemisphere—except Australia and New Zealand, and they are so very Anglo-Saxon." She was repeating, not so much with conviction as with a simple absence of question, things which she had been taught. "Here," she went on, "Señor Montoya can feel at home." This was coy, though not unbecomingly so; they were at present in the garden of her father's Manila home, hung now with lanterns and decorated with strolling guests.

Montoya's Annamese grandmother had had more to do with his everyday childhood than any other one person; and though he had been baptized and confirmed a Catholic, his memories and his sympathies were more importantly Buddhist. He had nothing, he felt, from his Spanish grandfather but his name and a kind of hereditary license, if he chose to exercise it, for a certain arrogant touchiness. In fact he was silently exercising it now. How often he had said, to explain his differentness, "After all, I am Spanish!"—just as he said, in other situations, "I am French" or "I am Vietnamese." All the time he had never felt Spanish. Now, listening to Josepha, he felt indignantly, 'Why, I am more Spanish than this little *mestiza*. At least my grandfather was a real Spaniard."

"My family came from Castile," she was saying. "Where did yours originate, Felipe?"

He did not like to be called Felipe; but he was too prudent to tell her that and thereby give her the power of annoying him deliberately in future. "God knows," he said. "The Garden of Eden, perhaps." He lifted his arms, inviting her to dance.

"Oh, *that's* why you feel at home in a garden!" She went laughing into his arms. The music was pleasant, and after all Josepha Sandoval was pleasant to him also, neither stupid nor vicious.

"You and your family must visit me soon," he said.

For Philippe Montoya, though he had never formulated it, one simple principle guaranteed freedom. In his complex, precarious life, balanced within an intricate network of connections, he had remained essentially uninvolved. His self was not entangled. Therefore he was free to make his choices without consulting the necessities of any other entity—human, institutional, or divine. It gave him an incorruptible integrity of will that was very useful in business dealings. He behaved always as if he had nothing to lose.

In sleep, the oracle's face was soft, childlike. In sleep, perhaps, she thought, he found the blessing of uncertainty. He would feel it wash around him, over his face, into his nostrils and through his hair, a sweet clear flow; the caked crust of knowledge would dissolve. Cool, the touch of freedom. She watched tautly in the dark. What good was it, then, if to master knowledge brought only this need to escape from knowledge, to lose it in sleep? But another time she thought, swallowing once and nodding, Yes, it was good, then; he had mastered knowledge, he held it in leash when awake, and asleep he was free of it and could forget. But she was never free; she fought it or fled it always, light and dark, or crouched, dreading, and waited for its claws.

CHAPTER 5

He bent over her chair, leaning his hands on its arms, to set a small, comfortable kiss on her cheek. These martial kisses, which would have surprised her if she had not been too preoccupied to think about them, were Montoya's spontaneous offering. As he straightened up, he announced, "I'm going to take you south. Soon."

Now she startled, and lifted her big-eyed humorless gaze.

"It's time for you to get better."

By which he meant, at present, merely that it was time for her to learn to leave this house. She took it in a deeper way, and leaned forward, frowning, abstracted. "But . . ." she said; then, "Yes, I know." She raised her face again, but her eyes were so intently inward that they crossed a little. "It's stupid. It's stupid. Because, you see, I didn't really find out anything new. So why is it killing me? Why does it make a difference just because it happened to *me?*" Her gaze refocused. She looked pathetic to him, childlike. "I can't be that selfish, can I? I can't be that stupid. Seventeen-year-old boys get beaten to death every day, everybody knows that. If it's important, why didn't it kill me before? I mean, every boy is as real as every other boy."

"Everybody doesn't know it," Montoya said. When she moved, she trembled. She would have a bad night tonight, and he had been looking forward to sleep.

He would not have done this to her without reason. But it was impossible to think seriously of marriage while she was in the house, and he needed to give it serious thought—which would involve, for example, having the Sandovals as house guests. And in any case, he believed what he had told her: it was time.

Having decided that it was to be done, he took satisfaction in it. The house on Palawan was very private to him, like his boats—something reserved from the showcase of his Manila life. He would take there both his Renée and his child. Marie-Ange too must be removed from the sphere that Josepha Sandoval was to occupy.

Nguyen's job on Pagbo, though technically menial, was not without importance. He had been given a place in the crew of a kumpit that plied irregularly between Palawan and the southern reaches of the Sulu Sea. He had a useful facility with languages, and a suppleness that was useful on shipboard; but his chief function was simply to be among them, a presence from Montoya's own household, guaranteeing by his existence the involuntary, spontaneous loyalty of hand to head.

He admired the Moro seamen for their skill, their casual cheerfulness, their pride—qualities he had long admired, under other forms, in Montoya. He felt that he was already like them, but distinct. It remained only to demonstrate his likeness.

They would make the trip by water. There were airports of a sort on Palawan, but none closer than Puerto Princesa, thirty miles of imperfect road from Montoya's house. Besides, he felt protectively that it would be easier for her if she could make the whole journey enclosed, as it were, in a piece of his household. For this voyage he chose his personal favorite from his motley little fleet, a middle-sized Tonkinese junk, seaworthy and comfortable, not as fast as a prao on the open sea, but eminently maneuverable and as stable as a lighthouse.

There was a cove, over-hung with scents that swayed in the green air like flowering vines. Before they stepped ashore they were within the forest. The path they followed led gently upward, winding, then across a stream by a footbridge that she crossed with open eyes and closed heart. She walked slowly, holding Marie-Ange's hand. Birds were all around them, fluttering, calling. She had a new ambition, immediate and strong. She wanted to come out of the forest—not that it oppressed her, but simply because she wanted to see birds flying, flying in the open sky. The path skirted a dark ravine, turned, offered suddenly a blaze of openness. They stood at the edge of a broad yard, overrun with a low, many-leaved plant. The house faced them, low, long, wide. She lifted her eyes to the brilliant sky.

Montoya was not casual about his dwelling places—no more than a ground squirrel about its burrow. Before he showed her her room, he explained her escape route. (In Montoya's experience, there was always an escape possible, if you had either foresight or luck.) The Moros of these waters moved among the southern islands like birds in a forest. No one, not the Moros, had ever counted the islands of that rich sea, still less charted them. Every prao's skipper had his own secret paths and places, and the gunboats of the Philippine Constabulary moved harmlessly among them like large blundering balloons. If the need arose (it was well not to limit your thinking by being too specific about what the need might be), any of Montoya's household would be safe with his Moro crews. The only difficulty would be in reaching them promptly; and for that he maintained a one-armed Moro called Mako. Ostensibly he was a gardener. In fact, his function was more specialized.

As the other had been a house of birds, so this was a house of vines. There were other plants as well, large and small, inside and out; but it was the vines that were, for her, characteristic. Here it was not enough for a plant simply to grow; there was a gush, a flow, of vegetation— fountaining leaves, stems that flung themselves wide to grasp and climb.

Spurting green flowed down the window, an emerald coruscation. Slowly her eyes began to focus on the curtaining vine. The leaves condensed toward solidity, then toward clarity. A little to one side of the center, where a branch twisted slantwise, she made out the shape of a bird, jewel-like and still. Her brows drew together a little as she forced her eyes through the final notches into clear focus. The bird rested motionless, its head turned away from her. Then, on the instant, with a motionless jerk, it was not a bird. It was the knuckles of a hand, yellow-green, grasping slantwise along the vine, and as she leaped, panicking, upright, the leaves beside it broke into a face, not human, green with reflected light, and moved, and the face broke again into leaves. She sat still on the edge of her bed and thoughtfully selected a cigarette.

Montoya smiled fondly. He liked to see her thus, unhurried, idle, at ease in the green asylum of his protection. He did not know that urgency beset her. A kind of swelling bubble divided her life. Above, cut off from the depths, insulated by the nothingness of the bubble, a layer almost of merriment, of quick, disordered flights, idle, content in truth as in appearance. But below was where she lived.

She knew now the anxiety of the dying. *Is there time?* was her continual question to the oracle. "Yes," he would answer; "yes, but you must hurry." She did not dare to ask, *Have I strength?* She could not forget the leafy in-

truder at the window, when for a moment reality had
flickered. That, she knew, was madness, the loosening
of her weary grip. She smiled idly back at Montoya.
Inwardly, below the bubble, she trembled like a leaf, a
bird among the vines. Before, she had been afraid that
she might not die; now there was another and worse fear,
that she might die too soon.

"You are alive," the oracle said. "I knew you would
live in this house." Yes; she was alive; therefore it was
not simply the house of the birds that had sustained her.
Something more inward fed her life.

Here, in this house, she had not faced the dragon.
Yet it was here; it prowled, it stalked, it waited. She felt
its bulk moving, somewhere underfoot. Now and again
the floor quivered as it scraped beneath. But of course it
was here, below her, rising from the bottom of the world.
All houses, all streets were built upon the same crust,
over the same center.

One sign, as it seemed to her, of her approaching death
was a progressive weakness. As she pushed further into
the dragon's night, she had grown not stronger but more
skilled. Her technique improved; she coped with horror
more adroitly. At the same time she felt herself debilitated,
reduced to a raw skeleton whose naked bones buzzed and
quivered with pain at a fly's touch. Sometimes in the great
heat of the day she would lie wretched, whimpering with
refusal, whipping her restive head this way and that in
hopeless jerks. She who endured the dragon's claw could
no longer endure the simple, senseless heat. It had not
oppressed her so in the beginning.

But there was a technique for this too. After a time—
always longer—she would rally her scattered forces, col-
lect herself, and cease to struggle. This was the great
secret of the heat: accept it, and its misery was tolerable.
Sweat collected steadily on the high points of her face and
body, globed, trickled ticklingly downward. But it was
only by vigilance that she could maintain even this
squalid imitation of repose. Something in her vibrated
sporadically, trying to escape once more into the irrespon-
sibility of panic. The heat was tolerable, yes; but tolerance
was a level of strength, and something in her longed to
slough off the last of strength. "When?" she whispered.

"Later," said the oracle. "It will be cool, cool. There will be rain. The wind will blow."

Not a hair stirred, not a leaf. Everything hung limp, clung damply. Every breath lifted the great weight of the air a tiny space, and sank again in collapse. "Soon?" she asked pitifully, angrily.

"Soon."

In this spiraling lushness, she felt herself shrink. Perhaps, after all, the other house had been her protection. Montoya, too, would leave her, perhaps tomorrow, perhaps next week. He had stayed already, out of silent consideration for her needs, longer than his custom. She was shriveling, wilting. Dread inhibited every movement of her spirit. She grew cunning. If the past was what she must know, then let all the future be a blank. She could endure, perhaps, so much knowledge; she would not burden herself with more.

Pagbo was a way station, a rendezvous and transfer point, a halt between stages of a journey; sometimes, for a short time, a depot. It had the inherent privacy of islands, and it had one artificial improvement, a wooden house or shed that was clearly different in origin from the airy architecture of these southern regions. There was no other wood on Pagbo but driftwood, just as there was no fresh water but what the rain and the transitory inhabitants brought. Flat, naked to the wind, the island lay beneath the sun, one among many, the sand and coral cays scattered in loose clusters down the coast of Palawan. She had never seen Pagbo. She had no cause to think she would ever see it. She would not have recognized its name.

The oracle's face was shadowed, haggard. He had a beard, soft and close to his face, tracing its hollows and salients like pencil shadings. "You don't ask," he said fiercely. "Why not?"

"Why are you angry?"

"Because you don't ask. I know why not—you're going to tell me in a minute—but I don't like your not asking questions. Why don't you ask me what's going to happen?"

"I don't want to know!"

"Why not?" he cried, pushing closer out of the darkness.

She had pressed her flat hands over her ears, her shoulders hunched forward, her elbows protecting her breasts. "Because," she whined, "if you *know* what's going to happen, it's inevitable."

He struck her hands away from her ears. He was strong, stronger then she had imagined. "No! Nothing is inevitable!" He grasped her arm, her wounded arm, in both hands, and his face twisted cynically. "I *choose* to do this," he said, and squeezed, twisting his grasping hands in opposite directions. She screamed. (Ah, that was a luxury she had here, she could scream here in the dark.) He dropped her arm.

"Why did you do that?" she cried raggedly. "Why?"

"There was no reason," he said drily. "It was not inevitable. I chose to do it. But I knew that I would choose to do it."

"You did it because you knew you would do it!" she accused.

His face flashed with anger again. "No! No!" His voice was bursts of thunder. "I *know* because I *did!*" Her head swam. You could faint from unconsciousness into deeper unconsciousness, just as you could rise from pain into keener pain. "Do you think time is important?" he roared. "*Act* is important! You know what happened to your son in Djakarta. You know what happened to you on that island. Does that make what happened inevitable?"

And she was writhing, spitted on the dragon's claw, her head, her whole body in the gape of its gullet. Vomit dribbled from her mouth, blood and excrement from her loins; her nails scrabbled at her body, at the horror around her; her mind rolled and twisted in swift jerks, knotting itself into itself. "Yes," she heard herself whisper, rapidly, clearly, so close that the whisper filled all the space of sound. "Inevitable. It was inevitable. Otherwise it could not have happened. Inevitable. It was inevitable. Otherwise it could not have happened. Inevitable." The dragon crunched. Its teeth closed around her; in the stifling, stinking dark its ridged tongue wiped her against the furrowed roof of its mouth. "It was not inevitable," the oracle's voice said softly. She fell into Montoya's arms.

CHAPTER 6

Montoya had heard the car coming, and stepped out onto the long, veranda-like porch of his house, alert. He was accustomed to making the traffic on this road himself.

Senator Sandoval emerged, waved to Montoya, paid off the driver (hired, no doubt, in Puerto Princesa), and helped his daughter out. They stood amid a threatening collection of luggage.

Montoya had come slowly down into the yard to greet them, framing an unenthusiastic smile. He was displeased. He did not enjoy anyone—least of all the Senator—looking over his shoulder so assiduously.

Josepha laid her little hand on her father's arm, laughing. "It's my fault, Philippe. I wanted to see your house. Besides, I wanted to see how a bachelor from Manila lives on Palawan."

"You'll be disappointed," Montoya said. "On Palawan, I only have time for business. If you want excitement, you should have stayed in Manila."

"Maybe I'm tired of excitement. Besides, Papa wants to talk business. May I see your house?" She released her father's arm with a pat, and moved across the porch, tossing her head coltishly. Montoya moved swiftly to reach the door first. He was good at tight-rope walking—ushering them in as he clapped his hands and issued instructions in Vietnamese, delaying them with hospitality in the front of the house while the old nurse got her charges under cover. This house was his sanctuary. He would not have his family (so, in effect, he thought of them) driven from it. But he rejected the idea of Josepha seeing or touching them, as simply and vehemently as his stomach would reject an emetic. This was not quite consistent of him; Josepha had met them both already, and even hugged the little girl, who had slipped out of the embrace like a wild bird, shaking her arms as if to settle the feathers. But Josepha had been only a dinner guest then. She knew, of course, that there was a legally adopted child among his waifs and strays; but her father had given her to understand that she would not be expected to function

as a stepmother, and that the little *mestiza* would never be
a threat to her own future children. There was even to be
some legal arrangement to guarantee that. All this was
absolutely as Montoya wished it. He would not, for any
consideration, knowingly subject his daughter to a sena-
torial family's condescension; and he did not want to place
Josepha in a position that would make him resent her. He
was quite willing to provide for Marie-Ange by an independent settlement, and breed new heirs of impeccable
legitimacy. Only let there be no interference!

The Senator had been considering a *pied á terre* on one of
the southern islands for some time. He had accumulated
money that called for investment, and he felt the need for
added solidity and protection to comfort his declining
years. There had never been so good an opportunity as
Montoya offered (offered, as it happened, involuntarily);
there would never again, he felt, be a better moment to
catch that opportunity. He and Montoya knew each other.
They were, now, like two traders haggling in the market,
watchfully circling each other's wares, assessing possibilities of profit and loss, offering with one hand and withholding with the other. It was a kind of work they both
enjoyed.

"Yes, I envy you," the Senator announced. He stood
upright, his elbow on the high porch railing, his small,
plump hand resting with complacent pats on his stomach. He surveyed the grounds before him, turned a little
to survey the line of the house front. "You have everything here that I have wanted for my retirement. And you
a young man! This is wasted on you."

Montoya laughed. "A base to work from, that's all.
You would find there are no comforts here."

"Even a retired person," said the Senator, "needs some
interest to occupy his time. And, of course, a little income.
I have been thinking about buying a boat."

"What kind of boat?" Montoya asked politely.

"One of the same type as you use. If, of course,
I could be sure that it would be handled as profitably."

Montoya smiled lightly. "No one can guarantee a
profit."

The Senator's chuckle was paternal. "I didn't say 'profitably'; I said '*as* profitably.' If we were partners in the
operation, I providing the boat, and you the skill . . ."

But the Senator had hit upon the one type of business venture for which Montoya felt real distaste. All the effort of his life had been directed to being, first and above all, his own man. The generosity for which he was known was premised on the satisfying awareness that what he gave was his own, won by his own labors. The pleasure he took in his vessels and his houses was the pleasure of unencumbered ownership, the powerful sensation that he could set the torch to them at will, as he had done, with less legal justification, to the rubber plantation in Annam. "Well," he said, "you came to the right place. This coast is full of boats, and men who know how to use them."

"I prefer to keep this kind of arrangement in the family," the Senator said, reprovingly. He lit a cigar, offering one to Montoya. Montoya declined; instead, he lit an American cigarette (he always carried a fresh pack, though he so seldom smoked them) and leaned on the railing, gazing forward toward the unseen sea, the cigarette projecting from the fingers of his clasped hands. "You know, of course," said the Senator, "that I am a member of the committee which is now investigating smuggling in the southern islands."

"I read the newspapers," said Montoya.

"In fact, that is one of my reasons for coming to Palawan."

This was unfair. The range of Montoya's business interests was not unknown in government circles already, and the Senator himself had expressed interest before now in the possibility of arrangements for mutual profit. But Montoya took the threat in good part, as legitimate under the rules of the game. He smoked for a time in silence before he spoke again. "I like the Moros," he said conversationally. "Some people say they are too excitable to be trustworthy, but I find them very reliable. They are touchy people, though. If someone offers them a bribe, they take it as an insult—just as if it was a threat. They are like the Spanish in that way."

"Yes," said the Senator thoughtfully. "Perhaps that is why Spanish culture took root so readily in the Philippines."

Montoya straightened and put out his cigarette. "A boat is a risky thing to put your money in, Senator. One storm can sink your whole investment." He gestured toward the sky, as if he were casually invoking a storm god. "And if you want a house to retire to, why not pick Mindanao, where there are no typhoons?"

"There are no typhoons on Palawan," the Senator said obstinately. "And Mindanao is full of Moro rebels."

Montoya drew in air through his teeth, a silent whistle of private exasperation. There were typhoons on Palawan, although not every year, or even every other year. As for Moro rebels—he was aware that Manila did not recognize danger signs on Palawan, any more than it had recognized them on Mindanao. He himself had good reason to be sensitive to angry stirrings among the Moslem Palaweños; he was, potentially at least, one of the objects of their resentment. What had set off the still-seething rebellion on Mindanao was an in-flowing of Christian outsiders, bent on taking everything they could. Montoya realized well enough that he was part of the same process on Palawan, although personally he did not feel very Christian, and less an outsider here than in Manila. But the Senator was only a senator, and could not be expected to grasp all this; therefore Montoya spoke to him patiently. "Did you hear the radio this morning? Unless the typhoon turns north, it will be here within three days. That's why I need to go up the coast in a hurry. I have things to take care of before the storm hits."

"I am prepared to pay cash," said the Senator. "At this moment."

Montoya did not pause in the movement he had begun, turning casually toward the house door; but he was interested. If the Senator had come with cash in his pocket, it was because he meant to make a deal, and one not wholly suitable for transaction on paper. That meant it would be an unusually large amount of cash, quite enough to buy another house and another boat. Also, Montoya's liquidity was, at the moment, not all he could wish; this cash was decidedly tempting. "Let's have a drink," he suggested.

Nguyen lay half-propped on a roll of matting, contemplating the sky. A wall of clouds stood in the east, and it seemed to him that it was slowly advancing.

His first Sulu voyage—now that all its awkwardnesses were past—had filled him with a boiling, eager pride. It was pleasure simply to lie on the hot deck, feeling himself from inside, nothing of his bubbling restlessness showing through the somnolent pose. There was nothing to do on Pagbo; and on Pagbo they were to stay until word came from Palawan. So he lay in the sun and watched the sky; and the clouds advanced.

"Well, have you finished your business discussion?" Josepha asked lightly, brightly.

"We discussed the weather," Montoya said. "And the Moros."

Josepha laughed, a rich chuckle. "I think that sometimes you're a Moro yourself, Felipe." She stood very close to him, bending her head, touching his shirt button with one fingertip, so that her deep, black hair brushed his chest; with a very slight tilt she would have been leaning against him. His chest expanded toward her; but they stayed separated, joined only by that breathlike touch of hair and finger. Looking down on her dark head, he felt a painful swell of tenderness, a feeling much like incest, as if he were looking in this way at a child of his own; she was so small.

Palawan—though Montoya was hardly conscious of the fact in such terms—had become in his eyes somewhat of a private preserve. His feeling was less affectionate than proprietary. Palawan: a long, ungainly island, hardly more than a straight ridge of forested rock, stretching away at a south-southwesterly slant from the main body of the Philippines, as if it were the archipelago's walking stick. In the whole length of the island, there was only one major road, fifty-odd miles from northeast to southwest, lying along the southern coast with the town of Puerto Princesa at its center. From the airport at Puerto Princesa, small planes irregularly connected with the teeming international terminal of Manila. There was no manufacturing here, no agriculture beyond the patches of rice and sweet potatoes scraped in the thin soil along the coast, no evidence of mineral wealth waiting to be tapped. Nevertheless, to Montoya as increasingly to others, Palawan appeared a fertile field, to be sown and reaped. One industry, at least, was both prosperous and legal. The little fishing fleets of the coast—above all, from the bay of Taytay, at the northern tip of the island—shared the rich fishing grounds of the southern seas with the more modern trawlers from Manila. Four of the shabby-looking vessels

operating out of Taytay belonged to Montoya; he hoped
to add soon a refrigerated ship that would give him an
advantage in the ravenous Manila market. These fishing
boats of his were also suitable for delivering other goods,
usually after a rendezvous with swifter vessels from south
in the Sulu Sea.

But his most enterprising ambition was on land. The
forests of Palawan were, by Philippine standards, thin and
poor; but they included the archipelago's only commercial
stands of ipil, which its admirers billed as the world's most
useful wood; and Montoya had quickly noted that they
were absurdly underexploited. He had begun by buying
one of the small existing sawmills. What he envisioned
was no less than an eventual lumbering empire. Such a
base on Palawan would give him leverage in the already
savage competition on Mindanao—and Mindanao was the
most likely field for his next expansion. Mindanao, indeed, had already been swept by so many waves of
speculators and settlers that the native Moslems, suddenly
reduced to a minority, had risen in furious revolt. The
revolt seemed to have settled into an interminable low-
key war (Montoya smiled drily; he had seen the theme
of these variations elsewhere), and the settlers and speculators were turning toward Palawan. Before the waves
broke there in earnest, Montoya meant to be firmly established.

CHAPTER 7

She had not seen Montoya since the Sandovals' arrival.
She had been told only that he would be busy with visitors, that she and the child could occupy themselves in
the servants' quarters. She understood from this that they
were to keep out of sight, and for the first time since
Montoya had washed her wounds in the cramped cabin, a
spasm of simple fear touched her, like a cold hand among
her entrails. "Will they find me?" she asked the oracle.

"Yes," he said flatly.

The cold hand clenched. For a moment her own hands
opened spasmodically, the fingers drawing back as if the
tendons were suddenly tightening. But her son was dead.

Her son was already dead, they could not kill him. The relief was so real that she smiled, a little wanly, and drew herself together.

"Why don't you ask who they are?" the oracle inquired. His voice was patient, distant, and amused. That would be how you survived, if you knew everything that was going to happen to you. Patience, distance, amusement—what else could there be, other than raving frenzy? It was all she could do, to cope with the single fact that she would be found. Her flesh twisted on its bones, not yet with pain but with grim anticipation. The cold hand had become a hundred vises, closing on her muscles. *Well, well,* she thought wryly; *after all, it's not important.*

"Why not?" he insisted.

"Oh! All right, who are they?" Irrelevant. That was one thing she had deeply learned: it didn't matter who they were. There was nothing unique about a street in Djakarta. Those were *people* who walked and rode it. People; she knew—she and her son had spoken with them, laughed with them, dickered with them. They had seemed different then, unlike people in her own country. Later, what struck her was their likeness, their overwhelming humanness; just as that strange, different street was overwhelmingly a street. So it did not matter who they were. They could all wield rifles, or other weapons, whatever street they came from.

"Then how can you trust anybody?" the oracle asked curiously. Trust would be a difficult concept for him to grasp, as difficult as knowledge was for her. There could be trust only where there was an unknown; and where there was an unknown, there could be surprise, therefore betrayal; so that trust could never be certain, never quite trusting. You could only trust where you could be betrayed.

"Because," she said sturdily, "everybody is good to somebody." Montoya was good to her—at least, good enough. She did not inquire whether he was good to anyone else.

"'Because' doesn't answer 'how,'" the oracle said, a little vexed, like a teacher bored with correcting minor errors of grammar.

At siesta time, they gave her a place to lie down—not really a bed, as Montoya's bed had defined the word for

her. The heat lay like wet bandages. Montoya came and
sat beside her; she turned on her side, to fit the curve of
her body to his hip. "I'm leaving now," he said. "I should
be back the day after tomorrow at the latest—tomorrow,
if I can. You must stay here, in the servants' quarters,
until the old woman tells you to come out. Understood?"

"Yes." She watched his face darkly, patiently.

He touched her cheek, a gesture of exasperation. "Why
don't you ever ask a question?" She smiled helplessly,
and he laughed. "It looks as if we'll get some of the typhoon. I should be back before it gets here—but if I'm
delayed at Taytay, I may have to wait it out. Nobody
will bother you here." He picked up her hand, considering for a moment whether to give her an important trust.
"Take care of Marie-Ange," he concluded.

"What is it like to know?" she asked. "How can you live?"

The oracle's ravaged face drew back, drew nearer. His
eyes were wild with dizzy pain. "Only by knowing that I
will live," he said, his voice thin, brittle, ready to break
into the shards of hysteria. "Only by knowing that I *will*
live, and therefore I *can* live."

"*Must* live," she corrected quickly.

"No!" His face rushed forward out of the dark. *"Can*
live and will! *Can* live and will! There is no 'must.' " He
threw out a laugh, cracked and feverish. "Do you think it
would be hard to know something inevitable? Christ!" It
was a trembling cry, shaken with too many feelings. "If a
thing is inevitable, then only stupidity can keep you from
knowing it. And to know that something is inevitable is—
is peace. It must happen; you are a cog in the machinery;
that is easy to understand—easy to know." He used the
word *know* as she did, with a special emphasis. It meant
not only *know* but *accept*. "But to know that something is
not inevitable and yet *will* happen—you could alter it but
you *won't* alter it; to know *that*—that . . ." His frantic
hands sank to his sides; his face collected, calmed; he
stood straight. "That is an accomplishment," he said with
simple dignity.

Her son was dead. . . . She lay with open eyes. Strange,
what a difference a perspective could make. Here was the
simple fact, now, that for the first time she saw something
good in her son's death—he would not have to die again

—and that simple fact made the whole world liveable. Or, at least, unveiled, like a rising curtain, the possibility that it might be liveable.

She took a proud, shuddering breath, and announced clearly, "My son is dead." And closed her eyes, to let the tears come unopposed. My son is dead.

So there it was, the first possibility of a path, the first clearing in the tangle. With a small, flat smile she felt the overgrowth of coiling horns swell from her brow; not her hands but her mind slit and spread a narrow opening in the cramped mass. She shook her head—a heavy, painful toss—sitting upright now on the raised pallet. She could not yet shake back that hideous mane, but she could hold her head straight up despite it. The soles of her feet curled and tingled; below, the dragon was stirring. God is not mocked, she thought. No, nor dragons.

Nguyen had known typhoons. Islands like Pagbo were new to him; but it did not require personal experience to visualize what a typhoon would do to this island. His opinion of the Moro seamen changed abruptly. The very fact that a house had been built here showed that they either did not expect typhoons or did not respect them. In either case they were wrong, dead wrong. And why should he let himself be governed by people who made such mistakes? No, he would leave this island while there was time; and since he could not sail a kumpit alone, some at least of the others must go with him. He rose lithely, and approached a group of his shipmates around their leader —"captain" would be perhaps too strong a word—adding a little swagger to his walk. It was necessary that they should know he was not a coward.

CHAPTER 8

It was dark night; the sky solid with the canopy of the coming storm. She startled upright, alert. The oracle opened sleepy eyes, and she relaxed a little, sharing vigil with him, however reluctant. "Who is it?" she asked. "Who's coming?"

"Do you want to know?" he asked cynically.

"Yes." She trembled too much, she felt the dragon rouse to her trembling. But she said yes.

"Don't worry, it's just a little revolution." Her son had said that to her, putting his arm around her playfully, when they heard the first shouts in Djakarta. For a moment she thought it was her son's voice again. Then she sprang up; her bare feet felt, through the slatted floor, touches of scaled skin as she ran. "Take care of Marie-Ange!" the oracle called after her.

That was her whole intention. For a horrible time, seconds long, she skittered, lost and confused, half a dozen false starts in false directions. Then the dark focused; she knew where the child and the old nurse slept, and knelt beside them, squeezing the nurse's arm. "Wake up! *Lève-toi!*"

The old woman was attuned to sudden alarms; her reactions were simply practical. She thrust her old feet into their slippers and reached for the child. They had hardly gotten farther than that when the alarm was raised. Other steps were running in the house, dogs barking outside. She shook the nurse's arm. "We must wake the others." Her eyes seemed at once to darken and to grow luminous. "Yes, the others—Mr. Montoya's guests." But someone was already running to do it. She stood hesitant, like a bird poised on a branch, holding Marie-Ange's hand.

Someone had brought the alarm from farther down the coast. No one could know yet how extensive the uprising was. It was not even clear whether Puerto Princesa had been taken. Only one thing was certain: the rebel leaders were explicitly threatening to kill or expel all Christians and other foreigners, and calling on all the native population to join in that great purgation.

She turned to the old woman. "Take Marie-Ange and get dressed. Hurry!" Through another door Josepha Sandoval appeared, sleepy and uncertain. The Senator followed. Wrapped in their expensive dressing gowns, they looked alien among the milling servants, vulnerable in their ignorance. "You are in danger here," she told them sternly. "You must put on your clothes at once."

"What about yours?" Josepha retorted pertly.

She stared, astounded that this unknown person should waste time in flippant argument. "We must all be dressed in five minutes," she said, and started away.

"Do we know each other?" Josepha asked suddenly. "I'm Philippe's fiancée."

Before she answered, she gazed for a piercing moment. "Yes."

Josepha turned. "I want you to meet my father, Senator Sandoval," she said decisively. "Papa, this is Madame Delisle."

Her fingers fumbled at her clothes, her shoes. "Five minutes," the oracle said sardonically. "Five minutes is too long."

"I'm ready!" She found Marie-Ange, fled back to the long front room where the household was gathering. Coming from the other door, dressed already, quick with excitement, Josepha Sandoval met her, and touched the child's head. "And where did this pretty thing come from?"

"This is your fiancé's daughter," she said firmly.

The Senator was decisive. There was a post of the Philippine Constabulary at Puerto Princesa. If they hurried, they could reach it before either the rebels or the typhoon struck them. There, they would be safe, and the PC would arrange their transportation back to Manila. He would not trust his daughter (or his money, though he did not mention that) to the protection of the local police; these southern provinces, in his private opinion, were not far removed from barbarism. But the PC was a national body, with a proper respect for national legislators.

She listened with growing dismay. There was so little time; and now, with these people, without Montoya, she stood so alone. She pushed herself forward. "No." The Senator did not recognize her objection in the general low hubbub. "Senator Sandoval!" She gripped his arm rudely, which captured his attention. "Philippe left very precise instructions for a case like this."

"What instructions?"

"We are to go with Mako. He will see that we get safely to one of the praos."

"One of the praos?"

"Yes. We will be perfectly safe at sea."

"Safe at sea in a storm? In one of those primitive canoes?"

"Yes," she insisted. "Safe at sea. Or on one of the islands."

"The offshore islands? I have no intention of subjecting my daughter to being trapped in that pirate nest. Who is this Mako?"

"There he is." She pointed out the one-armed man who stood, slender and tranquil, in the doorway—the patient, fluid calm of a rippled knife blade.

The Senator snorted. "Yes, a Moro! No, thank you! We are starting at once for the post at Puerto Princesa." He felt the thick layer of bills in his belt as a pregnant woman might feel the child in her womb—precious, vulnerable, and dangerous.

So, for the first time in a year, since Montoya had asked her his last question on the prao, she had decisions to make. More than that, a responsibility and a field for judgment. Take care of Marie-Ange—that was first; but also, she judged, he would want the Sandovals to be taken care of. Yet nothing was simple. Was this really the emergency for which he had provided the one-armed gardener—or was it indeed foolish to take to sea in the typhoon's teeth? Her mind dodged away into the dark. The oracle's face met her reprovingly.

She whirled, clapping her hands. The nurse stood ready with Marie-Ange. She steered them to the door and out. Mako moved like a flat spring. She held him. "Tell Montoya I have gone with these people . . . " she pointed at the Sandovals . . . "to the PC at Puerto Princesa." For a moment she had to stiffen her legs; otherwise she would have fallen on her knees to clutch the child against her body. There was no time. . . . She pushed past the crowding servants, calling for the car, for a driver who knew the road to Puerto Princesa. Three or four volunteers urged their qualifications. She chose a middle-aged man with a wizened face. The younger ones had more flair; he had a different sort of assurance. She steered Josepha and the Senator, startled, to the car. They wanted their luggage. "Get in!" she shouted.

It was still two hours, perhaps, before dawn. The wind blew in long gusts, almost lifting the little car from the road when they caught it at the wrong angle. Sometimes the gusts carried rain. Riding in the runaway dark, with the jerk and plunge of the pell-mell road, she sank back against the seat, silently into the roar of motion. "I could have hugged her then," she thought contentedly.

They got no farther than the first checkpoint. The oracle found it extremely funny. She had asked him, "What is the best way for us to get through?" and he had answered, "How should I know? I only know which way you *will* go." But she had grown cleverer at extracting information from him. "If we follow this road, will we get through?" "No."

That meant that they *would* follow this road, and would not get through. For the oracle did not lie, and the oracle only knew what would actually happen; if they were going to follow a different road, he would not know the fate that awaited them on this one. But this time she did not accept what she had been told. She did not want that future; she would find a way to prevent it.

"Stop!" She turned to the driver, laying her hand on his shoulder. The car jerked and stopped, tossing them all forward. "Is there another road?"

The driver's nutlike face gleamed in a lightning flicker. "Yes, ma'am. When we get to Rizal."

"How far is that?"

"Beyond the checkpoint."

"Then we must leave the road now."

He tapped the window, where now the plunging rain beat ceaselessly. "No, ma'am."

Her forehead itched strangely. He was right, of course. It would be impossible to drive across country in this. Perhaps one of the younger men would have tried it, and stranded them axle-deep in muck, or wedged among rocks and trees. "We can walk," she said.

But Senator Sandoval had had enough. He thumped the driver's shoulder. "Drive on!"

Inside herself she dodged and twisted, trapped. She fingered her head dizzily, shouting her arguments as they drove through the rain. "They'll take the checkpoints first of all! We've got to stay away from the checkpoints!"

But to the Senator, checkpoints meant hope, security, contact with legally constituted authority. He did not notice when the driver took a pistol out of his jacket front and laid it on the seat beside him. But she noticed, and drew away from it as if it were an obscene thing.

In the rain, they hardly saw the checkpoint before

they reached it. For the first moment, everything looked normal. Even the flashlight in their faces was reasonable during an insurrection. The Senator was pulling out his wallet, reaching it across Josepha toward the driver's window to display his identification. At that instant she snatched it; over his surprised protest, she broke into a torrent of loud French. The flashlight had already been turned off; with a force that, it seemed, could lift impossibility, she yearned to know that the Senator's gesture had not been seen. The sentry's face was lowered to the window, the sentry's hand was on the door handle; but the door was locked. "Get out!" he ordered.

In the little car, drowned in the rain—at this rural checkpoint, there was not even a roof to shelter the cars that stopped—the pistol report was ear-splitting. They were all deafened, a spotty deafness that blotted out segments of reality. For a moment it seemed as if they were blinded in the same way; the sentry had simply disappeared from the window. The motor roared, suddenly gunned; but before they were aware of movement, a second explosion burst, less loud. The car lurched once and died. The driver thumped against her, an instantaneous sideways shove that ended in limpness. She had thrust the Senator's wallet between her legs; she twisted, reaching into the back seat to grab a handful of his clothing and Josepha's. "Shut up! You are French! Don't speak!" she hissed cuttingly. "Give me your purse!" That to Josepha, who clutched her little purse reflexly. She lunged violently, tearing it from Josepha's hand. The driver's body slumped and slid, leaning heavily on her. For a small man, it was strange how much space he took up. She hurled herself awkwardly back around at the door on her side, shaking him off, and scrambled out into the rain, with the same impetus flinging purse and wallet down the embankment into the streaming dark; and whirled dizzily to address herself over the car hood to the weakly gleaming lights of the checkpoint box. "We are French citizens!" she cried. "What is the meaning of this?"

A shouted command answered, incomprehensible. It would be either *Come here* or *Stay there*, she thought. But in fact she was not afraid of bullets. At the moment, it seemed tremendously absurd that people should let themselves be commanded at gunpoint. A gun butt was much more intimidating.

They had gotten the door on the driver's side open, and hustled the Sandovals into the rain. She decided on *Come here* as more probable, and came around the front of the car. Someone pulled the driver's body out, into the light, where someone else was already stripping the dead sentry. They had only one uniform, and now it was damaged. "You forgot guns," the oracle said. "If you had each had a gun, you might have fought your way through this. They have no vehicle." She was looking down at the driver's body. "He had a gun," she said.

"We are French citizens," she kept repeating. "I am a resident of Manila. These people are my guests. We are only visiting Palawan." They stood sodden in the rain. The Sandovals had resigned themselves provisionally to silence. At last someone listened to her, motioned them into the box, asked for identification. She showed her papers. She had no purse—she never went out—but Montoya had impressed on her that these should always be within her reach, and she carried them in a little flat pocketbook that included a small sketch pad and a pencil stuck through a loop. While they studied the papers, she faked a little confusion with the Sandovals, talking quick French with gestures, magnifying their hesitations and murmurs into conversation, "discovering" that they had left their identification behind. This was the story they clung to, for what seemed like a very long time in the windy night. She introduced them as Jean Dubois of Paris and his daughter Josephine (grasping for names that they could all remember), and—now that their lives were committed to it—they played their parts well enough. Their captors were themselves not very fluent in English, so that their assumed accents were largely wasted; by the same token, their transparent phoniness went unnoticed. All three of them reiterated passionately their simple story, until it became an article of faith with them and they were heartily amazed that anyone could doubt it. The man who held her papers kept gazing around their little misshapen circle, Renée Delisle to Josephine Dubois to Jean Dubois to the papers in his hand, his broad Malay face gentle and distant. Perhaps the phrase "French citizen" did not mean much to him.

Nevertheless it was, so far as she could see, their only

defense. She tried another tack on the same course, insisting that they be taken to the French consulate at Puerto Princesa. She did not know if there would be a French consulate at Puerto Princesa, but she thought it best to have a destination of her own choosing. The man with her papers seemed to consider. They had moved the car a little, so that it no longer blocked the road. There had been no other traffic. At intervals, the rain stopped or slackened suddenly. The body of the sentry had been brought into the little police box with them. There was no room for it to be disposed at ease; instead, it was crowded half upright behind the leader's chair, so that the dead sentry seemed to be sitting against the wall in his ragged underwear, with his blown-open head hung down. At last the leader turned abstractedly, speaking in a soft voice. None of the three understood the local language, but they all had the impression that their story was being accepted, and that they were to be either released at once or delivered to French authorities. But there was a last requirement to be met, a final search to confirm the negative results of the first hasty frisking in the rain. These people seemed very gentle revolutionaries; they did not want to handle the women rudely—who, in any case, it appeared obvious, could not have anything very bulky concealed about them. The scrutiny fell on the car and the Senator.

Something like an electric shock went through the Senator's consciousness when the searching fingers (slender, almost childlike) touched his money belt. The women had not known about this cash, and they were too evidently surprised when it was pulled out and displayed. But the Senator had not traveled so far in life without becoming accustomed to shocks; he righted himself instantly. Since the money could no longer be saved, his immediate hope was to make use of it. Rebels, he supposed, were as subject as anyone else to human needs and aspirations, and therefore bribeable. If he gave them the money, they would not need to murder him. Staying as well as he could within his rich-French-tourist role, he made his offer. The rebels seemed not to understand. They were, however, clearly impressed by the money. After some discussion, the leader scrupulously copied information from her papers onto a page torn from her sketch pad, returned the papers to her, and turned to give instructions to someone else.

She took the papers absently, holding herself very tall, looking steadily at the Senator. She had understood the purpose of the money; but though she had learned so painfully to accept so much of outrage, she could not, for the moment, accept this. That these intruders had driven her from the house of birds was bad enough; that they had pursued her to this island, armed with money for the express purpose of taking away her last refuge, was intolerable. She stared at the Senator with haughty contempt. What right had he, he and his ignorant daughter, to interfere in her life and death—hers and Montoya's?

Hands bumped at her elbow, her back, turning her, steering her. They were not unlike the hands that had tended her in Montoya's houses—officious, diffident, kind —except that these were clumsy, rough with inexperience. The sensation was so familiar, and her mind was so much on the Senator's treachery, that she did not realize at first what was happening. They were being herded out into the rain, across the road, down the embankment on the other side, up a long slope into the forest.

In fact, the money presented a problem. The leader of the group at the checkpoint had really been on the verge of releasing them as harmless tourists. But this impressive cache of good Philippine pesos not only cast some shadow on their story; it was, above all, tempting. A home-grown revolution could not afford to throw away such a windfall. On the other hand, this Frenchman, if he was a Frenchman, might be too important to tamper with. These people, with their money and their documents, would have to be passed on to a higher authority for decision. And the higher authority was in the hills.

All this indignity and hardship the Senator accepted with a stoicism that would have surprised many of his colleagues. He was a reasonable man; he would save his indignation for a time when it might do some good. For the present, he was fully occupied with survival, with minimizing discomfort and maximizing the possibility of coming through without serious damage to himself or his daughter. But his indignation was very great;

sooner or later it would find expression. These insurgents
were not merely animals who threatened his physical
safety; they were spoilers, destroyers; their existence was
a throat to the integrity of life as he knew it. It was not
simple courage that sustained him (though in his pudgy
body he had his share of that) so much as a sense of
moral outrage.

CHAPTER 9

The typhoon had stabilized. It was one of those elephantine storms that could hang almost motionless for days,
bearing its whole crushing weight upon a single island.
The heart of the storm, as it happened, was still east of
them, over the sea, drawing a little more strength from
the water, hesitating ponderously there until some tilt
of balancing forces should set it underway again westward, or northward, or even curving to the south. For
the present, the hills of Palawan would feel nothing of
its real power, only the rain, the inexhaustible rain.

Even the rain was not steady. The grey sky was
streaked with slots of blue. She lifted her head to see it
through the branches, whenever the rain eased. They
plodded on through the sodden woods. Their little column
had lengthened. Early in the morning they had met two
men armed with bolos. She had braced herself for sudden
movement—this would be the chance to escape, and
there might be fighting—but the oracle had stopped her
with a laugh: "They are rebels too." Their guard had
talked to them briefly, explaining, and then all had fallen
into line together.

The Senator was distressed. With the guard from the
checkpoint he had felt almost secure. If it was necessary
to fall into the hands of rebels, then it was good that they
should be scrupulous rebels. They had not killed him,
they had not even taken away his money. And there was
always the hope that the three of them could overpower
or escape from a single guard. But these new two had
an unreliable look about them. Furthermore, they were
outlanders here almost as much as he, for they spoke
Tagalog, the language of Manila and the north. He had

heard most of their conversation with the guard, and there had been no mention of money in what he heard; that meant, he believed, that the guard did not trust them either. Also the looks he thought he saw them cast now and then at Josepha sent jets of horror through him, like injections of ice water in his limbs and belly, so that at times it was difficult to walk.

Philippe Montoya felt no moral outrage. His principles were simple, and in no sense moral. What he had was his; what was his he intended to keep, or dispose of at a profit. The rebels were his enemies not because they were wrong, but because they threatened to take his property and interfere with his business. He did not feel that they were under some universal obligation to respect his system of livelihood. The world as he knew it was too unstable to have given him any such conviction.

He had already started back from Taytay when the news of the insurrection broke. His first concern, and for some time the only one he recognized, was for his property. He did not believe the Philippines were ready for a serious revolution, or even, in these parts, a serious guerrilla war—he had seen revolutions, and felt confident of recognizing the signs—but it was certain that there would be damage done. His family was not much on his mind. As terrorists, these Filipinos were the merest babies; he could not help feeling a good-natured contempt. Mako would take care of Marie-Ange and Renée; and if the Sandovals were in danger, that, he thought savagely, was their problem. Let the Senator see what sort of retirement haven he had tried to buy.

It was, though, he admitted, as he followed the news by radio, unusually extensive for a Philippine uprising. The airport at Puerto Princesa had been seized, and checkpoints throughout the island were being taken over by the rebels. Government forces were reacting, but their first priority was the airport; it would take them at least a few days after that to restore road traffic. Meanwhile houses were being robbed and burned; capitalists and landlords were being kidnapped, killed, mutilated. Montoya's lips hardened into a private smile.

In fact, he found the situation stimulating. More than once he had been faced with the prospect of rebuilding his life from nothing; it never failed to give him a sense

of relief and excitement, such as a dragonfly might feel
when it cracked its pupal skin and crawled out of water
into air. This was a lesser thing; but the possibility was
in the atmosphere, and his skin tingled with it.

The rain had grown heavy again. Their captors, after a
little discussion, had cut branches and made a leafy lean-
to under which they all sat or squatted, their hips and
shoulders touching. The Senator had contrived to maneu-
ver Josepha between himself and Madame Delisle. The
shelter was far from waterproof, but it made the difference between downpour and dribble. They faced the open
side, looking point-blank into a curtain of rain whose
fringes laced their legs and faces with swift, delicate
sprays. They did not speak at all.

The typhoon was impersonal, as an elephant is impersonal to an ant. It rose from its own causes, pursued
its own path, and ceased in its own time. There was no
choice; what stood before it, bowed. It is like God, she
thought.

"What God?" the oracle asked derisively. "What is a
God?"

She wet her lips. She knew an answer; its dry ammo-
niac stench (outriding tendrils stirred from its unquiet
lair) burned her shut eyes.

CHAPTER 10

When Montoya disembarked in the little cove that was his
private harbor, it was earliest morning, and the rain had
paused. For hours he had been pushing his boat straight
down the throat of a southwest wind, and the land felt
disconcertingly stable and quiet under his feet, so that he
laughed as he took his first step on it. His next step was
backward, as automatic as an animal's sudden bristling,
for a figure rose from the edge of the woods not two yards
in front of him, silent, gleaming wet. But it was Mako.
The trees under which he had sat most of the night had
broken the pounding force of the rain, and he had not
thought it necessary to shelter himself better; he was

soaked to the skin, but he carried his drenched garments with comfortable grace.

"What happened here?" Montoya demanded.

Mako made an interesting gesture, tilting his head sideways toward his shoulder and his shoulder up to meet it, a movement like a large, impersonal wink. "They came. I took the little girl and the old woman to Pagbo."

This, as far as it went, was as it should be. But it did not go far enough; Mako should have taken Renée as well to Pagbo, and delivered all three on board the kumpit that would be waiting there. "What about Madame Delisle?" If he had not been startled by Mako's failure to mention her, he might have asked whether the contact with Nguyen's kumpit had gone according to plan.

Mako pointed. "Puerto Princesa. PC. Ramon took them in the car."

"Puerto Princesa! Why?" At last report, Puerto Princesa —except, precisely, for the Philippine Constabulary post —was in the hands of the rebels. It was not a tremendous feat militarily, since that metropolis of Palawan was an otherwise undefended town of eight or nine thousand people, but it meant that the airport was unusable and the PC at least temporarily neutralized.

Mako made a negative gesture with his head. "She went with the others. The fat man says, 'Puerto Princesa, Puerto Princesa.' "

Montoya felt a pang of alarm. What had possessed her —his haughty, pretty lady—to involve herself in the Sandovals' foolishness? "When?"

"Yesterday morning. Three hours before first light." Montoya was already turning back toward his vessel; the one-armed man sprang forward almost soundlessly, to stay within his vision. "She told me to tell you that. I didn't see them go."

And with the unpredictability of his Renée, there was no knowing what had happened. He felt that she was capable of much. Half a minute more of conversation told him that Mako had not returned to the house, and in fact had no knowledge of the rebels' movements. He had fulfilled the single commission for which he had been hired —at least, he had fulfilled it as well as he could in the circumstances—and had then sat down and waited to report.

It was imperative, then, for Montoya to go back to the

house, to find out for himself how things stood. He gave
instructions. His crew would stay with the boat, making
ready to cast off again instantly. Mako was dispatched in
his own prao—the same tiny vessel in which he had delivered his charges to Pagbo—to alert certain men of a
settlement a few miles down the coast; if it was necessary
to sail for Puerto Princesa, a larger force would be useful.
Montoya himself, with an automatic pistol under his shirt,
started on foot for the house. He foresaw no need of as-
sistance; if there were rebels at the house, he would observe and withdraw.

Montoya had survived this long by adhering scrupulously
to the tenet that his own skin was worth more than any
amount of money or extent of real estate. He had no
patience with a selfishness so short-sighted as to be self-
destructive. He was annoyed, too, that the Senator had
refused to trust his arrangements—not so much insulted
that his integrity was questioned (that was normal
enough) as vexed that the Senator was too stupid to see
that trusting Montoya had been his best hope. It was
more agreeable to him, somehow, to think of the Senator
with anger than to think just now of Renée Delisle.

Under the trees, the floor of the forest was clear and open
for long stretches. Darkness changed slowly, becoming
light. She lay with open eyes, on her side—sprawled and
limp, as if she had been let fall from a little height—facing
away from the others. Their wrists and their ankles—hers
and the Sandovals'—were bound with twisted fiber. Captors, captives, all slept. Their breathing was quiet, irregular but steady, like the ceaseless dripping from the wet
leaves. Immobile, almost inanimate; after the tumultuous
night they lay, all, unwilling to wake, not so much resting
as dormant; as if, having achieved immobility, they would
maintain it indefinitely, because there was no force to set
them moving. It hurt to lie like this, awkwardly disposed
on the hard ground, one shoulder jammed under her chin,
and all her flesh numb with wet chill; but it would hurt
more to move.

"He is coming," the oracle's voice said in her ear. "He
is on his way."

She watched, waiting. Birds stirred in the leaves. In the
sparse underbrush something scurried. The light was infi-

nitely soft. A creature emerged with stately steps into the open ground, shaking off a few drops of shining water. Its long toes stretched forward at every step; it carried its small head observantly, crowned with a delicate spike of shining green that trembled faintly when it moved. Directly before her eyes it stood still, and began to preen, drawing its beak slowly down the length of one feather and then another. Suddenly it thrust its near wing out and down, spreading the feathers until they skirted the ground, and sank its beak among them.

The glade was very quiet. The drops fell. The sleepers lay breathing, unmoving. The deep-green gleam of his mantle was like a dark light on the forest floor. He stretched and closed his wings, turned and stretched to preen his back. His sheafed peacock tail quivered; flashes showed in the mute light. Then he lifted his neat head; lowered it once to scratch his chin, and walked tranquilly on and out of her sight. She closed her eyes and slept.

The landing where Montoya had set foot with a laugh was, like his house, on the north side of the little river that fed into the cove. But between the landing and the house, a narrow stream cut down from the hills, crossed the path, and plunged into the river. The footbridge that spanned it had been a pragmatic structure of sapling trunks and withies—stronger than a foreigner would have expected, but not strong enough to support the advance guard of a typhoon. Soaked by the rain and torn by the swollen current, whole sections of the stream bank had given way, sometimes carrying trees and rocks with them. The little bridge was gone. The very aspect of the stream was altered, so that it might have been another watercourse in another landscape, newer and more unsteady. Here and there the water was thrown into folds by large stones, or driven foaming above the lip of the near bank. Elsewhere the stream was half-bridged by tree trunks or masses of brush. Everywhere the bank had an unstable look, with raw earth showing between down-beaten stems. Montoya ranged quietly along it, in search of a bridging log or a good place to ford. He would have avoided the bridge if it had been there—it was so obvious a spot to guard; and in normal seasons it was easy enough to ford this stream. But now the logic of the altered terrain funneled him back toward the path where the bridge had been. There lay the only means of crossing without a full-scale struggle against the current and the crumbling banks: a downed tree, half-submerged and insecurely wedged slantwise across the channel.

He would have crossed elsewhere without hesitation if his life were at stake, or if there were no other way; but the situation was hardly that urgent; and it would have meant—aside from a slight risk of drowning—getting his pistol wet. For a time he squatted in the obscurity of the trees, watching the other bank. Then he rose, and essayed the fallen tree.

He was more than halfway across, his feet underwater and feeling for purchase on the smooth bark, his hands grasping branches to brace himself against the current that ripped at his ankles, his eyes testing the further bank, where the tree's roots were lodged, for signs of giving way again—more than halfway across, almost within leaping distance of that treacherous bank, when the shot spun him off his footing and he crashed into the torrent. But the bullet had barely notched his right shoulder—which, at such close range, and he so slowly moving, was probably deliberate—and he had not even lost his left handhold. His feet were on a rock, and the water boiled around his waist. But the upheaval had loosened the tree again, and he felt it throbbing and trembling in the current, pushing against his hip (for he had fallen downstream). He did not know yet how much of a wound he had received, whether his right arm would be useable; but he had stooped automatically—the tree's branches gave him some sparse cover—and with a spasmodic effort, driving determination into all his right hand's muscles, he pulled out his gun. There was no sign from the bank so close in front of him. He loosed his hold, gingerly felt out his wound, and was gratified; nothing disabling. But two or three yards away (it could hardly be farther, judging from the sound of the shot that had dropped him) someone was watching him with a gun. He crouched carefully lower into the water, and began to work his way backward along the tree. The stream was deep enough here, but it was too treacherous to try to swim—full of shallows and obstructions and vicious turns of current. If he could back up to where the tree trunk was out of water, he could duck under it without wetting his pistol and without entangling himself in branches or debris. And he wanted decidedly to be on the upstream side of the tree-trunk.

In the woods in front of him, some bird suddenly raised an alarm call, harsh, insistent, reiterating. Montoya took a breath, ready to duck his head on split-second notice. A scatter of raindrops sprinkled the water, instantly lost in its churning surface. It was just then that the tree trunk broke free.

Loose, it was like a wild thing in fury, ponderous and yet quick and malicious. He fought to keep his head and arms up, above, not to be dragged down, forced under by the threshing branches. The mid-trunk struck an obstruction with a shock, and it pivoted, the brushy head wheeling him downstream and into a curve of the bank, the bank where his enemy waited. He tore loose, plunging ashore in a muddy scramble. His hand was numb; he had to look at it to discover that his pistol was gone.

The man on the bank had run downstream to meet him. For a moment they saw each other through a screen of leaves. Montoya plunged headlong behind a tall stump, collecting himself quickly into a crouch; the other had dodged behind a tree. His hand and arm felt like slightly animated mud. A bullet tore the moldered top of his stump. Another. It was time for negotiation.

Montoya called an inquiry, using the Cebuano lingua franca of the southern islands, and, after a moment, received a cheerful response: "Do you have a weapon?"

"No." He hoped the other had not seen the pistol before the tree beat it out of his hand.

"Come out."

"Not if you're going to shoot at me," Montoya said reasonably.

"Why should I shoot you?"

"Why did you shoot me already?"

This time the response was a volley of shots. Montoya crouched close while chunks and slivers of his stump rained about his head and shoulders. "Now," the voice announced triumphantly—it was a youthful voice—"if I don't return very soon, my friends will come. They are many."

"Return where?" It was perhaps illogical, but Montoya felt himself once more on the offensive, a more congenial position.

"To the rich man's house."

"I'm coming out," Montoya said. "Don't shoot. I'm

already wounded." This was true, and he let a little pain into his voice to prove it. He eased himself out into view.

The young man stepped from his own cover, leveling a carbine—U.S. Marine Corps issue, Montoya noted, but at least ten years out of date. He held the point of aim steady at chest level for a moment, then slowly lowered it, and fired a single shot into the ground at Montoya's feet. A very nice touch on the trigger. Montoya smiled, as involuntarily as he had jerked at the sound of the shot. The young man laughed delightedly, and motioned him back upstream to the path.

Before they reached the house, Montoya had learned all that his escort had to tell. If this boy knew what he was talking about, they were, he thought, rebels of a child-like simplicity. Their violence was directed not at the Government in Manila, but at rich men, foreigners, and Christians—categories that overlapped considerably, especially when "foreigner" meant anyone not native to the island of Palawan. This particular band of rebels was one of many—more spontaneous vigilantes than revolutionary cells—now busily expressing their disapproval of landlords, squatters and entrepreneurs in an eager wave of burning, killing and mutilation. It was not totally unlike the spirit in which he had set fire to the rubber plantation.

The question that had sent him here was not answered until they had almost reached the grounds. "And they say," his captor pursued, "there were two ladies and another rich man at the house, but they ran away before we got there." He paused to laugh. "They didn't run far, though. Our people caught them at the checkpoint. They're taking them up to headquarters in the hills. They'll know what to do with them there."

It was raining lightly but steadily now. Montoya, plodding two or three yards ahead, felt the aim of the gun at his back as physically as if the barrel were pressed to it. A new sense of nakedness was chilling him. His boats were of no use to him now; his route lay urgently to the hills, and speed and silence would be more important now than force.

They were approaching a spot where the path ran along the edge of a ravine. Montoya's intention was to drop over the edge. Then, assuming that quickness had saved him from a bullet in the back, he should have an acceptable chance of catching the boy when he came in pursuit; and at hand-to-hand he anticipated no difficulty. Or perhaps the boy, not seeing any importance in him, would not try to pursue. In any case, it would be a better chance than he could expect to find at the house.

But it did not happen like that. The boy had been right; his shots brought reinforcements. Not, indeed, many; but two were enough to turn the probabilities upside down. Montoya's face hardened. He followed silently through the rain. It would be too bad, he thought, to be killed in the house that had been his refuge, his sanctuary. It would be too bad to be killed for being a Christian. He had always considered Christianity the most unreasonable of religions.

Slowly she turned up her face into the rain, quivering a little with the strain of holding against that wet force. It was so heavy, so pendulous; it must be pulling down the sky. The world was closing. The sky up there, somewhere, above her blinking, gasping face, was sagging, tearing. She lifted her hands to shield her face from the rain for one solid breath. *My son is dead.* She could not quite go further yet.

In the rain, in the yard in front of his house, armed men crowded around Montoya curiously. He did not look like a *patron,* in his blue laborer's clothes; but then, he did not look like a laborer, either. And in this country his face was distinctive. A man with a pistol seized his arm and jerked him around for a better view. The others crowded nearer. "It's the half-Chinese from Manila!" (By this inaccurate title he was known in some circles.) The man with the pistol contorted his face in an exuberant sneer. "Come on, señor, let us introduce you to the customs of Palawan!"

The little crowd opened, like the two wings of a gate, so that he had an unobstructed view through the quiet rain to the house front. At the end of that short vista, at the top of the porch steps, stood a man with a bolo in his hand. Montoya saw that there was blood on the blade already.

The sky was darkening to night, though she had forgotten that night still came. She thought rather that it was only the thickening rain, lower and darker, the whole sky drawing forever centerward. They had stopped for the night, but she did not know that; they had stopped often all day. Here at the edge of some sort of man-made clearing or broad track, the men with bolos were constructing another shelter. They were all drenched, sodden; the women's breasts stood out through the plastered layers of their clothes; their hair streamed like dark water. Josepha, she noted with distant contempt, did not even know enough to be afraid.

She bowed her head. There were rifts in the wet air. *Marie-Ange is alive.* She could not say *safe.* There was no safety. Life was enough for gratitude. She smoothed back the wet tangles from her forehead. It was possible, it was likely, that some of the water streaming along her face came from her eyes.

In the darkness, where, until now, she had seen only her oracle, Philippe Montoya came to her. He wore a barong tagalog, the formal shirt of the Philippines, and its lacy white against the cool olive of his skin enhanced what had always been present in his face and bearing, a certain angelic remoteness. Here in the darkness, for the first time she was able to question him. "How can you live?" she asked eagerly. "How do you bear it?"

He moved closer, not explicitly smiling, but all his face and body, his very hands, expressing something of a smile. "It's not hard," he said.

"Tell me."

"I've always known," he said, "—no, not always, but since I was a child—I've known that we live on quicksand . . . on the side of a volcano . . . on an earthquake fault. You know that any minute of any day or night the roof can fall on your head, the floor can open between your feet, the earth itself can suck you down. And somehow when you *know* this—when you know you always live surrounded by unappealable forces so much stronger than you—then you are not the slave of those forces. When you must build your house on quicksand, you don't count on its standing. You find your security in yourself; because your self is all you have. And if you're a Buddhist you know that even your self is quicksand. In a way I don't exist, I'm an illusion. This self is only an accumulation of particles and forces interacting, clinging together for a second or a century. But this accumulation, this tension, this equilibrium that I call Philippe Montoya—this is all I have. When it falls apart, then Philippe Montoya has no more problems. But until then, Philippe Montoya exists—and what difference does it make what happens outside? Philippe Montoya exists."

Philippe Montoya could never speak to her like that in the flesh, she knew. But if he could have spoken, that was what he would say. Now he smiled, and put out his hand to touch her—his warm right hand, hard-fleshed, smooth-skinned, the hand that could knead away the taint of horror. But something withheld the touch. She yearned toward it, leaning and reaching, but he was farther away than she had thought. She needed that touch. Leaning, needing—and he was reaching, stretching toward her, but farther away, always farther.

He was gone. She curled, pulling her knees against her forehead, balling her body hedgehog-like. But she lacked the hedgehog's bag of prickled skin; on her skin, all the prickles pointed inward, and as she tightened herself she felt them drive and bore into her muscle and bone. She tried to lie quiet, motionless in mind, as she had learned to do a year ago. She was cold, very cold in her sodden clothes. Dumbly, she felt that it was harder now than it had been then. Why? The burden now was less, much less, and she had grown expert in carrying it. The thorns or claws drove deeper. *Then* she had been free—free like the smashed worm on the pavement, exempted from all considerations but the absorbing writhing of what remained of her mutilated life. That had been aloneness; this was aloneness with obligation. Philippe Montoya could not reach her now; and on what she did, said, failed to do or say, on how she looked, on what she contrived, remembered, correctly or falsely calculated, on these things hung the future—life or death, more pain or less—of those whom Philippe Montoya had left behind him.

But Marie-Ange, she remembered stubbornly, *Marie-Ange is alive.*

CHAPTER 11

"Renée." The word was not whispered—a whisper carries—it was only breathed into the still air, light as down. She thought for a poised moment that it was a word without a voice, without a speaker. *Reborn,* it hung in the air beside her ear. Then she remembered that this was the name Montoya had given her, the name that, for the present, had perhaps kept them all alive. She turned her head. He must be very near; but the night was so dark, she did not make him out until he moved, a broad formless shadow soundlessly leaning to her. "Not a word," the shadow breathed, so close this time that she felt the breath on her face, a warmth rather than a movement. She lifted her hands and touched woven straw; he was wearing the wide, flat hat of a Filipino farmer. "Not a sound," he breathed. "Tell them."

She rolled carefully onto her other hip, leaned and reached, closing her hands tight on Josepha's wrist and a piece of the Senator's shirt. He grunted, startled; Josepha held silent, though her wrist jerked. "Not a sound," she breathed. "Not a word." The point of Montoya's knife was already working at their bonds.

They had not been trained for this. They made noise. But Montoya kept them closely in hand, touching them with short, firm pulls and pushes, timing their movements to coincide with the wind's. Once he stopped them, pulling all their heads close together, to breathe the quiet threat, "Not a sound. One mistake and we are all dead." He wanted to keep them frightened. It was, of course, impossible to keep them perfectly still; but if they believed the danger greater than it was, they might stay quiet enough to escape the real danger. Which, certainly, was danger enough.

At the edge of a different blackness, he stopped them with a touch. Josepha had been waiting all this time for a chance to throw herself into Montoya's arms. Somehow, in their cautious progress, the opportunity had not arisen; there seemed to be always someone else between them. But when she understood that they were at the water's edge and must step down into a boat, she pushed past Madame Delisle and pressed herself against him, slipping both arms around his neck, whispering "Felipe," lifting her face for a kiss that did not come. He held her gently but without eagerness, enclosing her for a moment in a one-armed embrace, before he said softly, "We'll be all right now. Come on, get in," and shifted his hand to a grip on her upper arm, pulling her firmly away from him. He got them all placed to his satisfaction in the boat— Josepha in the bow, the Senator in the middle—before he stepped into the stern beside Madame Delisle. She turned to him like a released spring, flattening herself against his chest, and he wrapped his arms around her. "There's a pole beside you, Senator," he said. "Use it."

The Senator said nothing. His weary muscles quivered with indignation, but he was aware above all else of the money belt still intact about his waist. He had poled boats as a boy, on the canals and ponds of his family's estates. This was a workaday dugout banca the size of a rowboat, slow and quiet on the still water. He felt for the pole, and a silent jubilation rose through his veins.

She clung without a whisper of sound, only her quiet breath. Montoya held her awkwardly; there was something wrong with his right arm. After a time he cleared his throat and said quietly—it was a thing that had to be said—"They cut off my hand. I'm a little weak."

She shuddered once, and again, and again, until she contrived to quench all shuddering by plastering herself still tighter to his chest. He held her like that, his truncated right arm, bundled in thick wrappings, pressed lightly against her back, his left hand holding the back of her neck tightly, opening sometimes to caress her shoulders with a gesture as if he were smoothing her against him.

Josepha crouched in the bow of the boat, facing them. The consuming anger that had occupied her since Montoya had embraced the other woman (an act more sensed than seen, in the darkness) shielded her, for a moment, from the shock of his remark. Even when the shock came, she rejected it. No; she did not want to feel sorry for Philippe Montoya. More than that; what had happened to her so far she could accept as an adventure, but she did not want her life to be touched by real horror. Her

eyes squeezed shut; her mouth opened in a little voice-
less cry of repugnance, refusal.

"How did it happen?" the Senator asked sharply. He
was puffing a little from his efforts, but the boat was moving smoothly now through the dark water. He was aware
of a bank on their right, and kept it close alongside. The
air, that had been calm for a little, was stirring more
briskly now, again and again.

"They wanted to make an example of a foreign capital-
ist," Montoya said wryly. "They would have preferred a
Chinese millionaire, but I was the closest substitute available. Believe me, I was lucky." Luck, in Montoya's
opinion, was an illusory phenomenon, but he was grateful for its workings nonetheless.

"Where are we going?" the Senator pursued. He had
lost, on this strange island, even his basic sense of direction—something the worst typhoon could hardly have
done to him on Luzon.

"To the sawmill. Mako will find us there. Then—it
depends. Mako has a radio." By this he meant that Mako
would know the current status of the insurrection and
the typhoon. "Probably we won't have time to get to
Taytay. Maybe Puerto Princesa. There's a French consulate there." All three of the others stirred, uneasy. Fantasy and reality seemed to have grown too fused. "I am
a French citizen," Montoya explained. "So is Madame
Delisle." He did not add, *I have no money. I need help.*
It did not occur to him that the Senator's money belt
could be still intact. Struggle as he would, his mind felt
drained. All the blood that had gushed from the pulsing
conduit of his wrist seemed to have flowed direct from
his brain. But it was necessary to hold out a little longer.
He moved a little, gathering his arms closer about her.
"I think it will be better to get married," he said to the
boat at large. "It will give her Philippine citizenship rights.
And I can arrange for her to have joint ownership of
everything. That way, there won't be any problems. If
anything happens to me, she owns everything already. No
taxes, no bribes."

The Senator poled mechanically. The situation had
grown too outrageous for him to grasp. By all logic,
Montoya could be talking of marriage to no one but his
daughter. But obviously his daughter was not in need of
Philippine citizenship rights; and obviously a man does

not talk of marriage to one woman while he holds another in his arms. But neither does a man propose marriage to another woman in the presence of his virtual fiancée and her father. Not even Philippe Montoya. And yet . . . The Senator groaned unconsciously, as spontaneous a sound as he had uttered since babyhood. In the bow, Josepha sat rigid.

Montoya had acquired, with his sawmill, the traces of some previous entrepreneur's hopes for a lumbering empire. At the foot of a logging tract on the hillside, a stream had been regularized into the form of a canal, down which logs could be floated to a holding pond. Beside this pond, and sheltered from the wind by the bulk of the mill itself, stood a small square structure actually built of concrete blocks, with wooden shutters and door and corrugated metal roof. Nothing could have looked more anomalous in this landscape. Montoya had taken a fancy to it at once. Its very ugliness had seemed to guarantee utility.

Given the nature of the uprising, the terrain, and the weather, it was eminently reasonable that the military authorities—rather than seeking unnecessary battles to fight—had dispatched two or three patrol boats down the southeast coast of Palawan to check on the welfare of the wealthier residents. Such a boat had found Montoya's house gutted, a few servants remaining with the wreckage. These had reported that Montoya had been released alive, and that he was likely to turn up, if he turned up anywhere, at the sawmill.

When the banca came out among the floating logs on the sawmill pond, an officer and three men from the patrol boat were clustered beside the blockhouse in the grey morning drizzle, laying idle bets on the next move of this wild goose chase.

The Senator grounded the boat hastily and dropped his pole. "I am Senator José Sandoval," he announced, "and this is my daughter. We were kidnapped by rebels and escaped from them last night in the hills." His pudgy figure had reassumed authority. He felt the money in his belt, now, as an embracing circle of warmth. "My daughter is very tired. She needs to rest in a safe place, and I must communicate with Manila as soon as possible." He wanted very much to add, with a wave of his hand at Montoya, "Arrest that man. He is a smuggler."

But all that could come later. At the moment, it was better not to confuse the soldiers.

The officer nodded, accepting the Senator provisionally at his word, and turned more dubiously to Montoya and the woman. Whatever they were, they were clearly not Palaweños. "Will you come with us? We can take you to Puerto Princesa."

For the moment, Montoya could manage no answer but the expression on his face, a kind of sick sneer that said it well enough. He was experiencing a spasm of total repugnance. To go on board the same vessel with the Sandovals—worse yet, to take his Renée on board that vessel—seemed to him, now, too nauseating to be thinkable. And then, too, there was a bed in the blockhouse and the blockhouse, by its name, its structure, its appearance, was all solid, all motionless—an oasis of rest in the sick, moving world. Above all things else, he wanted to lie down on something that would not sway, or sink, or tremble. And he did not forget—though in his numbed brain he felt he had forgotten many things possibly important—that the typhoon's wings were still spread above them, poised for its screaming swoop. "Go on," he mumbled. "We'll stay here."

The soldiers conferred, the officer shrugged, they turned away. Neither the Senator nor Josepha looked back as they were helped on shore and escorted down to the patrol boat. For that matter, Montoya did not watch them go. He had turned immediately to the door of the blockhouse, holding his Renée with his good arm, an arrangement which yielded them both support.

One of the shutters was open, so that light fell acrross the bed—light still pale as dawn, though the sun must have been well up. For a minute they sat together in the light, looking at each other. It was the first time, for all either of them could remember, that they had ever looked at each other.

She could command her voice a second or two at a time; she spoke in quick little spurts. "I was afraid," she said.

He thought she meant in the normal way—afraid of dying, afraid of suffering as she had suffered before. "Of course," he said. "Everybody's afraid."

"Of the dragon," she said.

He drew back a little, to see her face better. "What?"

"Of the dragon. *Le dragon.*"

"Quel dragon?" he asked, puzzled, startled into amusement.

"At the bottom. Of the world." And she wept at last, shuddering, shuddering.

He held her off, still, a little, gazing at her with an unconscious frown. For the first time he glimpsed the dark scope of her life, the hollow depths on which she delicately trod. His right arm made a little, aborted movement; he had such a yearning impulse, at that instant, to stroke back the wet hair that was falling across her eyes. "No, no," he said carefully. "A dragon is a— is a nice animal. They make the crops grow."

She shook against him violently. The only answer he knew was to close his arms firmly around her, pulling her close; but it was the right answer. In a little while she ceased to sob, and they lay back together, like the limp debris that marks high-water along the shore.

The wind was rising. She thrust herself up on one elbow to gaze at Montoya. His face lay lax and sallow, washed, drowned with sleep. His lungs pulled steadily at the rich air. He had his freedom, she thought; and she, she had hers. It was true, then; it didn't matter how much you suffered, nor how many entanglements involved you—you could still be free. For the first time she was swept with a rush of love for him. What she had begun to feel in the dark boat on the still canal—the reality of him, as himself, this recalcitrant individuality, unique and total, so that everything he did expressed him, him and no other, the very flicker of his eyelash as he slept was Montoya— this feeling shook her now with its strength and endlessness. And, feeling that, she could feel love. She laughed with joy, a silent, open-mouthed laugh.

Mako came to the blockhouse in the rain. It was dark inside—she had closed the last shutter—but in the light from the door he saw them both asleep on the bed. He had come to report to Montoya—like the servants at the house, he had assumed that Montoya would surface here eventually if he lived—but Montoya was obviously sunk in a sleep too deep and deathlike for waking. The woman roused and stirred a little. Mako closed the door and settled himself beside it.

The oracle stirred wearily within her. His face looked drawn, longer, more narrow; he moved sickly. "The typhoon," he said, and his voice was a crusty sound, liable to crumble into nothingness. "It will come very soon. Marie-Ange . . ." and the crust broke, nothing lay beneath, his dry lips moved impotently. Dry—how could even fever parch him so, in the midst of the seething wetness of the world? Fumblingly she touched his face, and was pierced at once with fear.

"Marie-Ange—where is she?"

"Ask Mako." It was a whispered croak.

She looked at her fingertips, unsure whether they were burned or frozen. "Yes—Mako—where is he?"

"—about to die." It was hard, hard, to endure that writhing mouth, that broken husk of sound; and in his eyes she saw amusement still. Again he mouthed a silence, and heaved his arm against some deadly weight, pointing.

"Yes." Come, dragon; heel.

The one-armed man crouched like a household wraith beside the doorway. She knelt beside him. "My son is dead," she heard herself say. But no, it was not necessary to explain that to other people. She was here for a different reason. "Where is the child?"

"On Pagbo," he answered at once. He had been waiting for two days to answer this question. "No way we could get farther. Bad wind. Me . . ." He lifted the stump of his arm. "No men on Pagbo. No kumpit. Everybody already gone." He watched her face, dubious of her competence to understand, but he went on doggedly. "There's a good house there, wood. Nobody come there." He had finished.

From this she understood that he had sought one of Montoya's crews on an island called Pagbo and not found them, and had left the child and the old woman there in a wooden house because he could not sail them to a safer place unassisted in the teeth of the storm. "When the typhoon comes," she asked carefully, "will they be safe in that house?"

He moved his head in a strange way, sideward, as if he were bowing horizontally, as a leaf stretches sidelong in a gale. "That's a Christian wind," he said—by which he meant, among other things, that the great highway of typhoons ran north and east along the Christian islands, and only unorthodox storms strayed south and west into Moslem lands like this. It was, therefore, no responsibility of his. But his deep eyes were gloomy. He would have helped his charges better if he could. At any rate, he had fulfilled his obligation to put them out of reach of the rebels.

"Where is Pagbo?" she asked, and he rose immediately, reaching his one, taut arm to help her up with him.

"Three miles," he said. "Very near."

"It is not inevitable," she told him earnestly. He nodded, but he did not think he understood. "My son is dead," she said, taking an example. "That was not inevitable, but it happened. Now, *something* is going to happen, but . . ." But he did not understand; and there was no time. "But it depends on *us*." She paused only a moment by the bed where Montoya slept his utter sleep—so short a moment, Mako did not realize she had paused.

"Now," the oracle said. His soft voice rang unbearably, unblended jubilation and bitterness. "I am dying." Mako shouldered the door open, holding her arm with his hand, and they plunged together into the rain.

Philippe Montoya slept. The long rush of the storm did not wake him; and even when Marie-Ange crept onto the bed beside him like a small wet animal (her clothes had been wrung out as well as the old woman's strength could manage, but there was nothing dry to put on, and she crawled into the shelter of his arms almost bare, her skin adhesive with wetness), he only muttered in his sleep and shifted a little, huddling his body around her. There was no way to know what words he mumbled; the cry of the typhoon belittled all other sounds into nothingness. Later, when one of the wooden shutters broke with a crash, it was a crash to all intents silent, and the only change the ear could detect was in the quality of the storm-sound, sharper and more poignant. The shutter of the other weatherside window was taken away lightly by the wind, as if a child's hand plucked a leaf that was ready to fall. Through the unprotected openings the rain hurtled in broken masses, rushing and swirling about the room until the floor was ankle-deep in water and Mako opened the door to let it escape on the lee side. After a time the nurse had crawled onto the foot of the bed and squatted there, with her old arms wrapped around herself. Mako still stood, his back to one of the side walls. He would have joined the others on the bed, perhaps, but he did not like to wake Montoya. The wall throbbed and trembled against his back continuously, like a rough sound; sometimes it suddenly jarred, and the inescapable roar that submerged them was split for a moment by a shriller peal. It was interesting to Mako that as other sensations died one by one in the unceasing rush of wind and water, a pain was born and grew in the arm he did not have, so that soon he could trace out almost its whole absent length and fullness by the shape of the pain.

They did not notice at first when the storm slackened, they were so benumbed. Only when the rain had ceased to cannonade in thick volleys across the room, did they stir and swallow and look about them. The wind had fallen; in a very little while the rain ceased altogether, and the wind died to an angelic breeze. Montoya woke. The silence, and the throb in his truncated arm, combined into a single message: it was good that the typhoon had passed, because it was very necessary to reach a hospital.

He sat up, finding the little body beside him, and hugged the child with his good arm. She woke, but she did not answer his questions. He looked quickly to the nurse, and something in her grim old face made him turn to Mako, swinging his legs to the floor. "Where is she?"

Mako still stood against the wall, but now he shifted himself and squatted at its base. "She wanted to bring them back here. Too much typhoon for Pagbo."

"Pagbo?" Montoya repeated harshly. Pagbo was wrong, he knew, and yet for a moment he could not grasp exactly what was wrong with it. Something seemed to have been torn loose in his brain, and it was hard to re-establish the connections.

Mako raised his face. "Pagbo. No way to get them farther. No kumpit, no men. Good house, plenty of water, plenty of food. No way to get them farther." Montoya nodded; Mako was not to blame. Marie-Ange leaned her small head against him. "We got there before the big wind," Mako resumed. This was true in a narrow sense. The wind had not reached hurricane force until shortly after they had begun the return from Pagbo, he at the tiller, she bailing in the bow, with the child and the old woman flat under a canvas between them. "Then," Mako said, "the big wind came."

"Where is she?"

"The wind took her," Mako said. He did not lower his eyes. He had no apologies to make. He had passed very near to death himself out there, when the wind had flipped the prao almost over, outrigger or no, and they had fled like a scudding flake of foam. He had seen her go, her grip lifted as lightly from the gunwale as if her hand had only rested there a moment at ease. In the typhoon there were no rescues. One could only see and confirm: Yes, this is happening.

"Gone?" Montoya said, seeking his own confirmation. Mako nodded.

Montoya rose and went stiffly to the open door, looking out into the beaten landscape. Once his right arm moved a little, as he contemplated the hand he had lost for nothing. It, too, lay somewhere out there—underwater, perhaps, or wedged in the wreckage of some shattered tree—mouthed already, perhaps, by small survivors returning to the business of life in the track of the great storm. His mouth was dry with regret; he swallowed, to ease it. "She was—a nice woman," he said slowly. "She knew a lot."